Summerton

Lady Eleanor Mysteries, Volume 1

Becca St. John

Published by Winterbourne Farm Publishing, LLC, 2015.

This is a work of fiction. Similarities to real people, places, or events are entirely coincidental.

SUMMERTON

First edition. December 24, 2015.

ISBN: 978-1522758013

Written by Becca St. John.

Our Ancestors

By marriage and birth w Inspiring grand lives

Guiding through a legacy of stories

You are loved, missed, and honored

And to three fabulous women

Author, Beverley Gail Eikli

And readers extraordinaire: Liz Evans & Beverly Ross

CHAPTER 1 ~ The Bride

Alfred Henry Bertram Edgwater, Duke of Summerton, Earl of St. Martins, stood before the warm glow of the fire, studying the depths of his brandy. He sloshed it about in idle circular motions, coating the sides of the tumbler with rich amber.

A weak distraction, perhaps, but more suitable than pacing the room or indulging in his second occupation of the evening—glancing at the closed door to the duchess's chambers.

His duchess's chambers.

He could barely fathom it. Married.

It could have been worse, would have been if his bride had said no. Which she hadn't. Every lady wished to be a duchess.

Still, he fretted over his choice of looks and wit over breeding. He hoped to God he'd made the right decision.Of course, there was the dowry and, further, the pounds per annum. He mustn't forget the whole reason for the enterprise.

He downed his drink in one swallow, chastising himself. No need to be impatient. They had exchanged their vows, enjoyed a splendid wedding breakfast with a few guests. His man of affairs had confirmed that the funds were already in the bank.

No need to rush the bedding. A promise was a promise and he'd made his. Wait for the lady's maid to crack the door of the adjoining room and signal he could enter.

He set his glass on the table. Best not to have another. Brandy was a foolish means of wasting time.

Earlier he'd found diversion in his study, checking over the itinerary for a bridal journey he already knew by heart. He'd tried to read a recent book on traveling through Italy, but he couldn't concentrate.

Whatever doubts he held about this marriage—the taint of trade, a commoner for a wife—physical attraction was not one. Desire stifled all other diversions.

In the end, he left his study for his valet, Percy, before finally settling in the duke and duchess's sitting room. The fire, flaming perfectly when he entered the room, had died down to glowing red coals surrounded by ash.

No one took that long to prepare for the night.

Surely, the maid had forgotten to leave the door ajar.

According to Percy, his bride's bath had been emptied hours ago. He should tap on the door. Lightly. Except the duchess's bedchamber was on the far side of her sitting room, making it unlikely she'd hear it, and if she did, that he could hear her response.

Entering her sitting room wouldn't, exactly, break the promise.

In four long strides he faced the first barrier, hand hovering over the door lever. He withdrew it, uneasy for the hesitation. He was a duke, born and bred to be decisive, to have the last word.

That was the problem. He'd given her the last word. She had asked for his patience. Unlike her uncle, a doting old fool of a guardian, Summerton's beautiful, biddable bride had never asked for a thing before. Not anything in the whole of their brief courtship, or the six weeks of their engagement.

Mind you, in all that time, they'd seen little of each other and never shared a private word outside of one very short walk in the garden. Even that had been quickly interrupted. He sighed. The protection of innocence was a trying thing indeed.

Still, his impatience did him no credit. She was to be his wife, not his mistress. He'd do well to remember that. But how long could it take to brush out her hair? Arrange it in artful disarray? Don a wisp of a nightrail? Not this long, even if she wished to powder every inch of that delectable body of hers.

Restless, he took another tour past the long windows of his sitting room, pushed aside a heavy brocade curtain to find a world of silver and shadows. Eerie, even more so, for the constant howling that carried across the fields. Dogs and wolves loved a full moon. Good time for seeding fields as well.

A flicker of light at the edge of the woods startled him. He looked back. Nothing. Probably a town boy signaling to his sweetheart in the Hall.

Affairs of the estate flitted through his thoughts, nothing strong enough to linger. His steward, Tom, had the farmers plowing tonight. They would later plant clover, contrary to generations of traditional crops.

He thought of the pretty little mare he had bought for his bride, all high strung and prancing about. Hopefully, it would not be too much for her.

He smiled. It faded.

He was a husband. Although his bride did not strike him as high strung, she was an innocent. He had a duty to ease her beyond any shy skittishness. Young girls could be wrought with unnecessary fears of the wedding night, especially when they didn't have a mother to explain things.

Who knew what his bride had been told. Just like him, motherless from a young age. Missing whatever it was mothers provided. In this case, what to expect on a wedding night. Fears could escalate beyond reason. He'd heard of such scenarios.

It would do neither of them a bit of good to have her shivering and tearful beyond common sense. A bride's nerves were no small factor.

Prodded by worry, he opened the double doors to her parlor, stepped over the threshold, listened for sobs. Nothing. No voices, no footsteps. Quiet.

The blasted maid had forgotten.

Without any more hesitation, he headed for his duchess's bedchamber, fully prepared to give her maid a thorough set down if he found his bride's head buried in the pillows, stifling the sound of weeping.

Calming a distraught wife was not in his plans this night.

He stepped past the fanciful, gilded furniture favored by women ages past, crossed the Aubusson carpet. Décor his bride might well change.

But not before the wedding night.

Once more, he hesitated at a doorway, miffed by his own reluctance to act. A loud crash and curse swiftly changed all that. Without the slightest qualm, he thrust the tall paneled door open, strode into the chamber, and stilled, too stunned by the unimaginable tableau to move.

Thank God for his bride's lengthy preparations. A quick glance confirmed she was not there. No doubt still in her dressing room readying herself for the wedding night.

Instead of his bride, he found a filthy little urchin bent over an overturned table in the bedchamber. A shattered vase, bruised rose petals, and broken stalks lay strewn at his soggy feet. The lad had a huge bundle, nearly as big as he was, slung over one shoulder. The fabric, the only clean thing about him, was no doubt from the stripped bed.

His bed linens. By God, the imp was stealing from his home and using his sheets to carry the loot off!

In less than a blink, Summerton took it all in, but that slight hesitation proved enough time for the boy, initially as frozen as Summerton, to act first. One moment they stared at each other, the next the nimble rascal raced straight for the open French windows leading to the balcony.

Summerton roared to life, shouting, "Stay where you are! We've trouble out here!" to his bride, and charged after the thief.

The raggedy young scamp tossed his bundle over the railing. Summerton cringed in anticipation of the clanking crash of priceless candlesticks and crystal. It landed with a soft thump, softer even than the boy's final leap from the curlicues of stone.

He'd managed it all with agile deftness. Damn the imp. How many times had he climbed that wall?

Swift as a sparrow, the child abandoned his haul and pelted across the grounds, heading straight for the woods that surrounded St. Martins.

"George!" the duke bellowed for the nighttime groundskeeper, fully aware there was no hope for it. By the time George arrived, the rascal would be well and truly gone.

Alfred Henry Bertram Edgwater, Duke of Summerton, Earl of St. Martins, slipped off his finest damask dressing gown and stepped out of his Italian leather slippers to better scale the stonework. He, too, had practice, not with this particular wall but one very similar to it, having, after all, been a boy once himself. As long ago as that had been, he made good time.

Caught up in the chase, he forgot his bride, that he even had one, other than to chastise his own foolishness in dithering over whether to enter her chamber or not.

"George!" Summerton shouted again for the man whose job it was to ensure nothing like this ever happened.

Fueled by fury that anyone would deign to steal from him, Summerton didn't feel the sharp edge of stone or the prick of thistles.

He didn't hear George's shouts, or the barks of dogs let loose. He didn't even hear his own breathing. Determined to outdistance the scamp, he used his one advantage. Long legs. His little adversary did not have them, but Summerton did. As they closed in on the woods, he neared the boy and sprang, tackling the lad with a hard flying leap.

Their 'umphs' mingled. Summerton cursed the squirming boy—"Damn you, you little wastrel!"—as he wrestled to subdue him, avoiding some, but not all, of his determined kicks and pummeling fists.

"Stop it!" Summerton commanded, as he flipped the child over, sending his cap flying. A cloud of thick golden hair escaped with a billowing scent of lavender.

A familiar sensual fragrance, one Summerton was particularly fond of, but he had never been quite so finely attuned to it as now.

With this absconder.

For the second time that evening, both Summerton and his prey stilled, frozen as ice on a pond that teemed with life below the frigid surface.

"Caroline?" Incredulity blunted his words. "Caroline?" This couldn't be possible. It made no sense.

Up until eight that very morning, he had been *the* most eligible bachelor in the whole of England, failing finances be damned.

No, not the whole of England. The whole of the British Empire.

Every matchmaker, persistent mama, and giggling young lady of the ton had vied for his attention. He had been a veritable catch. A man chased from ballroom to country party to ballroom.

He was *not* some besotted fool left staring at the soot-streaked features of a fleeing bride.

Their movements mirrored each other, chests rising, falling, gulping breaths after the effort of the chase. Fury fanned like a blacksmith's bellows.

She had only needed to say no.

"What the bloody hell are you doing?" He slid off her, placing himself between her and the Hall before anyone could spot them. As he reached for the fallen cap, a massive bloodhound clambered up and wedged between them to slobber kisses all over Caroline's face.

Summerton recoiled, even as Caroline twisted and wrapped her arms around the beast. Those sobs Summerton had so feared surfaced as she buried her head in the plentiful folds of the dog's neck.

"Seigneur Baver, Seigneur Baver! You are alive," she wailed.

Summerton snorted. Lord Drool? Well-named. He swiped at a string of slobber that ran along his arm.

But why would she imagine her dog dead? Of course the bloody animal was alive. All the bloody animals she'd collected over the years were alive and faring very well, eating grain and meat in his stables.

Where had she thought they'd gotten off to?

Caroline pulled back, eyes on the dog. "How did you find me?" she asked, as if Summerton, who was perfectly capable of answering her question, weren't right there beside her.

"With his nose," Summerton said, thrusting her cap at her. "Put this on." And he held up his hand to ward off George, who'd just rounded the far corner of the Hall with half a dozen baying dogs on leads.

Caroline jammed her hair under the cap, filling the floppy fabric as completely as straw filled a rag doll. Summerton watched her as he tried to tamp down anger with reason.

No, she hadn't needed to marry him. If there'd been a lover, surely she would have wed the other man instead. Unless, of course, the cad was already married, in which case marriage would give her the freedom for an affair.

Fear of the wedding night, indeed! He never should have waited to enter her rooms.

He'd start were they'd left off.

"All your animals are here, Caroline."

Ah, that got her. Frozen as still as when he'd first found her surrounded by shards of broken vase.

"Every last one of your wounded, limping, hungry mongrels, as well as a three-legged cat, a mischievous fox the gamekeeper wants to shoot, and a number of nags so old, they'd starve out to pasture. Digger, the head groomsman, hired a new stable boy whose sole job is to hand-feed them gruel three times a day." She was definitely paying attention now.

"And what else?" He lounged back as if he had all the time in the world, eyeing his runaway bride, her eyes wide, wary. Resting his wrist on his raised knee, he idly tapped his fingers, drawing out the moment, giving her time to respond. She didn't. He pretended to search his memory. "Ah, yes!" He held up a finger, making his point. His wayward bride blinked.

"Mustn't forget the talking bird, which, undoubtedly, once belonged to a sailor."

She gasped.

"I tried to banish it to the servants' area. Cook is still blushing and Mrs. Beechum, whom you will find as accommodating as any housekeeper, finally sent it to the stables in a desperate attempt to protect the young maids from its verbiage."

He'd done quite a bit for this young woman. The problem was, she obviously had no notion he'd done anything at all.

The whole enterprise of taking on her collection of useless pets, which her uncle had suggested, was to be a surprise. At first it had seemed perfectly reasonable. What problem could a few comforting pets pose? Only there were far more than a few, and none of them were in any way comfortable. He'd regretted taking them on more than once.

"Where did you think they'd gotten off to?" he asked his silent bride. "Or had you not even noticed their absence?"

Wide green eyes met his, shifted aside, returned. She opened her delectable mouth, then shut it again, rather mulishly, and looked away, toward his home...*their* home. Concocting a story, no doubt, though it was too late for that.

Why hadn't he immediately recognized her when they'd stared at each other upstairs? Certainly, as a missish young lady, she'd never looked at him directly before, and the candlelight of the bedroom had offered only faint illumination to war against the shadow of her hat. No doubt the dimness had darkened those eyes, green as spring moss, or he'd have known them. Recognized the shape, wide, slanti-ng down ever so gently on the outside, with long, thick, straight lash-es.

He'd spent the first half of this night imagining desire in those eyes. Now he would always be watching for lies.

Her gaze veered toward George, who was now crouched down on the far side of the lawn, his dogs restless at his feet, waiting for some signal or word from Summerton. Lights were being lit all across the Hall, figures outlined in the windows, looking out. Curious ser-vants. He'd have to concoct a story of his own.

This wasn't the place for a confrontation.

"Come on." He rose and held out his hand to help her up.

Baver, her Lord Drool, had already lost interest in the reunion, drawn off by some elusive scent, as hounds were wont to do. "Let's get you inside and find out what this is all about."

George rose as they did. "Shall I go for help, m'lord?" he called out.

"No," Summerton called back. "It's the lad who used to care for Lady Caroline's animals. I'll take him up to see her grace."

Ah, if looks could skewer, he'd be pierced. Docile, he'd thought. He'd been wrong.

"Right oh, we certainly could use some help with those good-for-nothing critters," George groused. "If you have need of me, I'm near to hand," he promised and turned back for the kennels.

"They're not good for nothing," Caroline snipped, quiet but firm. She knew how to leash that temper. "They are as important as he is, as anyone is."

"She speaks," he pressed, wondering what would make the sparks fly.

"Of course I speak." She gave a haughty lift of her chin. "You've heard me before."

"Never like this," he said.

Of course she'd spoken, and he'd listened. Indeed, given his aversion to caustic, harsh voices and high-pitched screeches, his bride's voice had been one of many deciding factors. Caroline could lull a man to sleep with her soft deep intonations. Innocently seductive.

"I do have opinions," she informed him. "When I'm allowed to."

Before he could react, she pulled away and strode back toward the Hall.

When I'm allowed to.

God save him, his new duchess was no easy, malleable miss. He had troubles enough without having to deal with her. Worse yet, the delectable swing of her backside in trousers inspired a hedonistic lust, far too raw for seducing any bride, let alone a reluctant one.

Good Lord, he'd married the wrong heiress.

CHAPTER 2 ~ Diversions

Back stiff and straight, Caroline Mary Howlett—Caro to family and friends—led the way back to the Hall. A diversion, that was all.

She would not crumble. She was made of sturdier stuff.

Compliance was her best tactic for now, so she looked forward and marched, even as her mind raced for an escape. Jeremy was out there, somewhere on the periphery of the woods, but she'd not turn to see if he still waited. That would only give him away.

The Hall loomed ahead, a massive structure with more wings than a flock of birds. Where, exactly, did the duke want her to go? She hesitated.

"Around the back," Summerton said from behind her, like she was some prisoner. Which she was.

Damn the man. Damn his voice rippling through her, like a cat's purr. She scrunched her shoulders, and pressed her lips tight, protection against the seduction of his voice.

"There's a pathway, closer to the Hall, that leads to the back entrance." He moved up beside her.

"I'd like to go to the stables first." To see her precious pets. That was the crux of the whole thing. She could hardly believe they were alive, here. What would happen to them now, when she left?

Would he return them to her uncle? She shivered at the thought.

He startled her again, breaking into her thoughts with a voice as rich and dark as chocolate without any sweetening.

"Go to the stables tonight?" No hint of humor in his chuckle. "So you can run away before you've told me what you are about?"

She huffed, and waited for him to lead. He did not. "You stay in front," he ordered.

"I won't run," she snapped. She couldn't now, not until she'd made plans for her pets.

His response was caught between a chuckle and a sigh. In some odd way, he was enjoying this. She sensed the thrum of emotion woven into every sound he made; humor, anger, frustration, and confusion. Complicated expressions, though he'd barely spoken.

She fought a shiver of unease. Refused to let his voice sink into her, its barbed hook trapping her. She had things to do, people who needed her for more than a bank balance.

At the door, she turned, risking a look back over the path they'd walked, studying the edges of the woods. Even with the full moon, the shadows were too deep to see anything.

"Don't even think about it," he warned, as he reached around for the doorknob. He needn't have bothered. As usual, someone had anticipated his need. The door opened from the inside, revealing the housekeeper, Mrs. Beechum, and the butler, Hitches, on the threshold in their dressing gowns.

Summerton shifted, using his body and the dark of night to shield her. "Nothing to worry about. One of the duchess's stable hands came to see about the animals. I will deal with him. You may return to your beds."

The housekeeper held out a coat of sorts and a pair of gentleman's slippers. "Percy brought these down for you," she said.

Caroline blinked. She'd been so caught up in planning what to do next she'd failed to notice the duke wore nothing more than a thin silk nightshirt. How had she missed that? She bit back a laugh, imagining him climbing down the stone lattice of the balcony, his nightshirt catching on every twig of the vine dominating the structure.

Sure enough, snags marred the delicate red silk, pocking it. Bits of vines and leaves still clung. She might have felt sorry, except fascination rerouted all other thoughts. She'd never seen a man in so little covering.

Summerton was slipping into an asian banyan robe of striking blue, embroidered with heavy gold thread. Hitches held the garment in place as the housekeeper lifted the slippers for the duke to step into. He needn't even bend a knee, which was unfortunate, for when Caroline's gaze reached his face she caught him watching her, one eyebrow raised. She lifted her chin. It wasn't her fault he'd chosen to chase her with barely a stitch on.

Well, not entirely her fault.

He had released his hold on her as Hitches and the housekeeper dressed him, but she didn't dare try to run. He'd already proven he could outdistance her.

Plus, he had her animals.

"I hope this lad will teach the bird some better language," the housekeeper griped, without a single glance at Caroline. Servants could be a snobbish lot.

"Mrs. Beechum." Hitches's sartorial tone silenced her. "We shall leave his grace to this business." He bowed to Summerton. "We are at your service if you need anything. There is a candle for you in the hallway"

"We'll be in the study, Hitches."

"Will you need a fire, your grace?"

"No, I don't expect this will take long." Summerton waited, watching as the two headed back to their apartments.

"Well-trained monkeys." Caroline muttered, drawing a harsh, shaming stare from Summerton.

"They do not deserve your disrespect."

Her cheeks heated. Foolishness, belittling servants for her own frustrations. Her family was not that far removed from service for her to be anything but considerate to them.

Besides, there was no reason to fault Summerton's servants at this point. Not unless they became as intrusive as her uncle's tattling minions. And she could not really fault her uncle's servants. After all, they had had little choice in the matter.

The duke bowed and opened his arm to direct her to continue. "To my study."

Caroline sighed. "I don't know where it is."

"Ah." He nodded. "I suppose you don't."

He took the candle left by his butler and led her down a long paneled hallway, lined with pictures obscured by shadow. When he reached a doorway, he stood aside, silently inviting her over the threshold. He followed, his one meager candle in hand. On the edge of light she saw a mantle, the fire now cold. She crossed to it as the door thumped shut and a lock clicked into place.

Fate sealed, she didn't bother to look back.

She ignored the rustling and jostling, not really wanting to know what he was about, until a breeze shivered down her neck.

Summerton had drawn the drapes, opened the French doors, and stepped outside through the wide-flung panels of beveled glass. She crossed to them to see what he was doing. Was this her opportunity to run? He hadn't gone far, was even now returning, her abandoned bundle slung over his back.

If not for the finery of his garments, he would have resembled an ordinary worker. She turned away, disturbed, confused by a heightened curiosity traitorous to her plans. Had she not run, she would have known this man without any barriers, not even the silk of his nightshirt.

Back inside, he left the doors open and dropped the bundle near a bookcase before retrieving the candle from a side bureau near the door.

"It will do you no good to try and leave," he said over his shoulder as he used the candle to light sconces on either side of the fireplace. "You would not get away."

"I've already presumed as much," she admitted. He smiled, as though pleased. Whether it was in reaction to her honesty or common sense, she didn't know. His voice gave him away in some instances, but she didn't know him well enough to decipher his expressions.

What an absolute farce, that young couples could know so little about each other, yet be bonded for life.

Not wishing to dwell on that, Caroline took advantage of the light. They were in a study, decorated much the same as the rest of the Hall. A grand space with badly frayed furnishings. Like an old relative, once much loved, grown tatty and crippled through neglect.

Not that Summerton would realize such a thing even if he had the funds to make a difference. Men didn't, did they? It took a woman to care and there had been very little female influence on the Summerton line for generations. The duke's mother had died when he was just a boy and his father had never remarried. The same had been true for the previous generation. The Dukes of Summerton were well-established bachelors, preferring town life over country pursuits.

A woman might have changed that.

The last two Duchesses of Summerton had not survived long enough to make a lasting difference.

Caroline was not so superstitious as to consider this a bad omen for the third wife in line, but the situation had created a dreadful challenge. No doubt this duke meant to leave her to rusticate while he returned to the delights of the city.

This was not, after all, a love match. He knew nothing about her beyond her financial health. She, on the other hand, knew a great deal about him.

His city of choice would be London.

She needed to be in Manchester, soon.

If only she knew what he planned, having caught her running away.

Without thought, she reached to adjust the lay of her skirts as she took a chair near the cold fireplace. She wasn't wearing a dress. She blinked and just sat. Her trouser legs pulled uncomfortably. She ignored it.

Rather than join her, Summerton leaned against a large desk, deep in shadow despite the candles he'd lit. She waited, legs together, hands in her lap, pretending a calm she didn't feel. He remained silent, arms crossed over his chest.

Finally, his voice cut through the heavy silence, jerking her to attention.

"Was your abigail a part of this?"

She drew back, offended. "Alice?"

"I take it she wasn't."

"No."

He didn't ask any more questions. Just watched her.

"How long will it take you to change from," he gestured toward her, "those breeches you are wearing? And to clean your face?"

She'd forgotten about the coal dust. Running from the duke wasn't meant to be the end of things. She needed to travel across country without being noticed. No one paid much heed to dirty little urchins.

She rose to see if she'd dirtied the seat of the chair, only to realize that a bit of coal dust couldn't hurt a cushion nearly worn through.

"Well?" he asked, obviously impatient.

She turned toward him. "Not long if there's enough water. Do you mind telling me what you intend?"

He walked over to a wall of bookcases. "I haven't decided yet," he admitted, as he reached under one of the shelves. The bookcase moved. He swept his arm out, inviting her to lead the way into a yawning dark hole.

This she hadn't considered. That he'd lock her up in some closet.

"I don't think so." She tried to sound firm.

He looked beyond the opening and back, reached for his candle and went inside. The halo of light revealed a staircase. He came back out, but the interior stayed alight.

"Now, please, go inside. It's late and we have considerable planning to do."

Still, she hesitated. She did not like small dark places. "Are you joining me?"

"Yes, after I've informed Hitches that the lad is gone and that you require the services of your abigail and my aunt."

She blinked. She'd forgotten that his aunt was here. Another one of the reasons she didn't want to be married to him. He'd arranged for his aunt, as a companion for Caroline. No doubt to free him for pursuits other than getting to know his wife.

"Very well." She walked up to him. "But you'd best summon the others after I've changed." And sailed past him, stopping two paces into the narrow corridor.

Dust tickled her nose and a sticky spider's web stuck to her cheek.

She shivered and stepped back.

"Just wait here," he told her, plopping her bundle on the floor at her feet and shutting the door.

"Wait!" she shouted, but the closure was already well and truly shut. She searched for a lever, a knob, something that would open the blasted thing. She tried pushing. It didn't move, so she stood still.

Very still, and breathed slowly, methodically, trying to stem panic. She closed her eyes, pretending to be somewhere else, anywhere else, only to feel creepy crawlies on her neck, sneaking up her arms. Swatting at them did no good. Either they weren't really there or they'd gotten away.

Lips tight, she fought back a whimper. She must think. If she went up the stairs, she could end up anywhere. Anywhere was far better than waiting.

Voices stopped her.

"Your grace?" It was unmistakeably Hitches.

"The lad is gone, took off through the window," Summerton said. "Which makes me question whether he was really the duchess's man. Send George out with the dogs and place a couple of good strong lads below the duchess's windows."

Everything in her collapsed. Jeremy was out there.

Summerton continued. "Have my aunt go to the duchess's room. And see that the duchess's abigail waits in her dressing room."

"As you will, your grace," Hitches replied.

"I'll check on the duchess."

"Yes, your grace."

She could hear footsteps leaving the room. Summerton's, she presumed. He'd left her there. Hitches moved about closing doors and drapes, blowing out candles. All the sounds clear and distinct. Clear enough she could hear Hitches's footsteps as he walked out and moments later someone else started moving around the room. Whoever it was bumped into the furniture. She strained to listen, certain it couldn't be the duke, so at ease with the space she'd bet he could move around it blindfolded.

Shoulder to the wall, she pushed at the opening. Again, it didn't budge. She felt around, ignoring sticky webs catching her hands, the sleeve of her shirt. She must find the lever, free the latch. Surely there was one.

"Do you really believe I'd leave you here with the ability to get out?"

She spun around to the hem of his banyan and slippered feet on the stairs above.

"I wish you would stop sneaking up on me," she hissed, wondering if sound traveled into the study as well as it did into this little area.

He came further into view.

"Let's extinguish this one." He reached around her—*close, too close*—to blow out the light on the little ledge and lift the bundle from the floor.

"I don't like it in here."

"I'm not surprised." He smiled, but not with malice. "I didn't much like finding my bride running away."

She shrugged and edged past him to climb the stairs.

Once again, at the top, he reached around her, fiddling with a support beam, releasing something, for the wall opened without a creak. The scent of candle wax and leather and sandalwood mixed with other, subtler herbs, filtered into the secret space. Caroline stepped over the threshold. A bedchamber.

Summerton urged her further into the room as he closed the opening behind him. Everything in the chamber was heavy and strong, from the furniture to the picture frames. Masculine, a man's domain.

A huge four-poster bed on a dais stood directly opposite them. She stepped aside, not wanting to be confronted with the closeness of the bed or the intimacies it implied.

"You'd best wash off the dirt in here," he told her, as he opened another door. "I will gather your dressing gown and nightrail."

She'd never been in a man's dressing room before—other than her father's, that was—and she'd rarely been in there. This was better appointed than the duchess's rooms. Nothing threadbare or badly kept, though there was little beyond a clothespress, armoire, and washing table. One corner was screened off, no doubt, for the commode.

A chair sat beside a table with a bowl, towels, and an assortment of silver-lidded jars of beautiful cut glass. With a twist, she unscrewed one and put her nose to the opening, inhaling the distinctive lemon and spice scent so much a part of the duke. Carefully, she unleashed the straight razor from its silver handle, the polished blade glinting in the candle light, lethally sharp. She clicked it shut, set it down beside the matching silver soap mug and shaving brush, and tried not to think of the intimacy of a man at his toilet.

She distracted herself by looking around. The place was in sad need of modernization. No doubt the duke expected her to fund the update.

Surprisingly, the water in the pitcher was warm. It would seem Hitches had anticipated the duke's desire to clean up after running outside sans dressing gown and slippers.

She poured water into the bowl and scrubbed. One bowl of water was not enough. She dumped the blackened batch in an empty bucket by the washing table and started in with a fresh batch of warm water, using a lovely scented soap. Too spicy for a lady, but this was not a time for niceties.

By the time Summerton returned, the bucket was half full of black, scummy water, but Caroline was pink-cheeked with clean hands.

"Here." He held out her nightrail and a dressing gown of such delicate lace she could see his long fingers through the fabric. Awkward, the garments slipped as he passed them to her, floating down, forming a diaphanous pool between them.

"I'll leave you to it." His rough voice grazed her senses like a cat's tongue.

"Perhaps I should find something else to wear," she said, but he waved the idea away and left. Escaping without a thought to her sensibilities.

She couldn't greet his aunt in her lad's outfit any more than she wished to reveal herself in—she looked at the tumble of nothingness. Perhaps they weren't as bad as she imagined.

She stripped down, rolling the urchin's clothes into a ball and leaving them with the dirty cloths she'd used to wash. Careful of its fragility, she donned the nightwear and stood before a long mirror.

Every curve, every shade of dark and light, revealed in the glow of one mere candle. Impossible.

She went through the clothes press and armoire and found another banyan, this one quilted, lighter weight than the one he had on, with a mandarin collar and frog fastenings that hit the tops of her breasts. Far too long, but she fastened the upper buttons and flipped the extra length back to trail behind her like a train.

It would have to do.

Summerton stopped mid-stride as she entered the bedchamber. Heart thumping wildly, she waited, all too aware of the massive bed behind her.

"Good." He offered a perfunctory nod and held his arm, gesturing toward the door. She took a deep breath, wishing he'd say more, give some indication of his plans. He didn't. Just crossed the room to open the door to their sitting room.

The spice of his cologne had her turning her head as she passed. An urge to catch the full scent. She knew its source, the cut crystal bottle, but the scent from the bottle and the scent on the man were very different. The knowledge rippled through her, raising a heathenish instinct she fought to suppress.

She refused to be swayed by a man who counted her worth in pounds and pence.

"Thank you," she said, and stepped into a room softly lit by candles and a warm fire.

Beside the fire sat a strong-boned woman, neatly coiffed, clad in a simple day dress and shawl, despite having been called from her bed. She sat up straight without appearing rigid, her smile as enigmatic as the duke's. Like him, she commanded by presence alone.

She would be fair-minded, Caroline guessed, though neither she nor her nephew were the sort you'd want to get on the wrong side of.

Currently, she was on the wrong side of both of them.

"The errant bride, I presume," Lady Eleanor said. "Whatever are we going to do with you?"

CHAPTER 3 ~ Plans

His bride did not want him.

Face scrubbed to pink, hair a delightful tousle, dressed in his banyan, she should have looked like a child playing dress-up. The hem trailed ludicrously around her. She had to clutch the sleeves to keep them from falling to her knees.

No, not a child, a medieval queen walking into her court. How did she manage it?

He paced to the windows, unable to look at her. He'd let Eleanor ask the questions. His aunt liked such things, unraveling the chaotic puzzle of human existence. Of all the issues Caroline's attempted flight raised, only one haunted him.

His bride did not want him. Nor, did it seem, did she want to be a duchess. What woman ran from being a duchess? Or from him? Women fawned over him.

Or did they?

There was that incident when Lady Alyssa, poor girl, had swooned at his feet. An anecdote revived every year, with each new swarm of debutantes. He rather suspected the misfortune had more to do with the sweltering, overcrowded ballroom than it did with him, but the story must have been plausible, for it was repeated every season.

Wasn't it?

Worse, he wanted her. Badly. Even after she'd run from him, even though she was walking about in his clothes. This woman, who didn't want him, possessed more courage and backbone than any other woman of his aquaintance. Oh, yes, he wanted her, for so many reasons.

"Summerton?" Eleanor interrupted the useless path of his thoughts. "Do you have a plan?"

He had a plan, but needed more information before committing to it.

"Perhaps Caroline would explain herself?" He suggested over his shoulder before turning back to the shadowed landscape beyond. George was below, with a troop of men, lanterns in hand, dogs leashed. Not that the dogs would be of any help other than to frighten whoever was out there.

The light. While waiting to enter the duchess's chamber, he'd seen a light off to the left. Someone signaling. She'd most certainly had help.

He turned back, curious about Eleanor's hesitation. Caroline was taking the chair opposite his aunt. With a casual flip of the banyan, she transformed a burdensome hem into an elegant train neatly pooled at her side.

Eleanor's lips lifted a fraction at the corners—enough to let him know she approved of the girl.

"Well?" he asked, only to be interrupted by a scratch at the door.

Scowling, he crossed to open the door. If a servant had come with a message, he'd rather receive it at the door than admit another person into the room. They may act as if they neither heard nor saw, but they did both, and they also talked.

Hitches, uncharacteristically nervous, stood on the other side.

"Her grace's abigail is nowhere to be found."

"Gone?" the duke asked.

"No sign she was ever here," Hitches admitted.

Summerton dismissed him, closing the door quietly as he digested the information. Caroline claimed she'd left on her own, yet there'd been that light in the woods and her maid was missing. She'd planned this for some time.

Eleanor opened her mouth to speak, but he cut her off, suddenly too angry to hold back. "In the whole time before the wedding, you never once considered calling it off?" He stepped forward, looming over Caroline, disgusted with his outburst, the riot of his thoughts, but unable to hold back.

"You would be a duchess," Eleanor offered. Her quick glance chastised him for childish behavior. He stepped back.

"I would *never* be a duchess!" Caroline lifted her chin.

He snorted. "What? Are you holding out for a prince? Because, I must warn you, *they* are all taken."

This time Eleanor's glare took them both in. "Children," she actually said, stunning Caroline as much as him. "Bickering won't help."

"Well, I won't be a duchess," Caroline argued. "You know that, I know that, the whole of the ton knows it."

"Don't be ridiculous," he ordered.

She snorted.

"A most unladylike sound," he said, earning a bark of laughter.

"Perhaps that's because I am not a lady, your grace."

"Ah," Eleanor said, as if everything suddenly made sense, "you are afraid."

Caroline glared. He didn't blame her.

"Aunt, timid people do not run away into the night," he defended, promptly turning the tables by adding, "But strong people tend to stand up for themselves. So tell me, Caroline, why didn't you say something sooner?"

She looked away, offering an intriguing silhouette, all high cheekbones and straight patrician nose.

"Does it matter?" She turned to him. "I followed through, the wedding is over, and now you both have what you wanted. It is only fair that I'm allowed my freedom."

He sighed, pinched the bridge of his nose. He was a known negotiator, a mediator. He could get the Whigs and Tories to claim friendship. He could work this out. He turned to this stoic, obstinate woman. "You are the Duchess of Summerton."

"Trust me, your grace, you do not want me for your duchess."

"A bit late for that, but why ever not?" he asked, wishing Eleanor would step in and ask a few questions, but she sat back, offering no more than a wry smile.

"I do not care to spend my days pouring tea and discussing the merits of a particular feather for a hat. I would fall terribly short."

Eleanor *tsk*ed and shook her head. "My dear, there is ever so much more to being a duchess than pouring tea."

"Oh, did I forget the witty gossip?" Caroline asked, smoothing the fabric on her lap. "Unfortunately, I am sorely lacking in that ability."

Eleanor appeared ready to say more, but he wanted to get back to the crux of the problem. "You could have refused my offer. It's as simple as that."

"Offer?"

"Yes." He scowled despite trying to remain calm.

"Do you mean the carriage ride, where you informed me that my uncle had accepted your proposal?"

"Exactly." *Informed*? Surely he'd asked.

"Yes, of course. That was the carriage ride we went on after having danced twice at two separate balls. And then, of course, there was the dinner at Lord and Lady Beldons'. I believe you smiled at me from your place across, and considerably up, the table from where I sat."

He cleared his throat, disquieted by her version of events. She couldn't know just how keenly he'd observed her before making his approach, or how closely he'd listened when others spoke of her, or of the thorough dossier his secretary had compiled.

He had not courted her blindly.

"Yes." He nodded. "You sat beside Lord Willhaven and Sir Buttlemen. They spoke highly of your wit."

"How kind of them to give me a reference. Very flattering that you remembered me at all after such short acquaintance."

He sighed deeply. "I'm sorry if I offended you, but you could have called it off at any time."

"I would have, had you appealed to me first. Once you spoke with my uncle, I could not...or at least I thought I could not."

"My dear," Aunt Eleanor broke in, "one cannot force a person to marry in this day and age. There are laws. Forced marriages are not valid."

Caroline's chin rose. "It was more complicated than that. In any event, your grace, I did try to call it off. The one time we walked alone in the garden. Before my maid arrived."

"Yes, I remember that. You asked for more time before the wedding." He nodded.

"Yes. Exactly. With more time, we could have, at the least, gotten to know each other. To see if we would suit."

"That's not crying off and my mind was set. You were the woman I chose to marry."

She lost her starch, throwing her hands in the air, turning on him. "Do you not see how arrogant that is? You 'chose to marry' as if you were the only one who mattered?"

Eleanor rose. "I will leave you to your discussion."

"But Aunt, we haven't made our plans."

"Make them, and inform me in the morning."

"But we need your assistance, as chaperone. If you leave, no one will believe." He gestured toward the duchess's room.

This time Eleanor snorted. "Really, Summerton. This entire household, the whole of England, already considers the deed done." She faced Caroline. "Like it or not, you are a duchess, but cheer up, my dear. I believe you will make a fine one."

"Aunt." He tried to get her to stay.

"No, Summerton. If it's an annulment you are alluding to, nothing short of a physical examination will give you the grounds. Humiliating for both parties and a black smear on this family."

Caroline stood, a steely glint in her eye. She would run at the first opportunity. He had to stem that.

"Eleanor, you already agreed to act as Caroline's companion. All I ask is that you do so as a chaperone." His aunt stopped, stood beside the door. "Give Caroline time to reconsider—"he shifted, "—her aversion to this marriage."

"I see." Eleanor watched them both. "Very well." She nodded. "You will not be the first duke to grant his bride a period of acquaintance. Just see that you do a better job of seducing than you did of courting."

"I will not be seduced." Caroline lifted that chin again.

Eleanor laughed. "We shall see, my dear. We shall see." She opened the door. "You may continue with your bickering now." And left.

Caroline stood by the fire, her long, narrow hands splayed for warmth. "We both know you chose to marry a purse, not a woman at all."

He'd offended her. That he could understand. "To a point, you are correct. St. Martins requires an heiress, but you are incorrect if you thought that limited my options. There are any number of heiresses keen to marry a duke."

"Unfortunately, I was not one," she shot back, leaving his side to sit in the wingback chair, no longer making a show of pushing the hem away. "I would prefer my husband marry me, not what my father provided."

He distanced himself, using the poker to stir the fire as he searched for a way around that harsh reality.

"I met your father once."

"Did you?" He'd surprised her.

"Yes, I was impressed. A crude and harsh man, at least that's how he was among other men. It would have been easy to miss the depths of his mind, but he was a business genius, and a hard-nosed one at that."

She relaxed, her smile rueful. "No doubt he impressed you."

"You don't believe me."

"My father was not an easy man. As you said, crude and harsh." Affection rang in her words. She'd loved her father deeply, despite his flaws.

"He was very smart."

She cocked her head. "He was brilliant," she admitted. "I'm pleased you saw past his rough exterior."

"I wish I could say the same of my father," he admitted.

His father had not been a fool, but he had been no businessman, nor had he been raised to be one. Two generations of dukes had come into the title as younger sons, ill-equipped for the demands of the position.

Summerton's father had claimed their holdings were well-oiled. Nothing to worry about. Nothing to do. Summerton had been a fool not to question him long ago. The enterprises of a duke were vast and complicated and, undoubtedly, overwhelming. They could not be ignored. His father had done just that.

Caroline sighed, bowed her head.

He crouched beside her. "You know, Caroline, we aren't so dissimilar."

She glanced at him without lifting her head.

"We've lost our fathers recently enough to still be wrangling with their legacies and neither of us has had a mother's love."

She studied him carefully, as if the slant of his eyes, the curve of his lips, could discern honesty or guile. She looked away. "That is not why you married me."

"You want to know why I chose you?" He moved to sit opposite her. "You are a beautiful young lady, very well-mannered. I'd not expected that, having met your father."

Her head snapped up and he realized he'd offended her again when he'd only meant to compliment.

"Well-mannered despite my background, you mean." She leaned forward. "Ah, yes. No doubt that would be a theme throughout the marriage. And you ask why I do not wish to be a duchess." She sat back, like a child in a snit.

He didn't quite know how to deal with that. "You are congenial company."

"Congenial company? Like an acquaintance you don't necessarily avoid?"

"You're bright," he offered, realizing he was losing ground.

"Oh, my, thank you for your faint praise. I shall cherish that keepsake forever."

"Fine. You want some godforsaken idyllic romance and I failed to provide it." He rose again, this time to pace. "If that's the case, why did we have to go through the whole masquerade of a wedding?"

She stared at him in disbelief.

"The money, of course. It's the reason you married me, and it's the reason my uncle forced me to marry you."

He threw up his hands. "As my aunt pointed out, no one can be forced to marry. All you had to do was say something."

"You are so naïve." She was back to her regal self, sitting rigidly upright, eyes so hard, he felt as though she were jabbing at him with her finger.

"For every misstep with you, my uncle promised to put down one of my pets. If the marriage was called off, he threatened to drown the lot and fire every one of my father's workers with more than three children and then refuse them a reference." She lifted her chin. "When I informed my uncle I would not marry you, Seigneur Baver disappeared. After I made one attempt to speak with you, Old Jake was let go from the mill. I would not put more lives at risk."

"Except," Summerton reminded her, "Baver is alive, and Old Jake and his family are in a tenants' cottage. So it appears we have been played for fools."

"Old Jake is here?" Again she leaned back, deflated. He frowned over the muddle of his own feelings. He rather liked the girl who dared allow herself to sit against the back of the chair. He needed a woman who did not.

"Yes, Old Jake is here," he confirmed. "I will take you to him tomorrow, but first, where were you going and who was helping you?"

"Manchester, by myself," she said, too quickly.

"That's a lie."

Regal as the queen, she said, "Why ever would you say that?"

Because someone signaled her from the woods and her maid has disappeared. He wasn't ready to admit he knew either of those things until tonight's search came to an end.

"A young lady does not travel cross-country without escort."

"I wasn't traveling as a young lady."

"You would need a companion. Someone to confirm your story. Otherwise you wouldn't have been able to approach a market stall for food or coachmen for tickets or whatever you needed without risking discovery."

She fussed over the closing of the banyan in her lap, tracing the design of the fabric. "I'm very resourceful."

"Humph." He sat back, watching her.

"What will you do with me now?"

"You heard what I said to my aunt."

She wouldn't look at him, her gaze on her long, delicate fingers caressing the silk binding of the robe, much as a child touches a favored blanket. "I'm not certain I understand."

He couldn't tell if she was being coy. "The bridal journey." Her head snapped up. "Surely, you were aware of the bridal journey before tonight."

"That's why she didn't unpack my things?" Her gaze shifted to the duchess's rooms.

"Your abigail?"

"Yes," she turned back, intrigued. "Normally, she'd be busy as a bee unpacking everything, brushing out wrinkles and the like. When we arrived, she barely unpacked."

"You didn't know?" She shook her head, no sign of coy ignorance. "I see. Well..." He'd never suspected she'd been kept in the dark. "We will remain here for three, possibly four days and then go on our bridal tour." This caught her attention. "A promise negotiated with the marriage."

A bloody nuisance with so much to be done here at St. Martins, but he would be paid handsomely to see this through. And see it through he would, especially after their catastrophe of a wedding night.

Which had never happened.

At least not the part he'd anticipated.

Or, to be fair, what she'd anticipated.

"My uncle's way of getting me out of the country and out of his way."

"Do you think so?" he queried. "I was told that your father's greatest wish was for you, his adored daughter, to have the same opportunities as a gentleman on the Grand Tour."

"Oh, dear." She sat back, hand to mouth. "He did say that, quite often. But he was not well enough..."

He thought she might cry, so he looked to Eleanor to intervene. She merely shook her head and signaled for him to continue.

He cleared his throat and stared down at his boots rather than deal with such raw emotion. "The plan has always been to bring Eleanor as a companion." Caroline would need a companion when they reached Vienna, as he was expected to participate in the congress being held there.

He'd not taken his heritage for granted. He'd made a point of being actively involved in the government, preparing for his place in the House of Lords. He had a role to play in Vienna. The whole itinerary had been planned around that.

He looked up to see if she understood. She glared back.

It had been a long night.

"I'll see you to your chamber."

"Thank you, your grace."

"There is a footman stationed outside your rooms, another in the grounds below."

"Comfortable accommodations for a prison."

He didn't respond to that or speak of the dowry. A touchy subject. He wondered if she knew it did not come in one lump sum, but in three parts. The first had been delivered today. An equal amount would be dispersed when they returned from the bridal journey. The third—well, if he failed to win her over by the end of the journey, he would have to consider the very real possibility of not receiving that last allotment, or the promised yearly annuity.

After gaining her promise to marry and negotiating the marriage settlement, he'd worked night and day to design a scheme to rebuild his heritage. All the dominoes were lined up.

During this bridal journey, his men of affairs, secretaries, and stewards had explicit instructions.

A mere start to his plan to save his lands, improve his holdings, and ensure his tenants prospered. His plans stretched far into the future. They would take time, but he'd made them with an eye toward benefitting both husband and wife, and their progeny.

After this fiasco he'd either be a bride-less fool or a foolish groom.

Neither held much appeal.

CHAPTER 4 ~ First Day Welcome

"Summerton!"

Like a gong announcing Caroline's entrance, a large silver serving lid clattered to the floor. The reverberating crash echoed around the dining room.

Hitches scowled at the poor startled servant, as if Caroline's shocking display had not caused the upset. She'd charged into the room like some sort of fishwife.

Embarrassed, but determined not to show it, she stopped halfway to the table and smoothed her skirts with righteous dignity.

Summerton set his paper aside and stood with the utmost solemnity.

Of course he would. Elegant sophisticate. He knew how one behaved. Not a glimmer of reaction to her behavior. Probably expected as much. After all, he'd met her loud and crass father.

She knew better, knew how to behave. Mostly. She'd been trained to keep her early common years neatly tucked inside. But evidence always managed to slip out, in the worst possible ways. At the worst possible times. Especially when she was tired or upset.

It had been an awful, sleepless night. She'd listened to the baying of hounds, watched the sway of lanterns moving through the woods. Summerton's spurious search party, rousting men from their beds to go out, searching, fully aware there was no one to find.

Only, she knew what they didn't. She knew about poor Jeremy. A city lad, spooked by the country. He didn't even like picnics in broad daylight, let alone being chased by a team of hounds and scores of local country men through the woods at night.

Chin lifted, she placed her hands firmly on her hips, arms akimbo, just like that same fishwife. Let him see just how unsuitable she was.

"I hadn't expected to see you, my dear." Summerton bowed, shooing a footman away from pulling out the chair at the far end of the table.

My dear, indeed.

Tired, anxious, and cranky as a toddler without sleep, Caroline crossed to the offending piece of furniture, pulled it out herself, and took a seat. She slipped her serviette from the table, focused on placing it, just so, on her lap.

"You've dismissed my abigail, ordered that I be dressed in a riding habit, and now you forbid me from leaving the Hall?" She looked up then, to meet Summerton's solemn gaze. "You do know that a riding habit is totally inappropriate for breakfast?"

Eyebrow raised, he tilted his head toward the seat beside him. "Would you mind joining me at this end of the table? Preferable to visiting with miles between us."

It was a long way.

"Hardly miles." She stood, with all the regal stature of the top student she had been at St. Ann's Academy. "But as you've dictated so much of my day, who am I to argue with one more edict?"

He refrained from replying, proving himself the better of the two. One never argues in front of the servants.

Drawing nearer, she noted the dark circles beneath his eyes, the weariness. He was as exhausted and pained as she.

"We had a late evening." He pushed in her chair as she sat. "I rather thought you would sleep late this morning."

Caroline cleared her throat, gathered her anger. "Why ever would I do that?" she asked. "You were awake as late as I, and you've already been up and about and seeing to business."

"Ah, yes, well—" he nodded to Hitches, "—if you will serve her grace this morning."

"Of course, your grace." Hitches excused the other servants, taking a cup from a footman, who'd been about to put it in front of Caroline. "We were informed you prefer coffee in the morning," Hitches said, "but if you would like..."

"No." Caroline stopped him, surprised anyone had gone to the trouble of learning her partialities. The duke certainly hadn't. Or had he? "Coffee is perfect."

She breathed in the heady scent before the cup even reached her hands. One sip of the rich dark brew proved Hitches knew more than what she liked. He knew how she liked it. Heaven.

"We favor our coffee strong." Summerton frowned.

"Yes, bracing."

"Too much so?" he asked.

She looked at him sideways, certain he must be joking, before she remembered his comment about expecting her to sleep late. She put the cup down. "Do you imagine that all women are idle and prefer weakly flavored food?"

"No."

Behind him, Hitches moved about the sideboard, preparing a plate. She hoped it was for her. Sleep deprivation made her exceedingly hungry.

Summerton continued. "You are far too intelligent to be idle or to lack the adventure of strong food."

Hitches returned with the plate. "I took the liberty, your grace, of serving you a little of everything but the kippers."

"You are wonderful, Hitches." She held her hands in her lap as he put the plate in place, pretending she did not want to grab the silver and tuck in immediately. "You know my appetite better than I do myself."

He bowed.

"Would you care for more coffee, my dear?" Summerton's expression revealed nothing more this morning than it had last night.

"Yes, I dare say I would."

"Hitches, if you leave us with a small pot, we won't need anything further."

"Your grace."

Eggs, sausages, tomatoes, mushrooms and toast. Caroline made a point of cutting small bites, taking her time to savor what she would rather gulp.

Rather than pick up his papers, Summerton watched her.

"I would not be insulted if you care to read, Summerton," she said as she took a bite.

"I've read enough, thank you."

"Then perhaps—" she smiled sweetly, cutting her sausage, "—you can keep me entertained by telling me why you released my abigail without first consulting me." She popped the bite into her mouth.

He caught her gaze as she slathered marmalade onto a toast point. "Or why you sent strict instructions that I was to wear a riding habit, but refused me the freedom to ride?" She chewed and swallowed.

He lifted the coffee pot and reached for her cup. "Eat your breakfast, my love." He placed the full cup before her.

"Perhaps not." Neatly, carefully, she placed her silverware on her plate. "Aside from the fact that I am not 'your love,' I have a very bad feeling about what you are going to say."

He nodded.

Hunger fled.

"Who is it?"

"What?"

"Who has died?"

"No one has died, Caroline." His much larger, much warmer hand covered hers. "And I did not release Alice. She left."

Caroline pulled free. "But why? When?"

"I sent for your maid last night. Do you remember the interruption during our discussion? That was Hitches arriving with word your abigail has vanished without a trace."

Caroline sat back. "But why?"

"You are certain she didn't know you planned to leave?"

"No," Caroline shook her head. "No. She was my uncle's servant, not mine. She might have suspected I would release her, but I would have given her a reference, seen that she was safe until she found another post."

She felt his scrutiny, looking for truth or lies. It made her clumsy. Made her hands tremble, as though guilty, when she knew she was not.

"Would she have reason to doubt that?" Summerton took her hand again, his thumb brushing the back of it in circles meant to soothe. They did not. Caroline pulled free of him.

"No, I don't think she would doubt that. I'm known to be fair to all employees, even those I do not favor. One must be when employing so many. Otherwise, resentments build."

"I see." He drummed the table. "There is more, Caroline, but I do wish you'd keep eating. You barely touched your dinner last night."

Famished a few bites before, she wasn't sure she could eat another bite.

"Just tell me what it is."

"I did not mean to dictate what you wore, but rather thought to save time. I would like you to ride the estate with me."

"And if I don't ride?"

"You own a riding habit, Caroline, and I trust you are not the sort of woman to waste your time wearing something merely for the sake of appearances."

Perhaps he'd taken more notice of her than she'd realized.

"Thank you. I would like to ride."

"After breakfast," he amended, adding, "And, just so you understand, I did not forbid you from leaving the Hall. The footmen were instructed that I wished to see you, to discuss our ride. They weren't meant to bar your way."

She popped a buttery bit of egg into her mouth, smiling. His defensiveness had put them on more equal footing.

"I will enjoy the ride." It would help her get her bearings. Perhaps they would visit with Old Jake and she might catch sight of Jeremy. He'd not be with Old Jake; bad blood there. Jeremy had wanted to let him go as well. She'd stopped him.

She sighed, wondering if she would have time to pen a note and leave it somewhere for Jeremy, but where? How?

"While we are out, we will look for your dog."

"I beg your pardon?" Caroline asked.

"Seigneur Baver."

She looked up, startled. "My dog?" She blinked.

"He's a bloodhound, Caroline. You know how they can be, following a scent, any scent. He failed to return last night."

"Did he go out with the other dogs?"

Summerton sighed. "He took off before George could get him."

"Baver always comes back," she insisted.

"No doubt you are right," Summerton agreed, "but this is a new home for him. If you call for him as we ride, it might help us find him."

Caroline frowned. He was a bloodhound; scent drew him, not sound. Not calling. It would make no sense for him to run away.

Alice had left and Baver was missing. Neither was a good thing.

She put down her serviette. “I take it my other animals are in the stables. Do you mind if we see them, before we ride out?”

Summerton frowned but nodded.

He escorted her through a grand hallway, beneath a towering foyer and out wide double doors. She’d seen it all the night before, but the scope, the height and greatness of his home, had been diminished by lantern and candle light. The view from the entrance had been hidden as well.

Two stairways curved away from the front porch, arching down, arms reaching as if to embrace anyone walking through. When they’d arrived last night, they’d driven under a portico and then entered on the ground floor. They now stood on a balcony above that portico, looking down at the sweeping view of the drive and parkland beyond. Great tall winged beasts, carved out of stone, loomed over them.

“Goats,” Summerton told her, patting the cloven hoof of one of the statues. “A family beast, signifying victory by negotiation and policy over might.”

“They are on your coat of arms as well.” Her uncle had tried to get her to study the history of her future family. Instead, she’d studied ways of escaping, though she had learned Summerton’s coat of arms by default; it was emblazoned on everything connected to him. “Persuasive speech is in your heritage, then?”

He offered a rueful smile. “Which I failed to employ when I courted you.”

“And the wings? I’ve yet to meet a goat with wings,” she said, instead of reminding him there had been no courtship. Just an announcement of marriage.

A tickle of awareness was her only warning before he moved closer, coming to a stop just behind her. “If I did this with wings—” he wrapped his arms about her, whispered against her ear, “—I would be protecting you.”

Trapping me, she thought, fighting the panic. Not fear of him, but of her. That she liked the feel of him against her, the fence of his arms.

She stepped forward, breaking his hold.

"The grounds..." She cleared her throat, amazed words could escape at all. He really shouldn't stand so close. "Quite extensive."

He moved beside her. "We will ride across the land, and later we can take a carriage to show you the rest." He gestured as he spoke, his long, strong fingers so casually expressive. "This, before you, is merely the entrance park. The drive on either side leads to the north and the sound ends of the village of Hillside."

"I see." She didn't, but needed to move, to distance herself. She headed for the stairs to her left.

He took her elbow. Tilted his head toward the other side. "Stables are this way."

She hurried. He merely lengthened his stride, no doubt a more comfortable step than if he'd had to match her normal pace. "It would have suited us better to go out another door," he admitted, as they walked around a corner without a stable in sight, "but I wanted to give you an idea of St. Martins and her lands."

"It's beautiful." It was, all golden stone.

"If we'd gone the other way, you would have seen the original twelfth century hall. I'm afraid it's in rather bad repair."

"Will it survive?"

With her money, of course. It would take her money.

"One would hope. It bridges the two wings."

On their ride from London the day before, the duke had told her about St. Martins, its history, the family's history. She'd listened, more curious than she would have liked. Today he pointed out actual places he'd referred to.

"Do you remember what I told you of the last battle waged at St. Martins?"

"You said horses grazed in the field now, but artifacts, bits of arrow, shards of pottery, still work their way to the surface."

"Precisely," he pointed, "out there."

Interested despite herself, she looked at a fenced area surrounding rich green grass and animals, their muzzles to the grass, scattered throughout. Lovely and peaceful and...she stopped, tilting her head, startled by an entirely different 'old thing' in the paddock. Fingers pressed to lips, she whispered against them. "Socks?"

Her old pony lifted its head, as though it had heard the bare breath of its name. Caroline whistled, lifted her skirt and ran to the fence.

"Look at you, old boy," she crooned, hanging over the fence rail, tears in her eyes as the old pony made his arthritic way to her. "He was my first, you know." She deigned to look over her shoulder, offering the duke a fleeting moment of consideration.

"He's been about a few years, then," Summerton said, straight-faced, smiling and backing off when Caroline swatted at him.

"Socks is still a good animal."

"No doubt," he allowed, though he didn't look like he believed it.

If she left—without Socks, without Parrot, without any of her animals—he would probably have them sent to the knacker's yard. If she went on this bridal journey, she might be able to negotiate for him to keep them. Especially if she didn't quibble over her dowry. She had no need of it.

A flouncing bundle of strawberry-blond curls rushed up to her, jumping and wagging its rump.

"Goldie?" Caroline laughed, kneeling down. "Goldie!"

The cocker spaniel burrowed against her legs. "I thought you were gone."

She looked at Summerton. "Goldie was the third animal my uncle took."

The duke merely raised an eyebrow. Of course he would know which animals had been sent and when.

She crouched down for a good cuddle. “Oh, pew! You stink,” she murmured, and pushed the dog away, standing up, brushing residue from her hands and skirts. “She lives indoors, your grace. The outdoors offers too many ripe situations.”

“Does she? I don’t think she minds being in the barns. The horses tolerate her and the grooms, it seems, rather like her.”

As if to prove his point, Goldie darted off to be greeted with enthusiasm by a stable boy.

“She only has one ear,” the duke remarked.

“What difference does an ear make?” Caroline asked.

He didn’t bother to respond, but gestured to a pretty little mare. “And what of this mount?”

Caroline didn’t move at first, just looked.

“She’s yours,” Summerton assured her.

“She’s a beauty.” It was an understatement. The mare had a glistening caramel coat. Caroline approached slowly.

“She’s right good-natured,” the groomsman promised.

“No doubt she is.” Caroline reached up, her hand on the mare’s forelock, and stroked the long muzzle.

Summerton came up beside her. “She is good-natured, but spirited as well. She won’t be dull, but you should be able to handle her.”

“Thank you, she’s wonderful.” Caroline pulled a bit of sugar she’d hidden, offering it to the mare. “Is this like breakfast?”

“Breakfast?”

“Someone has already looked into how well I can ride, into what I can handle?” she asked.

“We wanted to make you feel welcomed. Do you find it intrusive?” he asked, genuinely curious.

“No, not in the least,” she lied.

"Do you want to get to know her better, or shall we go?" he asked.

"Oh, let's go!" More and more she realized how brilliant his suggestion had been. A good bracing ride on a beautiful day. She followed the groom to the mounting block. "What is her name?" she asked.

"That's for you to decide. She's my wedding gift to you." Summerton explained as he mounted a large black stallion.

"Wedding gift?"

A shrill screech rang from inside the stables. "Lift them skirts, girlie!"

Wide-eyed, Caroline hurried up the steps of the mounting block, refusing to look at Summerton, and settled into her sidesaddle.

"And he popped into a hole, hehehehe."

She slid a glance at the duke.

Eyes sparkling, he bowed from atop his mount. "Your parrot," he explained.

"I see." Which she did, indeed. She knew this bird and its litany of verses, a little too well.

With serious hauteur, she said, "Should you have any young ladies in this vicinity, I would recommend a blanket, your grace."

"A blanket?"

She nodded, facing forward. "If you cover his cage, he thinks it is night and will quiet down. We've employed that method any number of times."

"I'm quite certain you have," he agreed, as the parrot trilled, "and he popped into a hole. Hehehehe."

Caroline spurred her mount forward.

CHAPTER 5 ~ Death Comes to St. Martins

They rode up to a small group of ramshackle buildings. Summerton shifted in his saddle, shamed even as he was determined. He'd had no choice but to bring Caroline along. He could only hope she'd ignore her surroundings. Ladies of his acquaintance would accept these 'cottages' as something so far beneath them, they needn't pay attention.

Except poverty was no distant beast for Caroline. Her father may have left it behind him, but a man's history sticks to his shoes. His child would know of it.

If they'd had a proper wedding night, he would have excused himself, leaving Caroline to adjust to being a wife, a duchess, in the comfort of the Hall. But they hadn't had a wedding night and he didn't dare leave her alone. She wanted courting. Unfortunately, that meant having her accompany him on a visit to his tenants.

Caroline reined in the mare she'd named Boudicca, stopping just outside the large communal yard. "Surely these are not your tenants' homes." And smiled, as if she'd asked a foolish question.

His lips tightened, neck muscles bunched. She lost her smile.

Fine, let her know what she would leave undone, if she ran. "You fault me for considering your dowry. Tell me, what would you do?"

Boudicca tossed her head as Caroline's fingers turned white, clenching the reins.

A group of young girls stood around a well at the center of the yard. Small windows, tidy yards and side gardens disguised the decay, but only to a point. Caroline saw beyond that. "I've seen better chicken coops," she whispered for him alone. "Your people deserve to live in better conditions." Her harsh words sliced deep.

"Yes," he admitted, "they do." Because they did. He knew that.

That was the crux of the matter. He needed her money, needed to keep this marriage together, when his pride wanted nothing more than to send her packing. After all, she didn't want him. But he would have to live with that because he needed her for his tenants, to improve outdated farming and animal husbandry.

To provide a future for his children.

Their children.

He settled in his saddle once again.

Men pulling braces up, tucking in shirts; women holding babies on their hips; children clinging to their mothers' skirts, stepping over thresholds, walking down short paths to the area around the well.

The men would have been up and out, working at dawn, back for their morning repast. Summerton had hoped to catch them exactly at this point. Well awake, satisfied from a meal.

"Your grace." The men doffed hats. The women offered curtsies. Summerton dismounted, helped Caroline to the ground.

"I'll hold the lead, your grace," one man offered. Summerton nodded, turned to introduce his bride, but she was already on her knees, risking her cashmere skirts in the dust and dirt, coaxing a little girl to come closer.

"And who are you?" The little one cringed back, thumb securely tucked in her mouth. When that failed to get a response, she turned to a young boy. "What's your name?"

"Tommy." He kicked the dirt, and a chunk broke loose and hit Caroline.

"Here, now!" a woman chastised.

"No harm done," Caroline said, as she stood, swiped the dust from her skirt, looked about the swarm of people. Again, she cut off his attempt to introduce her by leaning down to the boy.

"Tommy, I wonder if you could help me? You see, I've lost my dog. An old hound, far more skin than body, and long droopy ears."

"A dog?"

"Yes." Caroline nodded to the woman who had scolded Tommy. "Is this your son?"

The woman curtsied. "Yes, your ladyship."

"Your grace," Summerton corrected, earning a quick, censoring glance from Caroline. "This is my bride, the Duchess of Summerton." He'd let her scowl, but she wasn't doing anyone favors by pretending to be someone else. The people would feel abused by such games. "We were married yesterday and she insisted on meeting you today."

That wiped the scowl away. Caroline held her hand out to the woman. "And you are?"

The woman curtsied again, staring at Caroline's hand as if it weren't real. "Betty, your grace. My Tommy can help you find the dog. He loves dogs."

"Caroline," Summerton interrupted, handing her a bundle of peppermint sticks wrapped in a cloth. "For the children. To celebrate our marriage." Winning the parents would not be so easy, but candy worked miracles with children.

Even the shyest of them squealed and crowded in on Caroline. She laughed, the first time he'd heard her do so. The sound was as rich and warming as her voice.

"Your grace." A man stepped forward, breaking through the excitement. "I heard howls when I went to check my traps. Early this morning."

"Traps?" Caroline asked.

"All legal, with the duke's permission, like. Trap game for the big house," he explained.

Caroline wouldn't care about poaching, but she would care if her dog was caught in one of those traps.

"Did you hear this anywhere near your traps, or was it in the distance?" the duke asked.

"No, your grace, it was a fair good walk. Told Old George when he came through asking about the hound."

"Ah, well." He gestured for Caroline to remount. "We will go see what we can find."

"I can take you," the man offered.

"Good." He didn't ask if others might have been trapping further in the woods. Of course they would poach. The valley was hungry. The Summertons had brought this down on themselves.

One of the boys waved his candy stick and shouted, "I heard howling, too. I went with me da. It's out in the woods this way." And with that, he darted toward a path.

"I heard it, too," Tommy cried, following him. "Petey and I was together."

As Summerton formed a cradle with his hands, to help Caroline back into the saddle, she leaned close. "Sweets do not a belly fill."

"I'm well aware of that." He lifted her up, too high for whispered words. "Apology for a late start."

She gave him a quick bow, tipping her neat little top hat, and turned her mount to follow the mass of children now leading them down the path. Although an older boy, Jack, offered to give him a boost, he decided to walk with the men. It appeared the whole neighborhood had nothing better to do than follow.

"Old Tom, the steward, says we're to build new cottages," one hunched old man said.

Summerton nodded. "Yes, that's right. He'll bring in some men from the village to help."

"With indoor pumps?"

"That's right."

"Who are these cottages for?"

Summerton stopped. "For you, of course." He looked at the solemn faces around him. "For all of you. Your cottages are barely standing, the roofs are leaking, you've no water inside..." but he stopped. One woman buried her face in her apron, and the men held their caps in front of their chests.

"After the farms are improved?" someone asked.

Tapping his leg with his crop, Summerton tried to explain. "There are changes to come, yes. One step at a time."

Of course, if Caroline were to leave—and he thought she just might—he'd lose all but the first payment of her dowry. He'd filled his part of the bargain, so he'd not return the funds that had been allocated with the wedding. But the rest would have to be forfeited, and he would not be free to find another heiress. He and Caroline were married, after all. Her leaving would not change that fact.

An annulment, divorce, would mean years of legal battles. Expensive legal battles. Without the rest of the dowry and the promised annuity, there was only so much he could do for his tenants.

At least Caroline seemed open to going on the Grand Tour, which would secure him the second installment of the dowry. Improvements to the tenants' cottages would have to wait until then. Without the farm working properly, there would be no point to tenants' cottages at all—it was simple as that.

One of the farmers spit. "Aye, I'll admit, you've been fairing things up. But your father had a way of making nice promises and then nothing. We'll see," he said, and turned back the way he had come. "Time will have the truth of it." The others studied him for a second before stalking off, too.

He recognized their needs, something his father and grandfather had failed to do. He stopped, reins in his hand, and turned to follow them, but a shout had him looking back.

"Baver!" Caroline called.

Then he heard it: a low, eerie howl.

"Caroline," he shouted, stunned she'd ridden so far ahead.

The men may have left, but Jack, the lad, had not abandoned him. He stepped up, offered his cupped hands. Summerton used them to leap onto his mount. "Caroline, wait," he spurred his mount on. "That could be anything."

She slowed, but he suspected the low branches she had to maneuver through were the cause, rather than his request.

"That's coming from quite a ways off." He gained on her.

"No, not far, *weak*." She urged her horse on, calling, "Baver, Baver!"

The loud clamor of children grew dim as he and Caroline moved swiftly along the narrowing path. They took turns and curves, following the hillside. Both had to duck under and leap over branches blocking a path rarely used and then only for walking.

He wished she'd slow down, but he knew she wouldn't. She was a woman of action.

The dog's wail was akin to someone shouting with a sore throat, as if he'd been baying for hours.

Caroline rounded a steep bank, out of his sight, and let loose a wild cry, worsened by the wrenching whinny of her mount. Each silenced in a heartbeat. He made the bend, dismounting in one, to find Caroline standing beside a nervous prancing Boudicca, George barring her path.

Quiet, but for the heavy blowing of Caroline's mount, its hooves stomping at the dirt path.

The dog's howls were louder in the silence.

"Where is he?" Caroline demanded. "Where is Baver?"

"Youse can't go further, m'lady. I'm sorry." George waved his arms about, hat scrunched in one fist. "You must stop her, your grace. It's not for a lady. Then youse best come with me."

"What is it?" Caroline commanded. "What has happened to my dog?"

"Your dog is fine, lass. Worn out by calling for help, but fine nonetheless." As if to confirm his words, Baver, ears flopping with his jolting movements, rumbled up to Carline.

George sidestepped the reunion, twisted his hat. "It's the lass what's dead," George bemoaned. "There's naught you can do, but his grace had best come see."

"Someone's dead?" Impossible. He'd heard wrong.

"Dead?" Caroline pushed forward, but Summerton stepped in her way, raising an eyebrow at George, warning him not to say another word.

"Nobody's dead. An old cow we've been missing, that's all." He hoped that was all. "Baver needs you. Poor old boy looks done in." He studied the lay of the land. "With all the rains lately, the creek has some water." He pointed to a thin trickle running along the path. "He needs a drink. I'll see what this is about."

Her concern for her animals might actually induce her to do as he asked. At least, he hoped it would.

He followed George up the gentle rise of the embankment to a flat lay of land, overlooking the road.

A young lady lay in the small clearing, beneath a huge oak. Her skirts, bunched up as though she'd fallen. Not hiked up, so no suggestion of interference. Not that he'd ever seen a dead woman, let alone one with an odd tangle of skirts.

Multiple skirts. Thick layers of them.

"George, is she wearing too many garments?"

"Looks to be so, your grace," George mumbled.

He knelt down and lifted layer after layer. The outermost was a cloak. Stylish, well-made, but far too heavy for this time of year, even with the cool temperatures. Below that were garments of finer fabric. Sheer muslin, fine silk, exquisite embroidery.

He'd seen that embroidery before, on Caroline.

"Your grace," George said, and pointed toward the woman's head.

A noose rounded her bruised neck, the length of it frayed and broken, probably by the weight of her. Her eyes bulged in her purple face, and her tongue was out.

A branch snapped behind him just as he laid his monogramed handkerchief over the girl's face.

"It is a dead body," his bride whispered. "How awful! Do you know who it is?"

He stood, took her by the shoulders, tried to turn her away. "Please, see to the dog."

She refused. "I got him to the creek. He's fine. He's done his work, getting us here."

"You don't want to see this," he warned.

She stood firm, looked at him directly. "If I can help, I will. I've seen the dead before, unpleasant deaths as well." The children's voices reached them, laughing and teasing as they neared. "But the children shouldn't see this. When they get here, we'll have them take Baver back, but they are a ways off yet. For now, who is she?"

He studied the bruised look beneath her eyes, the strain at the corners of them. She was exhausted, but not so weary as to let the regal tilt of her head slip or the firm line of her lips to soften. She didn't push or fight him, but he knew she would not back down.

"You said your abigail did not know of your plans," he said.

She sucked in a small breath, nothing more, and shook her head. "She did not know."

The evidence proved otherwise. He gestured to the corpse. "I believe this is your Alice."

"Alice? But that's not possible." Caroline pushed past him, past George, who looked aghast that he could not stop her from approaching the body. She crouched, her hand on the fallen figure.

"Are you certain she is dead?" she asked.

George grumbled something Summerton couldn't understand. He didn't ask him to elaborate anymore than he tried to respond to Caroline. She knew the truth of it, just needed a few moments to reconcile expectation and reality.

"Why do you think this is Alice?" she asked, frowning, studying the dress. "This looks familiar, but Alice is much smaller. She's thin as a rake."

Summerton hunched down beside her and lifting one hem after another, revealing finer and finer quality of clothes. Caroline fell back and sat on the ground, bewildered. Or doing a fine imitation of appearing that way. He wasn't quite sure what to believe.

"Those are my dresses."

"I rather gathered that."

"But why?" she asked, then gasped. "Oh dear, that does explain..."

He watched, waited for her to finish. "Explain what?"

She shook her head, moved to lift the handkerchief. He stilled her hand, felt the coldness she'd hidden. Whatever her plan had been last night, this was not part of it. She was fighting shock.

"You don't want to see," he told her.

"I want to be sure it's her," Caroline told him.

"It's not pretty."

"Brutal death rarely is, but as I said, I've seen my share—limbs torn off, workers crushed. Factories can be very dangerous places."

He held her hand a beat longer, to instill some warmth, then let go. She lifted the kerchief. Tears blossomed. Reverently, she lowered the cloth.

"I didn't much care for her; she was a meager-minded soul, but no one deserves to have their life taken this way."

"Hung herself," George corrected.

"No." Caroline and Summerton responded as one.

"Clear as the lines on my face," he argued. "See here's the rope, there's the rest of it up there." He pointed to a heavy branch above them, a length of rope coiled and tied around it. "She were too heavy, and it broke," he pointed to the frayed ends. "See?"

"I don't think so," Summerton argued, interested to see Caroline shaking her head right along with him. "She did not do this to herself."

"Why not?" George demanded, clearly baffled.

"Rudimentary, to a lady." Caroline explained. "She'd not bother to steal my clothes to kill herself. She had other plans."

"There is that," Summerton added. "Plus, her hands are behind her back. No doubt tied. It's not a natural way to land."

"Of course!" Caroline's hand went to her mouth, "She couldn't tie her own hands behind her back." She plunked down on her backside. "Summerton, this is terrible. Who would have done this to her?"

He put a hand on her shoulder. "Perhaps you'd best go back to Drool."

"Baver," she answered by rote, her mind fixed on her abigail's fate. "This doesn't make sense. Why would she have left in the first place? Surely a few dresses wouldn't have made her life any easier than a good reference and another position."

The men exchanged a look.

"What?" she demanded, with that regal air of hers.

He wasn't about to tell her how a couple of pretty dresses could help a girl enter the oldest of professions.

"At this point," he attempted to distract her, "It's all conjecture." He gestured to George. "Tilt her on her side, will you, let's see her hands."

George crouched down, hefting the stiff figure, tilting her on her side so she faced Caroline and Summerton. They kept her from falling all the way over.

"She's so cold." Caroline shuddered. He wanted to soothe her, but George spoke at the same time.

"You're right, your grace, hands tied behind her. Poor lass." The groundsman cut through the bindings. Caroline's lips pressed tight. "Fingers loaded down with rings, they are."

"Interesting." She was either stealing from Caroline or transporting for her.

"My rings, do you suppose?" Caroline asked, the strain disappearing as curiosity had her leaning over the body to see.

"She's stiff as a board, don't know if I can move them," George announced, laying Alice down on her back.

Caroline turned away, as if she couldn't bear to keep looking.

"The children should be here soon. Why don't you go wait with Baver?" he suggested.

"Yes," she said, meek as could be. She was starting to believe it had happened.

"I'll accompany you," he told her, "just let me give some instructions to George."

"Poor old hound's been howling all night, trying to get someone's attention," the old man said.

"Stay with her, George," Summerton gestured toward the corpse, "until Tom can come out here with some men and a cart. The magistrate will have to be informed." Summerton sighed.

"You might as well tell Lady Eleanor. She'll be in her element with somethin' like this."

"I dare say you are right," he agreed. Daughter of a magistrate, married to a magistrate, his aunt had been exposed to more than one murder and solved her share, though the men had always taken the credit. "She does have rather a talent for this sort of thing."

He only wished she didn't need to use it when he was supposed to be courting his bride.

The past two days had been full of surprises and none of them good.

CHAPTER 6 ~ Discontents

The rings were hers, though not her best pieces. Those would have been kept in her uncle's safe. Or had they been transferred to Summerton's keeping? Caroline brushed the thought aside. It was of no consequence other than as another piece of the puzzle.

Why would someone have killed Alice? And what had she been thinking, running away into the woods?

As Caroline herself had tried to do.

Summerton had not been shy of reminding her just how dangerous it was for a young lady to run—alone—into the woods. He couldn't know that Jeremy had signaled her with a candle. That she had Jeremy to keep her safe.

Except now, she had to wonder, if the signal had come from Jeremy...or someone waiting for Alice?

Summerton had a point. Perhaps it was a good thing her escape had failed. She looked at him, strong and firm despite the troubles that beset him. He would be a wonderful husband for some woman, even if he was a duke.

The magistrate had brought in the jewelry found on Alice, and Lady Eleanor was sifting through it on a table in the study.

Caroline meant to look, too, but Summerton proved the stronger draw.

He stood, so alone, hands clasped behind his back, looking out over the grounds.

She didn't have a high opinion of the aristocracy. She'd borne the brunt of too many slights and pranks at St. Ann's. Even more vicious for their subtlety, out in society. They dared to ridicule her father for his success.

Aristocrats who did nothing, yet expected all manner of toadying. All of them disdaining any sort of work, expecting others to kowtow to them. She thought not.

Summerton, darkly stoic, facing a world of worry, seemed so different from them. He recognized her father's brilliance. He saw through the stink of trade. But she would do well to remember he was part of the ton. The pinnacle. Her birthright would bring censure on them both.

A man could, would, ignore such things. She could not. The women of the ton would never allow it. She'd stepped beyond bounds by marrying above her station.

Their marriage would never suit.

She rather wished he weren't a duke.

Eleanor tapped her arm, pulling her back to the jewelry.

"That piece is mine," Eleanor exclaimed, holding up a small ring. She studied it, clasped it in her fist, held it to her chest. A dear, precious object. "I know it's not much—" her eyes misted, "—but Francis gave it to me one summer shortly after we met. Just a little trinket from a village fair. It is one of my favorites. However do you think the girl found it?"

Summerton turned, frowning. "One of the rings is yours?"

"Yes," Lady Eleanor nodded. "And another." She rummaged through the collection of rings and brooches the physician and magistrate had found on the body. "Is this yours, Lady Caroline?" Eleanor held out a linked group of silver bands. "It's a puzzle ring. Have you ever had one?"

Caroline shook her head. Eleanor twisted and turned the linked bands until they slipped together, forming a single ring.

"Alice has never taken anything from me before." Caroline hesitated, picking up a small pinkie ring. "Not that I knew about, anyway, but this looks like Louisa Peppy's ring."

"Do you keep a close eye on pieces of little value?" Summerton joined them. "Could she have been gathering things like that for a while?"

Caroline turned away. "I don't know. Louisa only visited once, after our engagement." She bit her lip. "If this went missing then, I never heard of it."

"But it's not an expensive piece."

"No, it isn't." Caroline shook her head. "Perhaps Alice thought I would let her go, without reference, once I married. That's all I can think. I've been distracted since the engagement, so she might have started stealing then. I wouldn't have noticed except..."

Eleanor harrumphed. "Summerton, you may think these are of little value, but such things are in the eye of the beholder." She looked at the two rings in her hand, then wandered over to a wing-back chair by the fire and sat down, awash in memories.

Caroline could feel Summerton watching her. If she found Jeremy, she might be able to get answers. He may have seen Alice, or spoken with her.

"Except 'what,' Caroline?"

She shook her head and dropped the jewelry. "Alice was odd last night, that's all. She told me it was tradition for a bride to soak in a scented bath for hours. Who stays in a bath for so long?" She threw up her hands, let them drop."But she claimed it a tradition, to relax a bride." Caroline had been determined to play the dutiful bride, rather than risk suspicion that she would run away. "I finally insisted on getting out." Alice had not been pleased.

"The water would be dreadfully cold."

"No," Caroline explained, "she kept water on the fire, heated it at any sign of cooling. While I soaked, she moved about the room, left a number of times."

She took a seat in the chair opposite Eleanor, but leaned toward Summerton to explain. "When I first saw my cloak, the dresses, I thought she'd designed her plan last night, as I soaked, but the cloak..." She sat back. "The magistrate said there were pockets, quite a few, sewed into the cloak. That had to have been made in advance."

"She filled them with these baubles—" Summerton gestured to the table, "—and other things. We suspect she was partially robbed."

"What makes you think that, Summerton?" Eleanor asked.

"She had the jewelry, but no money. Surely she would have taken her savings with her. And a couple of pockets were torn."

"Your search might have scared him off before he could find more," Caroline offered.

"If it *was* a him."

"Surely you don't think it could have been a woman?" Eleanor exclaimed.

Summerton pushed away from the desk so he could better examine the jewelry. "No, not really. But it begs to be answered whether it is the work of more than one."

"Oh." Eleanor looked at the fire. "Oh, I see."

Caroline bowed her head. "Poor Alice. Poor misguided Alice."

"It could have been you, Caroline," Summerton said, not for the first time. Not as a reprimand, but rather as if he couldn't quite fathom the idea. "Was she transporting your clothes for you? Your jewelry?"

Ah, the real question. She had been wondering when he would ask her. She sighed, because it didn't matter what she said. Unless they found another reason for Alice's actions, his suspicions made sense.

"No." Caroline shook her head. "No, I did not ask her to help me. It is as I told you, she was working for my uncle. She would have told him and something would have been done to stop me. He wants this marriage very, very badly."

"And what could he do, Caroline, if Alice had told him?"

She looked at the fire. "He would make certain Alice kept me here."

Eleanor lifted her head. "I met your uncle once. A charming man. Very congenial."

Caroline didn't quite know how to respond. She'd always rather liked her uncle, too...until recently. He made people smile and there was always a twinkle in his eyes. Ladies adored him, though he had never married. Her father kept him close, despite his lack of interest in, or acumen for, business.

But now that her father was gone, her uncle had taken over everything.

And everything suffered, especially the mills.

Too many hours demanded of the overworked, resulting in too many ghastly accidents. Money drained from the coffers. Soon they would be turning workers away, with heavier burdens on those who remained.

Caroline knew she could make things right. She knew how to look into the books, how to organize employees, find solutions. She'd learned at her father's knee.

But her Uncle Robert had chosen to honor a misguided promise to her father rather than listen to her. Caroline would be a boring lady of leisure, married to an aristocrat.

He'd go to any lengths to secure those plans. Desperate, even. Or so she had thought.

Caroline shook her head, more confused now than ever. Her animals were safe and well cared for, but her abigail was dead.

"Summerton," she said, deciding it was Summerton's turn to be accused, "the state of those cottages is untenable."

"I have to agree," Eleanor added. "The former dukes should be horsewhipped. Really!" she huffed. "I went down to see to Kip's wife and though she keeps that sty of theirs neat as a pin, it's in deplorable condition."

"Yes, I know. I saw for myself."

"Didn't you have any idea?" Caroline asked.

He'd returned to the window, his back to them. He shook his head. "Not until this spring. No idea," he murmured, barely loud enough for them to hear.

This was painful for him, she understood. He would not want to talk about this any more than she wanted to speak of her uncle, but at least they could have some hope of improving life for his tenants.

"Worse, they don't trust you." Her needling worked—he turned, but his face remained in shadow. She explained. "You know how the people followed...the body, Alice, back to the Hall? I was helping one of the little ones tie his shoes by the well. The women didn't realize I was there." She hesitated, knowing she'd have to tell him at some point, not quite ready to do it now.

"Go on."

"One of the women said you planned to start on the cottages in three years. Three years! Why ever would you wait?"

"We will get to that," he offered, "but what were their reactions? Were they pleased?"

Caroline rose and returned to the table to sift through the jewelry. "They didn't quite believe it," she told him, without conveying the contempt of their disbelief. *Three years from Doomsday?* one had asked. *Just like his father*, another said. *These cottages won't last that long*, the third quipped.

They hadn't been intimidated when Caroline announced her presence by standing up, nor did they attempt to apologize. And why should they? Their opinions had been hard earned.

"I'm afraid I made a promise to them," she told Summerton.

He stepped toward her, stopped, turned away before turning back. Obviously, he didn't like being cornered, though he refrained from shouting. Barely. His jaw flexed with the suppression.

Her father would have ranted and raved. She knew how to stand up to verbal bellows. She didn't know how to deal with Summerton's quiet resistance.

"Just what did you promise them?" he finally asked.

Caroline faced him head on. "I told them you were an honorable man and their homes would be rebuilt. I explained you were preparing them for the delay because it takes time to build new."

"You told them I am an honorable man?" He frowned. "This from the bride who ran away?"

Caroline sniffed and turned back to the table. "And I said someone would be down this week to look into the matter."

"Bravo, Lady Caroline, bravo!" Eleanor smiled.

"You think so, Aunt?" Summerton snapped. "And just how shall we pay this someone? And what will happen when we fail to follow through? Do you think they will be any happier about that?"

She jerked back, offended. He had her money. Money she could use herself, to fix the mess her uncle had created of her father's empire. "You did receive a settlement upon our marriage."

His mouth quirked up on one side. "I received a partial settlement," he informed her. "The funds will arrive in installments. The first will be used on the infrastructure of the farms. Without the farms, there will be no need of tenants or tenant cottages."

"That doesn't make sense." She shook her head. "Father secured my marriage funds, to be dispensed on my wedding day. I would not have left until that was done." Now she paced. "I knew you needed the funds. I thought once you had your money and Uncle Robert received his percentage, no one would much care what happened to me."

Eleanor actually gasped. "And what about an heir?"

"He married me for money. There was nothing said about heirs," Caroline reminded her. "Some other woman can provide those."

She didn't want to think of that, so she focused on the vein that stood out on Summerton's forehead. Restraint was not always a healthy thing. She shouldn't have been so blunt, but there it was. He was being married for a title and she was being married for her money.

But not an heir.

Would she have stayed if it had been the other way around?

It didn't matter. It was what it was. He had been promised funds that her uncle could not touch, no matter the state of the businesses.

Unless Uncle Robert had found a way to release them for himself.

But he wouldn't, couldn't, her father had been far more clever in such things than Uncle Robert. Surely the money was in trust. Summerton would have delved into that, or should have, but by the looks of things, securing finances was not a family strong point.

"So there is nothing in this arrangement to your benefit?" he asked.

"Very little," she whispered, not meaning to speak at all.

He turned from the window. "But there is something?"

"No. I really don't see any need for me to stay here. Uncle Robert's pressure couldn't be denied. He received a percentage, you see, the amount dependent on my marrying an aristocrat. He was very determined it would come to that."

Again, Lady Eleanor shook her head. "Be that as it may, you are married, Caroline. It would be a very ugly business to undo this."

"Surely, once the funds are dispersed, there is no need of me."

Lady Eleanor slapped the chair arm of her chair. "You forget the heir, carrying on the line."

"Stop, Aunt. I will not have Caroline put in an untenable position. We will come to that when we must. For now—" Summerton started to pace, "—your dowry is secure, Caroline. My men are assured of that. But your uncle insisted on three equal stages. The first was the marriage, the second was the completion of a bridal tour, and the third was the conception of a child."

"Good grief." Caroline sat back.

"If the third came before the completion of the second, we would be free to return immediately and all funds would be released to us."

Caroline tapped the arm of her chair and looked blankly at the floor. She would have to see the documents, look for holes. "What if I never conceived?"

She glanced up to see both aunt and nephew looking at her, he with his eyebrow raised. "Well, it does happen," she defended.

Summerton nodded, crossed to the globe, spun it as though that could dispel his worries. "There is a provision for that, but we need not cross that bridge at this point."

Her thoughts returned to his tenants' ramshackle homes, threadbare clothes, and deep hostility.

She thought of the mills, and all the people there who needed her assistance.

She could mend the problems at the mills and help hundreds of people.

She could take ownership of the problems Summerton faced, and help a whole village.

She couldn't do both.

"Did he give you enough to mend the roofs?"

There was another chair beside hers. Summerton took it, took her hand. "Right now, this is not your worry."

"Summerton," she demanded, without raising her voice, "do you have those funds?"

He sighed, his unfocused gaze on their joined hands, his thumb absently stroking hers, unsettling her.

She tried to pull away, but he firmed his grasp and looked into her eyes. "The tenants are my concern, and I take that very seriously, but I will ask that you not make promises out of hand."

"Summerton," Lady Eleanor stood by the fire, holding her newly found rings. "I suggest you talk to her about your plans. There is a distinct advantage to marrying a woman of her background. No doubt Caroline can hear of business without going glassy-eyed."

"Aunt Eleanor."

"Don't 'aunt' me. Do it." She turned to leave.

"Where are you going?" Summerton asked.

"To see if Jenny, my abigail," she clarified for Caroline, "might know how this Alice person could possibly get two of my favorite rings within hours of arriving at St. Martins. It's inconceivable." She opened the door for herself. "And then I will have my afternoon rest."

"Very well," Summerton allowed.

"And while I am resting, take your bride for a carriage ride while you explain your plans for improvement."

"Really, there's no need," Caroline argued. She did not want to be distracted from her course.

"Yes, there is," Eleanor informed her. "Your decision will affect many people, my dear, and you best see what that means." She started to leave, then twisted around and popped her head around the door. "And Summerton, be frank. There's no valor in skirting the issue."

With that, the door snapped shut.

CHAPTER 7 ~ Getting to Know You and Yours

The open wicker gig was clean—mostly—though a bit of dried mud clogged the corners and the seat was worn on the edges. Things Summerton would have ignored during past visits to the country. One must expect a bit of dirt when rusticating.

As if living in a Hall that had grown well beyond its medieval origins was rusticating. It shouldn't be. He'd not realized that until now, in his present company.

St. Martins Hall had always been the place he visited with his gentlemen friends. Here they were free from the demands of women and society. It was a place where a man could leave his cravat behind, ride with his hounds, and practice archery and fencing in an open shirt, sleeves rolled up. A place where a group of men could finish bottles of brandy over a card table deep into the night. No need to curb their language or navigate their way home when foxed.

With its square Norman core and Tudor wings, St. Martins had always been a temporary destination. The London townhouse was his true residence.

He glanced over at Caroline, the woman he'd chosen to live at St. Martins. He'd never thought of her changing things, but she would, if she stayed. Women were like that.

If she stayed.

She sat beside him, cool and straight backed without being rigid. Her gracious, regal manners were one of the things that had drawn him to her and made him believe her background could be ignored.

She'd been raised by two men as different as chalk and cheese. A socially offensive but brilliant father, and an undeniably common uncle, who could charm his way past social barriers.

Then there was Caroline—more aristocratic than the aristocrats. Yet she had no wish to leave the culture of her youth. If that had been the case, she wouldn't shy from being a duchess.

He maneuvered the gig along the tree-lined drive that would take them through the gates of St. Martins to the edge of the village, Hillside. He'd turn there, along the road that bordered the estate, to show her the vastness of his ancestral home.

He would see if that would win this green-eyed beauty. Or would she tilt that petite chin of hers, slicing him with a look over those high cheekbones of hers? Right now, her eyes were shielded by her thick lashes, lowered as she studied her hands clasped in her lap.

She hadn't agreed to stay with him. Not yet. Perhaps never. But she would join him on the journey. She would give him time. All he needed to do was find her weakness.

It wasn't him.

He held nothing of value for her.

The horse shied, so he loosened his grip, relaxing hands that had fisted with frustration.

Nothing of value for her.

Without her, he would be a duke in name only. That wasn't her fault. He'd been a fool to trust his father's claim that the estates ran themselves. He had appreciated the freedom to follow his interests at Whitehall while he could.

They lived well in London. His allowance was healthy and never delinquent. If he needed more, the funds were there.

He'd had no idea there were mortgages upon mortgages. That the whole estate sat on a precipice of loans.

New cottages? There would be no need for cottages if he didn't shore up the crumbling foundation of the whole damn thing. The Dukes of Summerton had estates across England and every one was too ravaged to sell without tremendous loss, too grand to hold onto.

They might be out of a home, all of them, even himself, if he didn't pay off the mortgages and get his affairs running profitably again.

There was an incredible amount to do before they left, even with just a third of the promised funds available, yet here he sat in a gig, riding with a woman who held the future of his estates, his workers, his name, in her hands.

And she didn't want him.

Worse yet, he respected her for it. She was strong and sensible and thought for herself. She'd make an excellent duchess. Unfortunately, the only thing he could offer her was the hope of a secure future and himself, as a man.

Any other time, he might have enjoyed that challenge, but he was too desperate to trust that 'he' was any kind of bargain.

"Oh, look." Caroline put a hand to his arm.

They were just leaving the gates of St. Martins. Hillside High Street was to their right, the path he wanted to take, to the left. The night before, when they arrived, it had been too dark for her to see any of it, or to even know Hillside was there.

"Do you mind, Summerton? Can we go into the village?"

He stayed the horses. "There isn't much to see, I'm afraid. Just a few shops with wares well below London standards."

"And a pub." She frowned. "It might do you well to have a drink with the locals, see what they have to say. Begin as you mean to go on." She turned to him. "Really, Summerton, you should get to know these people."

True, but not now, not with her. "I will go this evening."

She turned back in her seat, her regal icy shell coming down again. "Of course. Such a vulgar suggestion, too common. Do forgive me."

He sighed. "Not common, but we don't have time, not now." There was no telling what sort of reception he would receive. He didn't want to subject her to that, not when he still had to convince her to stay with him.

"I think it would be wise," she argued, "to develop a personal relationship."

He hesitated, looking down at the reins as he weighed her suggestion. "It might not be friendly."

"It rarely is when superiors, who have been absent for too long, decide to descend to the peasants' level, but they will respect you for it."

"Peasants?" He snorted.

She turned to him, a half-smile on her face. "Yes, peasants. They've been treated as such."

"Fine," he nodded. "For one drink, but you'd best put away that hard face if you want to win them over yourself."

"Hard face?" He'd startled her. Her smile broadened and the warm, rich sound of her chuckle rippled to his core. "Is it gone?"

She didn't want or need him, he reminded himself. He'd best remember that.

THE SMALL VILLAGE HAD old Tudor brick buildings, their upper stories jutting out, shadowing walkways, where a dozen men stood about in twos and threes, much as they might in London or Manchester. They even looked like town men. Cravats, frock coats, and tall hats, though not of the finest ilk, far different than a farmer's coarse woven shirt and baggy-bottomed breeches.

Surely, with so many about, this village should have prospered better. But building facades were worn, shop fronts bare.

She'd worried that Jeremy wouldn't be able to go near town. That such an obvious stranger would stick out among the farmers. But surely he would blend right in to these circles.

"Is this a major thoroughfare?" she asked Summerton, who scowled at the clumps of men.

"No, it is not. Nor is it usually this congested. There must be a market nearby."

"Ah," she nodded, just as confused. Markets drew people from the countryside. Not this sort. But then, what did she know of country life?

Summerton slowed as they neared a sign, swinging in the breeze, illustrating a coachman high atop a post chaise, cracking a whip. An inn, Caroline realized, The Coachman. Men stepped aside as they turned into the crowded coach yard.

Caroline squeezed her hands, stilled their trembling. She was made of sterner stuff, but Alice's death had stolen much of her pluck. She'd best find it again because Jeremy was here, she'd just seen him, at the top of the street, when they'd left St. Martins. He'd seen her as well. Had ducked into a shop, must have stayed there while they drove past. He would be watching. He would find her.

They needed to speak, somehow.

She waited in her seat as the duke jumped down and secured the horse, not bothering to unhook the gig. They'd not be there long enough to warrant it. A young stable worker stood leaning against a barn door, rake in hand. He doffed his hat. Barely.

Neither he, nor any of the others milling about in the stables, came to help.

Bad reception indeed.

Caroline put her trembling hand in Summerton's as he helped her down.

"Are you chilled, my love?" he asked, rubbing away a cold that wasn't there.

She wished he wouldn't call her *my love*, or *my dear*, or any of those endearments. She was nothing but a cash cow to him, no need to pretend otherwise.

And she wasn't cold, but it would be better for him to think so. She was frightened and determined and confused. "I'm perfectly fine," she hid the lie behind a smile. "Thank you, though."

"Your grace!" A small balding man, with a white apron strapped around his waist, came rushing out. "We're sorry," he said as he bowed, shouting to the stable lad as he rose. "See to his grace's cart. Come on now, right quick."

Summerton nodded as if the fuss was his due. It probably was, this and more, which made the lack of reception earlier that much more worrisome.

"We've been busy, your grace, men coming from all over. I 'spect the boy just thought you were another."

"Is that what we saw, on the high street? Men coming to Hillside?" Summerton asked. "Whatever for?"

"Don't know, sir, but we aren't sorry. They've filled the inn and just about eaten us out of food. But don't you worry, if you want..."

"That won't be necessary," Summerton told him, as he waited for Caroline to come abreast.

She waved him on, happy to have these moments alone, even if it was only a step or two behind. The door led them through a dark corridor. The scent of beeswax carried her past polished paneled sidewalls, across clean wood floors, centers worn pale by decades, if not centuries, of traffic.

The common, everyday sense of it offered a much needed normalcy against the sixes and sevens of her nerves. She couldn't risk Jeremy approaching her when Summerton was near. The duke would recognize him from the wedding. She didn't want the two to speak.

She just wanted to get a message to Jeremy, to let him know she had agreed to go with Summerton, for a month, possibly two. Then she would return to Manchester.

Nothing would keep her from that. Not even the duke—rude, arrogant man who had barely spoken to her before the wedding. Disinterested in anything but her money. She resolved to remember just that as she followed the two men.

Summerton listened to the publican's words with rapt attention, absorbing the news as if it were of the utmost importance. How had she missed that? He had a rare ability to look at a person without distraction and listen. She'd never noticed it before...and she had watched him quite a bit. In the days before his half-hearted courtship had started, she'd watched and admired without really knowing why, beyond his fabulous good looks. And, of course, he moved like a living, breathing piece of art without losing a smidgen of his masculinity. Caroline rather liked art.

That was before he had told her they were to marry. Before she had learned he needed an heiress. She had more pride than to settle for that. Even if the duke continued to reveal himself to be a different man than she had believed.

She could ill afford to have him get under her skin now.

The innkeeper's babble floated back to her. She ignored it, and pushed up against the wall as a maid scurried past with linens piled high above her eyes. When she stepped back into the hall, she wasn't in a hall anymore, but a foyer. The duke and his newfound friend stood on the threshold of a room to the right.

Head still cocked toward the man, Summerton's eyes were on her. She joined him at the entrance to the public room, amazed by the buzz of conversation. The innkeeper wiped his hands on his apron.

"Here we have it, your grace," the man boomed.

As though a curtain rose on a great stage, silence settled, sudden and thick. All eyes turned to them.

A hand on her back, the duke guided her to a bench in the inglenook, beside the fire.

"Warm yourself. I'll see about tea."

But he didn't need to go anywhere. The landlord was at his elbow. "Tea for her grace, then?" he asked. "Will you have the same, or something stronger, sir?"

She looked about. Heads turned quickly, pretending they hadn't been staring. She caught the odd peek here, a quick glance there, as people tried not to be too obvious.

The attention left her feeling awkward and gauche. No wonder Summerton hadn't wanted to stop.

The landlord had gone to fetch their drinks. She leaned in close to Summerton. "He said there were strangers about, but in here, do you think these people are local?"

Even as she said it, a group of town men barged into the room. Summerton ignored them for her, his keen attention as disconcerting as the rest.

"I'm afraid I've not spent much time here, not since my youth. Can't claim to know any except—" he nodded to three men at the end of the bar, "—I believe they are tenants.

They all looked to be tenants, or local country folk, with their untidy shirts, open at the neck, waistcoats without overcoats.

Even if she could slip out without attracting notice, she wouldn't dare leave Summerton now and risk undermining whatever tenuous respect these people held for him. He could ill afford that.

She smiled at a woman across the room, who'd been staring at the duke, startling her so much she stepped back and knocked into a man, causing him to spill his drink.

"Crikey, Edna!" he shouted. Only then did Caroline realize how quiet the lounge had grown.

Feeling like a specimen in a zoological exhibit, she determined to dispel the abnormality of their presence.

"Summerton." He turned to her. "I'm warm enough now, do you mind if we move to a table?" She rose, shaking out her skirt, addressing the couple on the other side of the nook. "I swear, if there's a fire nearby, the ash will find me."

"Oh, ain't it the truth," the woman responded, hastily adding, "your grace."

Caroline wrinkled her nose and leaned in closer. "I'm not used to the title, either. Seems an awful lot of fuss."

"Does it?" Summerton joined her, pulling out a chair at a table near the fire. "I rather think it suits you."

"A mouthful." She winked at the woman as she sat in the chair the duke held out. "But we all have our burdens to bear." Her dramatic sigh earned a chuckle from both the duke and the couple in the nook.

"Such a lovely place, so warm and welcoming," she said to the duke.

He looked around in apparent surprise. "Yes, I rather think you're right."

A woman pushed her way through a doorway in the back, tea tray in hand, as the publican brought a glass of ale for the duke.

The woman bumbled up to them and then unloaded tea and biscuits from the tray. Caroline noticed a man scribbling on some paper, while another appeared to be sketching the duke.

She pretended they weren't there, took a small bite of biscuit and smiled as she let the sweet buttery confection melt in her mouth. "Oh, Summerton! You really must try one, these are excellent."

When he did, he suggested, "Perhaps they'll share this recipe with our cook."

Caroline slapped his hand, ignoring his stunned expression. "Of course they won't! If we want these biscuits, we'll just have to sneak out and come here for them. It's very bad business to give away your secrets."

The air lightened as people nodded and chuckled.

"Well..." The publican rocked back on his heels. "We're pleased you stopped in."

The locals relaxed, turned back to their own conversations. The others remained focused on Caroline and Summerton. He leaned over, speaking softly. "I suspect they are reporters, here because of Alice."

"How would they have heard? To get here so quickly?"

He frowned, and she knew he was wondering the same thing. Word of the death would barely have reached the village, let alone town.

They drank their beverages and nibbled on biscuits. The duke covered her hand with his own, giving it a reassuring squeeze. Caroline offered a bright smile across the tumble of worries between them, wishing the warmth of his palm were not so welcome.

A week ago, she would have been flabbergasted to see the duke speak to a publican. He was far too high in the instep.

"You've changed." It came out as an accusation.

"Have I?" His eyebrow rose. She knew that look. It meant, *go on, tell me more, I'm waiting*. She didn't dare. She'd not meant to say even that.

"Shall we go?" he asked, rising and holding out his hand, ready to leave.

Caroline stood, leaned toward the couple in the inglenook, bidding them goodbye, unaware of the tension unfolding behind her. One minute she was saying, "A pleasure to meet you," the next Summerton took her arm, tugging her close.

She shot him a warning glance, miffed by his arrogance, but then she saw them. Stern-faced men, some of them she'd seen this morning, by the tenants' cottages. All farmers, by their clothing, circling them three deep.

It had been her idea to stop. Summerton had warned her it might not be pleasant, but she hadn't believed a gang would confront him.

He shifted, putting her between him and the couple in the inglenook. "Gentlemen." He bowed to the men. One stepped forward, doffed his cap.

The others followed suit, taking off their caps, bowing their heads slightly, shifting nervously from foot to foot.

"We'd like to thank you," the front man said.

Caroline released her breath. Summerton's shoulders relaxed.

The man turned and gestured to the others. "We'd all like to thank you," he said, "for lowering the rents, giving us a month free." Determined, but clearly uncomfortable, he stepped back into the mix of the others. A couple of the men bowed their heads, sniffed.

"Ah, yes," the duke nodded. "Well, raising the rents had been a misguided notion. My apologies for any—" he faltered, "—difficulties it has caused you."

Another man stepped forward. "And my Nettie says you're really going to build those cottages."

Summerton cleared his throat. "We spoke of that this morning. New cottages are the end I'm striving for." He brought Caroline forward. "Now, if you will excuse us." Summerton nodded respectfully. "We don't want to keep the horse standing too long."

"Sorry about the murdered gal," one man called from the back. "She was your girl, they say."

Caroline blinked. "Yes." She managed, clearing her throat. "Yes, Alice came with me." Tears pricked her eyes. "Thank you for your condolences."

"Right sorry we are about that, in our woods. Never seen the like before."

There'd been no mention of Alice as a real person, a young person, whose life had been taken from her. A young woman, alone, here at St. Martins, without any of her own here to tend to her.

"Thank you, all of you," Caroline told them, sincerely touched. "I will pass your kind words on to her family."

"Shall we, my dear?" Summerton bent to her, urging her forward.

The men parted, but they held up their glasses and toasted, "To his grace and her grace of Summerton."

They bowed their heads, receiving the accolades. Caroline was discomfited by the attention. If this was what it meant to be a duchess, she did not want the role.

They retraced their steps along that dark, beeswax-scented hallway. Only one servant stood in the hall, her back against the wall, head down, waiting for Caroline and Summerton to pass. The rest were probably upstairs, preparing beds for the surge of guests. An unexpected boon, thanks to Alice.

Poor, poor Alice.

An image of her came to mind, all battered and purpled, eyes wide open, horrifically red. Caroline blinked, looked at the maid, pressed against the wall, to distract herself. But she proved a poor distraction. The girl's very pretty face featured a nose that had been broken more than once, and an odd dip of one eye, swollen out of shape. Just a girl, Caroline fretted, even as the maid fell against her, taking her hand.

Stunned, Caroline tried to pull free, but then the corner of a folded note was pressed into her palm. Jeremy had found a way to communicate.

"Lucy!" the publican admonished. "You outstep yourself!"

"No," Caroline argued, "it was an accident." Righting the girl, holding her by her shoulders, aware of Summerton watching over her shoulder. "Are you all right?"

"She'd best respect your person," the publican snapped, grabbing for the maid, trying to shove her out of the hallway.

"She's just done in, is all," Caroline concluded. "You mustn't punish her."

The man sighed. "No, your grace. I think the girl's seen punishment enough in her time."

Ah, so he wasn't an abusive employer. She'd wondered, what with the state of the maid. "Good. I'm glad you understand."

No more was said until the duke helped her up into the carriage.

"That was deliberate," he said. "The maid, she meant to fall into you. Have you checked your jewelry?"

"You're wrong." She opened her reticule, as if to look in there, and managed to get the note inside. She snapped it shut. "She's no Alice and my jewelry is right here." She held out her wrist.

"Very well." He didn't argue, though he doubted her.

Perhaps that was why he went so silent. Falling so deep in his thoughts to be driving by habit, letting the horse take the lead. He didn't even notice the group of men turn down the drive to St. Martins. He continued straight.

Caroline leaned back to watch them. Reporters trespassing? Or the fellows investigating for the magistrate? She'd heard that he and Summerton had hired men from the village. They'd organized a search party and a few extras to watch the Hall and grounds.

The duke neither showed a reaction to her interest nor asked her to sit back, but tapped a single finger against the side of his leg. Just as he'd done the night before. Caroline took that as a signal that he was not quite comfortable with the affairs of the moment. She'd best remember it.

A horrid business, this murder. Earlier, when they'd waited for the magistrate and Lady Eleanor, Caroline had written a letter to Alice's family. There was little else she could do now, other than encourage the magistrate to release the body and send the poor girl home.

Summerton did push, to that end, when Sir Michael had arrived. Hopefully, it would be done soon.

She thought about chatting to distract him from studying those reins as if they held a world full of answers, but decided against it. He had important matters to deal with, and she'd just added to his problems.

Besides, it was a pretty, twisty little road. Sparkling from a rain that had fallen while they visited The Coachman. Daffodils just budding, crocuses fading along the side of the road.

The estate wall stood strong and tall to their left, while fields with tidy, freshly turned rows encased in smaller stone fences encompassed as far as the eye could see to the right. A musty rich scent hung heavy in the air. She breathed in deep.

"What are they planting?" she asked, regretting it even as the words slipped out. She'd not meant to disturb him.

He looked over at her, eyes focusing. "What was that?"

"It's not important."

"No, of course it is. I'm a poor host, to be so lost in thought. Forgive me."

Ah, that warm, kind smile, so absent during his courtship. He was not fair to turn it on her now. He muddied the waters, and she couldn't think.

"You are forgiven." She turned away from his smile, looked out over the fields. "You obviously have much on your mind."

"And you asked a question." He slowed the mare.

"Merely making conversation, but I forgot your habit of dwelling in your own thoughts."

He stopped altogether, so abruptly she turned to face him again. "I have been remiss," he said.

"Not at all."

"Oh, but I have, and for longer than I realized. Let me help you into my thoughts."

"No." She panicked. "No, really, that isn't necessary." Familiarity was a dangerous thing, at least with him.

"You have a right to know why I failed to attend to you before the wedding. You deserved better."

"There is no need, your grace."

He met her gaze, his eyes keen, focused

"You also have a right to know what you married, and trust me, there is far more to it than the man." He turned halfway, gesturing to where they were. "The village we just left is called Hillside by virtue of being on the side of the hill."

She nodded. He kept her waiting as he watched her. She managed to hold his intense gaze.

"Good." He pulled back, lifted the reins. "Now close your eyes."

"Close my eyes?"

"Yes, please, trust me."

"Fine." She closed her eyes, putting her hands over them, spacing two fingers enough to peek.

"No, no, not fair!" He chuckled. "Firmly closed."

She did as he asked, felt the gig move forward to, she surmised, where the tall stone wall lining the path connected to a much shorter one. She had wondered what lay beyond that wall.

The gig came to a stop. He put an arm around her.

"You may look now." And she did.

A valley sprawled out below them, the road cutting through a magnificent patchwork of fields, each field framed by stout stone walls. Trees dotted the land, and a river flowed down the hillside and through another village below. The view went on forever, possibly the whole breadth of England.

"Oh, my!"

He pointed. "And the village below."

"Yes?"

"Summervale. Because it is in the valley." He pointed to the high wall that ended abreast of them. "This demarcates the home grounds surrounding the Hall." He frowned. "St. Martins Hall, home for the Dukes of Summerton, sadly in need of repair, but that is a tour for another day."

"How did this happen, Summerton? How did everything get in such disrepair?" She'd assumed the money had been frittered away through a hedonistic lifestyle. One gaming debt could topple an empire in an instant.

But this loss was not instantaneous. This was a steady drain.

"Mismanagement," Summerton admitted. "Or no management. Unlike your father, the Dukes of Summerton have not shown good business sense."

"And you think you are different."

He shifted to face her again, when he'd been so studiously looking forward.

"Yes, I think I am. My mother's family were rather well suited to economics and I do carry her blood."

"Your mother."

"Yes, I like to think the affairs of the family would have been vastly different had she lived."

"It might have done." If his father had been willing to listen. Men often weren't. "An abhorrence of trade, business, does not work in your favor."

"Ah..." He traced her cheek. "This duke is very aware that he is the head of a rather large enterprise. Not so different than your father."

"My father built his, of his own sweat and blood."

"And I mean to rebuild mine, with whatever it takes."

"Such as?" *Marrying a woman who stinks of trade?* She waited, dared him, to say just that.

Mulling that over, his gaze narrowed, until some thought struck him and his eyes opened wide, trapping her in his answering smile. He shifted his attention to the lands spread out below them. Acres and acres of fields and pastures.

"What you see, my dear, is Summerton. Named for the farm or 'ton' of the land."

Caroline blinked.

"Rather magnificent, is it not?" he asked.

How could anyone take such a thing for granted?

"The front of the Hall faces the town. The one we just left?"

"This," his arm swept out, encompassing the entire view before them, "is not the whole of Summerton. If we were to crest the hill in the other direction, and take in that view there, everything before you would also belong to the Dukes of Summerton."

"And the towns?"

He snapped the reins and they started moving again. "A part of Summerton."

"And revenues?" Asking about money was not done, but she'd been raised to think of such things. She rather thought she had a right to ask, if he thought to bring her into his world.

"Yes," he said with a nod. "They pay rent, though the villages are far from prosperous."

"Because your father overcharged them."

His jaw worked, but he was honest enough to respond. "Yes, that is exactly what he did. He impoverished his own tenants without giving them the means to make up the difference in farming."

"So the corn laws..."

"How do you know about the corn laws?"

"I read, your grace, and I listen. Food is exorbitant because of those tariffs. They really must be repealed."

"Stop!" he exclaimed. "Those corn laws are all that's saving us from penury."

"Oh?" She sniffed. "I thought I was all that was keeping you from penury."

His mouth kicked up on one side, as though only half of him saw the humor. "No, my love," he whispered, with the sort of self-deprecating humor that could have won her over so easily. Far, far too late now.

"You are the key to turning the whole damn lot of it from bloody ruin."

He didn't stop to apologize for his word usage. His nostrils flared, the muscles of his jaw worked.

"One cannot teeter on the edge of poverty without eventually toppling in. You have the power to counter that balance and drive us away from the edge. You, Caroline, offer prosperity for every inhabitant of Summerton."

"How far?" She jutted her chin toward the view, needing to know more.

"All that you see and more. So, so much more, with other estates in other counties, plus hunting lodges and blocks of town."

"And it is all to let?" She couldn't believe it. More incompetence than her uncle Robert. "How far, if we'd taken the road in the other direction?"

"The same, north, south, east and west. I will take you to the tower, where you can see from on high."

The mills needed her. They employed thousands. Vast as Summerton was, it was not populated in the thousands. Or was it?

Once more he stopped the cart, and put his arm around her. "You asked me what I would do to regain prosperity, for the land, for the people?"

Oh, those eyes of his, clear blue and burning with fierce determination. "You, Caroline, that is what I would do for the land and the people. You. But not just for your funds. I married you because you would understand that this is a vast enterprise. An intricate business."

He took his arm back, adjusted the reins. "And that is why I was inattentive in town. Like your father, I was busy working, sleeves rolled up, poring over business scribbles, listening to experts on farming, trying to learn all I should have been learning when my father was alive. I was fighting to find a way to regain the Summerton name."

He clicked at the horse. They started on their way.

"Forgive my language earlier. Totally inappropriate. This whole situation has carried me beyond polite conversation."

She felt his glance, but refused to give him any idea of the wild thoughts buffeting her peace. His language? *The whole damn lot of it*, he'd said. *Bloody*, he'd said. Offensive words for a proper lady, but she was made of sterner stuff than that. She recognized just how meager words were to convey the vast scope of his responsibilities. She only had one thing to say in return.

"Damn you, Summerton. You do not make this easy for a lady."

"I sure as hell hope not!" He laughed and snapped the reins, propelling them forward.

CHAPTER 8 ~ Eyes Opened

They decided not to go all the way to Summervale. They'd nearly reached the village when Caroline reminded him the day grew short and she needed to prepare for dinner, so they'd turned about.

"Thank you," he said, as they headed down the drive to St. Martins.

"Whatever for?"

To his ears, she sounded truly baffled. He wanted to laugh. The whole ride, he should have been courting her, complimenting her beauty. He should have been promising to make her dreams come true. Instead, he had spoken about St. Martins, and the trials he faced.

They had been so caught up in their discussion, neither one had taken the time to admire the budding spring, the daffodils. She buoyed his ideas, added to them with thoughts and solutions of her own.

He was not alone. The future held promise. If only he could convince her to stay. Involved as she was in their discussion, he wouldn't blame her for throwing her hands up, saying it was too much.

He hoped to God she wouldn't.

"Look." Caroline pointed to a black buggy ahead of them. "Is that the magistrate returning?"

"Most probably." It was hard to tell, since black buggies were a fairly common conveyance and the hood was up. "It could be the doctor again, though he had a good look at the body earlier." Summerton snapped the reins. "Shall we catch up with the visitors?"

The two conveyances arrived at the front steps simultaneously, but the buggy did not stop. Sir Michael, the magistrate, knew St. Martins well enough to know of its deficiencies in staff. There wouldn't be a servant to wait on him there.

Summerton followed the black buggy around to the stables.

"Good God. Who are these men?" Summerton pulled in the reins as they took in the bustle of activity before them. A cluster of men, similar to the ones they'd seen in the village surrounded by workers, milled about near the stables.

"I saw some of those men," Caroline told him. "They were turning down the drive when we passed it earlier. I thought they might have been the fellows you and Sir Michael hired."

"But what's my aunt doing out here with these men? Strangers should not be wandering around the grounds."

"You'd better go and see," Caroline suggested. He snapped the reins again.

Sir Michael's buggy came to a stop, and the crowd broke up and reformed around it, everyone speaking and gesturing and pointing toward the stables. Aunt Eleanor directed a stable lad to stand at the horse's lead, and then made her way past the magistrate to meet Summerton and Caroline.

"What's happened?" he asked, jumping down from the gig. Rather than make him walk around, Caroline scooted over. She was a girl in a million. He took her by the waist and helped her jump down.

"Summerton," Eleanor was clearly agitated. "I'm pleased you have returned." She offered Caroline a weak smile. "We've had some unknown men wandering around the grounds. Strangers, all, claiming to be newspaper men."

"You said they looked like newspaper men," Caroline reminded him. "How ghoulish, to chase after poor Alice's murder."

"Yes," he squeezed her hand. "They have no business on our property, and can take themselves right off."

"I don't think you understand, Summerton," Eleanor warned, her tone stopping him.

"What do you mean?"

"They didn't know about the murder—" she looked over at the group of men gesturing and exclaiming to the magistrate, "—though they are quite fascinated now they've learned of that development."

"Then why are they here?" he asked.

Rather than answer, his aunt raised a questioning glance to Caroline. "Perhaps, my dear," she said to her, "you can explain."

"I don't understand." Caroline looked as baffled as he felt and quite convincingly so.

Eleanor nodded once, sharply. "We'd best go inside." She turned to the stable lad. "Inform Sir Michael that we will await him in the study."

"Have you already spoken with them?" he asked.

"Yes, of course I have. All but the few over there." She gestured at the group they'd seen upon their arrival. "The others are in the stables. I couldn't think of anywhere else to put them."

The duke nodded."I suppose it's best to keep them close at hand."

"When I sent for Sir Michael, I requested some of his men to watch them, so we needn't tie up your servants."

"I'll have Hitches hire some more." He glanced at the hub of activity. "At least the empty stables will prove useful."

"Three blocks of stables?" Caroline asked, heading for the house.

"Yes," Lady Eleanor offered. "And better equipped than some homes."

Sir Michael wasn't long in joining them. He and Eleanor sat next to each other in wingback chairs beside the fire, a small table between them. Caroline sat across from them on a King Louis couch. Summerton leaned against his desk in the shadows opposite the fire—arms folded over his chest, ankles crossed. From there, he could watch Caroline easily enough, while staying in the periphery.

Hitches oversaw the delivery of tea, which Eleanor poured. No one spoke until the last servant had left and Hitches bowed out the door, closing it smartly behind him.

"I received your summons, Lady Eleanor. What is this all about?" Sir Michael asked, saving Summerton the trouble of asking the question.

"The gardeners noticed strangers in the park. They told Hitches, and eventually their presence was brought to my attention. They are journalists. Most are from London, a few from Manchester." Eleanor took a sip of tea, sighed, set the cup down, and continued. "There's even someone from Cornwall. After I spoke with them, I suggested they take their rest in the stables until Sir Michael has the opportunity to interview them."

"Quite right." Sir Michael nodded. "And what did you learn from them?"

"A waste of time and effort over foolish gossip. I rather wonder if there wasn't one of those dreadful bets going on in some gentlemen's club." Eleanor's gaze shifted to Summerton, but he wasn't going to argue with her about men's clubs or men's desire to bet on foolish things.

"Just what sort of bet are you referring to, Aunt?" he asked.

Her gaze shifted to Caroline. "They were under the false apprehension that your bride *had* run away, and you were stepping straight into debtors' prison."

Past tense. They had believed it a fait accompli. They hadn't known about the murder. Having lost one story, the other was a feather in their caps.

"How could they know?" Caroline shook her head, as all eyes had turned on her.

"Know what?" Sir Michael asked, clearly baffled.

Caroline ignored him, pressing her argument to Summerton. "You must believe me. I meant you no malice, Summerton, truly I didn't."

"I don't think you did," his aunt agreed. "You were focused on escape, and it's harder, not easier, to do that with journalists sniffing the ground for you. Unless they were meant to help, and there's no evidence of that."

Something she said niggled at him, but he didn't pursue it. Had his bride partnered with someone ruthless enough to steal her away and destroy him in one fell swoop?

He'd managed to hold on to a deep well of rage over the past six months; his father's death, revelation of the crushing debt, even an unwilling bride. Now, he didn't dare move, certain this new possibility—that his reluctant, fascinating bride might be trying to destroy his reputation or colluding with someone else who was—would tip him over the edge.

He kept his arms firmly crossed at his chest, his feet tightly linked at the ankles, and his neck stiffly turned, as he took in the tableau before him.

Caroline watched him. He smiled back, or rather his lips quirked up at the corners in a semblance of a smile. His aunt also watched Caroline, and Sir Michael watched his aunt.

Caroline broke the chain to reassure the magistrate. "His grace and I shall go out and prove to them they've wasted their time."

She rose. Summerton still did not move.

"Just a moment, my dear." Lady Eleanor toyed with her teacup. "Perhaps we should attempt to isolate the source of their information before we apply to them for confirmation."

Sir Michael was already shaking his head. "No, Lady Eleanor, I do not believe that would be prudent. It is important to keep an open mind in these investigations. And if we suggest a potential source to them, they will not feel obliged to tell the truth."

"Yes," Eleanor agreed, again watching Caroline, "unless they were sent here to muddy the waters of a murder enquiry." She turned toward Summerton.

He broke his silence. "You don't think this was a random killing."

"No, Summerton, I do not."

Sir Michael argued with Eleanor. "Who would set out to kill Caroline's maid? No purpose to it. She's just a maid."

"No," Eleanor explained. "She was not just a maid to the killer."

Caroline studied the floor. Her voice, tremulous and weak, breaking through a distrust Summerton didn't dare release. "You think the killer planned to murder me, but found another victim when I didn't leave as planned."

"No." Sir Michael refused to believe it.

Eleanor challenged him. "The girl was wearing the duchess's clothes, was she not? And she had on her jewels. I rather think the murderer thought he was capturing Caroline, and when he found out he was not, he murdered the poor girl instead. He would have already summoned the press. The more strangers in the village, the easier it would be to hide his own presence."

Of course. That made perfect sense.

"You don't think it was done by a local or a gypsy?" Sir Michael asked, rather hopefully.

"I dare say we've had gypsies around Summerton for centuries. Things may go missing, but we've never had so much as a wound, let alone a killing." She sipped her tea, all eyes on her. "No, I think this was deliberately done."

"But why?" Caroline asked. For the first time he noticed that she sat on the very edge of her seat, hands clasped tightly in her lap. She was no calmer than he.

Each held their peace as Eleanor studied the dance of flames in the fireplace, waiting for her to speak. Summerton had already explained to told Caroline that his aunt had a talent for this sort of tangle. He just wished she didn't need that talent here, at St. Martins.

Eleanor finally responded to Caroline's question in a soft whisper, as though to herself. "I don't know, my dear. I haven't figured that out yet, but when I do, we shall know who killed poor Alice.

Caroline sat back.

The magistrate rose. "I'll go interview these fellows. Then, if you don't mind, your grace, you and the duchess should come out and speak with them."

"Yes." Summerton stood up, walked the magistrate to the door, and closed it smartly behind him.

"Caroline," he said, turning around, "Last night, you claimed to have run on your own, without help. It's time you told us the truth."

Her eyes widened. He'd caught her.

Neither he nor his aunt knew Caroline well enough to guess when—or if—she lied, other than by catching her at it. Her eyes said it all. Someone else had been involved in her escape attempt.

It was as simple as that.

He'd argued his point the night before. The whole adventure was far too complicated and she wasn't stupid. She would have known the risks, the challenges. She would have considered them all before making her escape.

"Summerton does have a point, my dear," Eleanor added, "in suggesting you had an ally, someone helping you."

Even as Summerton quit his pacing to watch Caroline, she rose, so obviously unnerved by the question that he felt a fool for not having pressed the matter earlier.

"Yes," she finally admitted, crossing to a table on the other side of the room. She shivered, having moved away from the fire.

Reluctant as he was to show her any mercy, he wouldn't have her chilled in his home. He took off his jacket and stalked over to put it around her shoulders, doing his best to ignore the scent of her, a gentle, alluring perfume.

He stepped back, but not so far he couldn't see her shift of expression.

"Go on," he encouraged, more gently now. "Tell us."

"It's not what you think." She lifted her bowed head, appealing to both him and Eleanor in turn.

"He's not a lover?" Eleanor asked.

"No," Caroline denied, vehemently. "No, nothing like that. He oversees the mills. He worked with my father from the time he was a wee lad."

"Wait," Summerton moved closer, something tickling his memory. "He was at the wedding, was he not?"

"Yes," Caroline smiled and nodded before looking away. "That's how he knew we were coming here rather than staying in London."

He remembered it now, Caroline's lively comments about traveling to the country to see St. Martins in Summerton Vale. "Why didn't you tell him before?"

"Because I didn't know where we were going. I barely knew when we were getting married, let alone where."

Of course she had known. It was her wedding. "Surely someone told you."

"You didn't. What makes you think someone else would?"

"Why?" Eleanor had risen.

They really should sit rather than have his aunt stand with them. "Come." He took Caroline's arm and steered her back to the settee. He sat beside her and Eleanor resumed her seat.

"So tell me," Eleanor leaned forward. "Why didn't you know where you were going? It seems a strange thing to have kept from you."

"I don't know." Caroline shook her head. "But that's the way he wanted it. My uncle was relieved you didn't spend any time with me. He preferred it."

"Well, of course." Eleanor sat back. "That makes perfect sense. He didn't want Summerton to know of your reluctance. But why he would keep the location of the wedding night a secret...?"

Summerton finished for her. "He knew you might run. If you didn't know where you were going, you couldn't plan."

CAROLINE OPENED THE French windows of the duchess's bedchamber, and stepped out on the balcony. Fresh air washed over her, but she couldn't delight in it, not with the men below. Guards to keep them safe. They would also assure Summerton that she couldn't run.

She wouldn't. Not now. She'd promised to go on the journey. But he didn't trust that.

She'd spoiled everything, upset Summerton, and quite rightly, too. He was no fool; far from it. The deception she'd played insulted him.

He hid it well. They'd looked the perfect couple when they'd gone out to speak to the newspaper men, but his smile had fallen away after he'd sent them off with a firm warning not to trespass.

What had Jeremy been thinking? Had he really talked to the press, or had he simply told the wrong person? That might be possible. He could easily have talked to someone who talked to someone who was then overheard, and...well, he should have known better. Thieves and kidnappers were everywhere. Her father had been forever warning her to be careful.

Words spoken out of turn had caused Alice's death. It couldn't have been Jeremy, Caroline was certain of it. Eleanor's suggestion made sense, but something was still missing in that scenario. Perhaps it was that she simply couldn't imagine anyone wanting her dead.

Surely no one did. If only she could talk to Jeremy...Jeremy? The missive, the note from the maid! Who else would have sent that? No one but Jeremy.

More fool her, she'd forgotten.

She found her reticule on the side table, and pulled out the message.

Meet me tonight, by the kennels

One simple line, no more. She threw it in the fire. Another secret from Summerton. But she didn't want him to worry about her meeting Jeremy. He had enough worries on his shoulders.

Because there'd been a murder on his home grounds.

It was dangerous out there. Too many strangers about.

She wouldn't worry. Surely the kennels were close to the stables, which weren't far from the house, and Jeremy would keep her safe.

The paper darkened, reddened, and curled, before disintegrating to ash.

If anyone complained about the cold spring, she would defend the weather. It provided the perfect means for destroying incriminating evidence.

CHAPTER 9 ~ Congenial Company

The evening proved surprisingly congenial. Sir Michael joined them, and they all sat comfortably in the family dining room rather than suffer miles of table in a drafty room.

Summerton rather liked this room, with its whimsical ceiling of robin's egg blue with fluffy white clouds and a brilliant sun during the day. By night, that same ceiling transformed in candlelight to the twinkle of stars and a shining moon.

Caroline sat opposite him, near enough that he could actually see passion in her every wave of expression, the keen, knowledgable light in her eyes as she discussed the dangers of the Luddites with Sir Michael. The magistrate had heard of the disturbances in Lancashire, but he knew none of the details.

"Well," Sir Michael said, with a nod, "the world is changing. They can't stop that, no matter how much of this...this newfangled machinery they try to destroy. Foolish of them to imagine they can. These Luddites will be caught, their lives will be destroyed, and the owners will rebuild and carry on."

"More's the pity because I understand their fears." Carolyn tapped the table as she made her points. "We must find other means for them to earn a living. As for the machinery, it is costly to replace, but it's also very dangerous for the workers when the machines are sabotaged."

"Terrible, terrible." Sir Michael shook his head, and turned his attention to the decadent syllabub before him. "The world is a changing place." He lifted an eyebrow to the duke. "Don't you think, Summerton?"

Summerton blinked. "Are you referring to my affairs?"

Sir Michael chuckled. "Yes. Precisely." He savored a bite of his sweet dessert. "Ah, you still have the best cook in the county." He stuck his spoon into the confection again. "Word has it that you are intent on changing everything from the crops that are planted to how they are farmed. The farmers are skittish."

The magistrate sat back, watching his host. "What is it your father used to say?"

"What was good enough for generations of St. Martins, was good enough for him. And look what that's done for us."

"You're changing the farming methods?" Caroline asked.

"Yes." He hadn't meant to snap, but this was a touchy topic for him. "We should have modernized in my grandfather's day. I can only hope we are not too late."

"You've looked into this?" she asked.

"Yes, that was another reason you saw so little of me in London. I was preoccupied with learning why the estates were faring so poorly, determining what had gone wrong." He ignored his syllabub, preferring the sweetness of dessert wine. "Farming techniques have evolved, gaining greater profits with less manpower. The Summerton holdings are as out of date as this hall."

"Oh, dear," Caroline said to Sir Michael, "you are absolutely right, sir, the farmers will balk, most of them anyway. No one likes change. It's difficult and awkward."

"Greater profits with less manpower?" Lady Eleanor asked. "Does this mean you're bringing in new machinery, too? Will we have the Luddites here next?"

Summerton didn't say anything. If his marriage were secure, he would be hiring far more staff for St. Martins. There would be plenty of work to go around.

If he had the dowry.

"Caroline, is that the only problem at the mills?" his aunt asked. "The trouble with these Luddites?"

"No," Caroline shook her head. "No, since my father passed away, the mills have been losing money."

"When was that, my dear?"

"Just over a year ago."

"And you haven't been able to correct the problem?"

Caroline shifted, almost squirmed. "No."

"Why not?" Sir Michael asked.

"My uncle is determined to deal with it himself. He won't even allow me to see the accounts."

"Then how do you know they are in trouble?" Sir Michael asked.

Caroline pleated her napkin. "Jeremy has kept me informed, plus Uncle Robert's personality has changed. Dramatically. I think he's frantic. And it worries me that he refuses to tell me anything." She met Summerton's gaze. "If you anticipated income outside of my dowry, I don't think you will get it."

"Just a moment, my dear," Lady Eleanor leaned in. "I would like to know how your uncle has changed, but first, tell me, do you think one of these Luddites might be responsible for Alice's death?"

Caroline's wine glass was raised halfway to her lips, but she set it back down on the table. "I doubt it would be them. They are local bullies, neither comfortable out of their own neighborhood nor with the means to go much beyond it."

"Hm." Lady Eleanor contemplated her answer for a long moment before asking, "And your uncle? How is he different?"

Caroline *tsk*ed. "He used to shout at my father behind closed doors, but he was never like that with me." She shook her head.

"Since my father passed away, my uncle has become, well, aggressive. He frightens me, actually, but that is probably because I'm not accustomed to this side of him."

"Caroline," Summerton interrupted. "I've met your father. Surely you are not intimidated by a man who reveals his temper."

"Of course not," she snapped. "But my uncle used to be charming to me. The look on his face, when I refused..." She shuddered.

Grimly, Summerton finished for her. "Refused to marry me."

"Yes." She studied her wine. "I never expected him to force me to accept a proposal for his own gain. He would never have done that in the past. He teased Father, mercilessly, for sending me off to St. Ann's. Claimed it would make me too high in the instep for my own family. And then he pushed me to marry you for a title? He's stretching for something. I just don't know what."

"And if you didn't marry Summerton? What would have happened to your wealth if something were to happen to you?" Eleanor asked quietly.

Sir Michael snorted. "Lady Eleanor, they are married, so what would happen..." His words trailed off when all three of them stared at him. "You did marry, did you not? In London?"

"Yes." Summerton bit out, "in front of God and witnesses."

Caroline blushed, a deep red, dark enough to be seen in candlelight.

"Summerton is giving her time to adjust to the marriage," his aunt explained.

"I see," Sir Michael murmured, "this has something to do with the gal trying to run away." When no one responded, he went on. "You said something about that earlier, in the study."

Lady Eleanor sighed and rose. "You might as well tell him the whole of it, Summerton. Caroline and I will leave you to your port."

"Aunt," Summerton reprimanded, as he stood. It was natural for Lady Eleanor, who had hosted for the previous duke, to take charge without thought, but Summerton did not want Caroline overridden.

If she *wanted* the role of hostess. If she knew what it meant. He had no idea whether or not she knew of the intricacies of a dinner party.

"My apologies, Caroline," Eleanor offered. "It was not my place to step in like that."

"You have not offended me at all." Caroline rose. "That is the least of my worries." The men bowed to them, and after a moment, she added, "I think I'll take a stroll, see to my animals. I won't be long in joining everyone."

"What an excellent idea." Lady Eleanor beamed. "Nothing better than a bit of fresh air after a meal. But let's wait for the gentlemen. You won't be long over your port, will you?"

"No, not at all," Summerton promised.

"I hadn't meant to trouble anyone," Caroline demurred.

"No, of course not." Eleanor patted her arm. "It's no trouble at all."

"Fine," Caroline agreed. "I'll just freshen up and get a wrap. I promise to be ready before you men join us." Turning toward Eleanor, she asked, "Would you like me to fetch something for you?"

Eleanor shifted the shawl she had on her shoulders. "I always have mine at hand." She waved Caroline off. "Go."

"Caroline," Summerton stopped her, "do not go out there by yourself. There is a killer at large."

"Of course not." Her smile was too bright for comfort.

He tapped the table. "Fine. We won't be long." And bowed, wishing he could trust her.

CHAPTER 10 ~ Danger Lurks

Caroline did hurry, but she did not return to the drawing room. She needed to find Jeremy—tonight—before anyone frightened him off. Summerton knew about him now, so he needn't hide himself anymore. It would be dangerous in the woods until they found the murderer.

Caroline avoided Hitches who, she was certain, would not have let her go out into the dark on her own. She wasn't at all sure what Summerton had said—or not said—to the servants, but she knew they were watching. She could feel it, as though she were a child heading for the hearth and about to get burned.

Perhaps she was.

Lantern light and men's voices—the extra men brought in by Sir Michael—spilled out onto the courtyards. By the sound of it, they were enjoying themselves despite the incessant baying of her hound.

Baver's howls haunted the night. The vigil he had kept last night and this morning should have exhausted the old dog, but he proved incessant. She'd settle him before she spoke with Jeremy

If she could. Baver loved a full moon. The moon would be near to full when it rose, but it hadn't risen yet. Other than the wedge of light from the stables, it was pitch black. She frowned, hesitated. Why was Baver baying?

She was near the Hall, and the kennels were just at the back. She would be within feet of the men in the stables. There was nothing to fear.

She set off again, walking briskly despite her silk slippers, better suited to a ballroom than a cobbled stable yard. They'd be ruined, but she'd been in a hurry and had no intention of taking any longer than absolutely necessary. She wanted to get back to the drawing room before anyone missed her.

Pulling her wrap close around her, she murmured a little prayer as she crossed the dark courtyard. She wondered just how far would she have to go before Jeremy would come to her.

A shadow shifted at the far end of a corridor between two stable blocks. She waited for Jeremy to call to her.

"Your grace." A young voice came from behind her.

"Blast," she whispered, and turned to find one of her minders, a young page who was always nearby.

"I'm going to the kennels to see my dog," she told him.

"Lady Eleanor requests your attendance."

She sighed. "Yes, I'm quite certain she does, but I'm almost there, and as you can hear, the old fellow is rather vocal tonight." Not that she meant to go that far. She'd already decided to leave Baver to George, the groundsman. The groundsman and hound had formed a relationship faster than she and Summerton had managed.

"I'll go with you," he answered, squaring his shoulders.

Caroline relented.

"Get us a light then, will you? Hitches should have lanterns." The distraction might give her enough time to meet with Jeremy without interruption.

When the lad reached the Hall, she turned to face the forbidding shadows. No movement. She stepped closer.

"Jeremy?" she whispered.

If he was going to show himself, he'd best do so now.

Another step and she was between the two stable blocks, on a narrow dark path leading to the kennels beyond. Gravel crunched further down the path. She heard it, despite Baver's racket and the cacophony of conversation from the stables. "Jeremy?" she said louder this time.

"Caroline!"

She whirled to find Summerton striding toward her. She ignored him, turning back. Someone was on that path, and his shadow loomed too large for it to be Jeremy. Her friend would have responded. This person was silent as a secret.

Her heart beat furiously, but she kept moving forward—slowly, so she wouldn't frighten him. If this was the murderer, she could not let him get away. Not before she saw who it was. Summerton grabbed her from behind. She almost crumpled with relief.

"What the bloody hell are you doing out here?" he snapped, turning her into a one-arm hold. His free hand held a lantern high, casting a halo of light.

Any other time she would have pushed him away, but not now, not tonight. She welcomed the hard, firm warmth of him, and the steady beat of his heart calming hers.

"Someone is there," she whispered.

He looked up, sharp, keen. "Just shadows, Caroline." His hold eased, loosened, but he didn't let go.

She looked over her shoulder. The shadow was gone. Or had it ever been there? Could it have been her imagination?

"It's dark. Easy to see things when you are alone in the dark." He allowed.

They stood like that, his comforting arm around her, their eyes on the far end of the path.

She felt foolish, looked up to tell him so, but said nothing, caught by his eyes on her. His thumb stroked idly along her side, where he held her against him. The same way he would caress her hand, but it felt entirely different, touching her deep inside.

Even in the midst of the baying hounds and jovial men, the slender space between them roiled with silent sensation.

His brow furrowed; his head tilted. She saw the question in his changing expression, when worry slipped away. His brow cleared, his eyelids lowered, and his mouth kicked up into a half smile.

"Why?" he asked, his warm hand pressed against the curve of her waist. He urged her even closer, as though there were miles between them rather than inches.

What was he asking? Why she was out here? Why she defied him? Or why he wanted to dip his head, brush his lips across hers—for he did that. His breath teasing her lips, he whispered, "I've wanted to do this ever since we met."

Her world dissolved, fear, anxiety, and the needs of others fell away. She melted into her first kiss with this man who had broken her heart by marrying her for her money. But her heart was already broken, what harm in reveling in this kiss?

She smoothed her hands over his chest, feeling safe, alive with tingling awareness. She rose, onto her toes, slipping her arms around his neck.

The crunch of gravel pulled her back to reality, to the path and the dark shadow beyond, not an illusion, for it had returned.

She eased away from him, but he merely shifted, pivoting so his back was to the end of the path.

Behind him, the shadow shifted in the gloom. Something glittered, caught in the halo of Summerton's lantern. It rose, catching the light in a series of quick glimmers and then, then...

"No!" She grabbed Summerton's arm and threw herself to the ground, pulling him off balance so he followed her.

It all happened so quickly—her shout, his curse, a whizzing sound, and then a thud. Summerton tried to take the brunt of the fall, twisting them, but he'd had no warning. He only managed to shift them both to end up on their sides, facing each other.

Her arm was crushed, at a bad angle, beneath him, but she didn't really care. They had to get away as quickly as possible. The lad who had offered to accompany her earlier was running toward them now, another light held as high as his young arms could hold it.

"Your grace!" He ran to get the lantern Summerton had dropped. "Are you a'right?"

Summerton lifted himself up. "Caroline?" He tried to help her. "What just happened?"

But she didn't have to speak, not that she could with all the wind knocked from her, for the lad was pointing. "Crikey! Your grace, sir, look at that!"

Above their heads, in direct line with where the duke's back had been, a dagger, still shuddering from the impact, pierced the stable wall.

His nostrils flared.

"I'll go after him," the lad proclaimed, jumping from foot to foot, but not moving forward.

"No!" the duke shouted, standing swiftly. "You," he ordered the boy as he worked his leg, "go get Sir Michael and have Hitches gather some men. I'll go."

"Absolutely not!" Caroline stood on shaking legs, holding her bruised arm to her chest. "No, I could not bear it. Please don't."

"What? Afraid I will hurt Jeremy?" he snapped.

"It isn't him, but whoever it is, he just tried to kill you. You mustn't go. Not alone. Please."

They stood for a long moment, his eyes flinty and narrowed, his chest rising and falling as if he'd already run. "Come," he finally said. Limping, he led her away from the path and into the stable, which smelled of hay, horses, and unwashed men.

Two stable hands sat on stools in the hall; six other men were on benches inside a stall. They all stood as the duke and Caroline entered. "You two, come with me," he said, gesturing to the stable hands. "The killer is out there." He turned to face the men in the stalls. "And you," he commanded, as he pulled one of the abandoned stools over and pushed Caroline to sit. "Watch over her. If anything happens to her, anything at all, you will pay for it dearly. Do you understand me?"

And he took his two men with him, into the dark of night, to catch a murderer.

She simply sat there, holding her arm to her chest, raw with worry. Who could have tried to hurt the duke and why? What was happening? Where was Jeremy? Why would Alice's death lead to an attempt on Summerton's life?

Sir Michael and Eleanor wasted no time in finding her. Eleanor encouraged her to stand, clucking over her arm, leading her back into the house.

The men tried to follow. "His grace says we're to protect her. If she's not here when he gets back, there will be hell to pay."

"Did he now?" Sir Michael asked. "She will be fine with Lady Eleanor. In the meantime, we need to get you out on the search. Liam, you take charge. See that they fan out. From what I gather, Summerton went north. I doubt the assailant would have gone south, given all the open fields and fences in that direction, so only send three that way. The rest of you search between the north and west."

"Will do, sir."

"And all of you, be careful! Call for help if you find the man. He's dangerous."

"Yes, sir," they chorused.

"And Jimmy, here, you ride out to the tenant farms to warn the people to lock up tight."

They looked at each other uneasily. "You don't think..." one man started to ask, but Sir Michael waylaid him.

"I don't think anything of the kind, but better to be safe, eh?"

"I will have Cook prepare some refreshments. No doubt, you will all be cold and famished when you return," Caroline promised, pulling herself together. This was no time to turn to jelly.

The moment she stepped indoors, Caroline went straight down to Mrs. Beechum's rooms on the lower floor of the Hall. The housekeeper opened the door, still dressed from the day, and offered a quick curtsy.

"Your grace," she said, as she rose, "you could have rung, I would have come."

"Yes, I'm sure." Caroline took in the cozy room beyond, the warm fire, a cup of tea sitting on a table beside a wingback chair. "Do you mind?"

Mrs. Beechum hesitated, but only for the blink of an eye, and then stepped back.

Visiting the housekeeper was not a normal arrangement; however, Lady Eleanor's comment about the servants' quarters had unnerved Caroline. She didn't dwell on it, but instead explained that men were out searching for Alice's killer.

"We need to make arrangements for some cold meat, bread, and ale, that sort of thing," she explained. "Better yet, something stronger to drink than ale, don't you think? For when the men return."

"Yes, ma'am."

They stood just inside the door, but the housekeeper offered no invitation to sit.

"And I would like to see the servants' quarters tomorrow. If you could arrange that."

The woman remained silent, but couldn't hide her widened eyes or the paling of her cheeks, which quickly transformed to too much color. Red, she'd gone red in the face.

She managed a sniff. "I will see to it."

"Thank you. It needn't be too early. No doubt we will all have a late night."

"Yes, ma'am."

"And the food as well, will you see to that?"

"Of course. I won't wake Cook, but I'll take care of it myself."

"Do as you wish," Caroline offered, "but I believe she is already in the kitchens. No doubt the whole hall is awake after...well, it is rather an upset."

"A footman said someone tried to kill his grace."

"We don't know that for a certainty."

"St. Martins has always been a peaceful place. We don't have murders."

"Let's see to it that it becomes a warm and welcoming place, shall we, Mrs. Beechum?"

Foolish, foolish to put the weight on the housekeeper. The poor woman had enough to contend with. Water stains on the walls, doors swollen beyond opening and the wavy warp of floors. And now her, a reluctant bride who brought misery down upon the duke and his people.

She didn't doubt Mrs. Beechum was right, that St. Martins had been a peaceful place before Caroline arrived.

If only she could offer them some measure of prosperity without being lost to the kisses of one man. She touched her cheek, felt warmth creep into them. An odd way to stave off the cold of fear.

CHAPTER 11 ~ Failed Search

Dawn hid behind deep patches of fog as the men trudged back to St. Martins, shoulders slumped with fatigue and the weight of failure.

The only person they'd found was—Summerton suspected—Caroline's Jeremy. Which would have made him look guilty as sin, except he was concussed and bleeding from a knife wound. At least this victim was alive and could be questioned.

George sent the hounds on the scent. Ridiculous exercises; they were never trained to track humans, just foxes and pheasant. So they kept returning to an area near the initial incident, drawn by the scent of Jeremy's blood. Nothing was found, not even by Baver.

The dagger that had been embedded in Jeremy's arm was another matter. Michael sent word that Hitches recognized the weapon from Summerton's own armory. Hitches would know. He was the only one who ever entered the armory, housed in the original great hall of St. Martins. A chamber closed long ago because the owners couldn't be bothered to visit enough to use them.

Or so he had thought. The truth, he'd found, had more to do with dry rot and damp and a leaky roof.

Hitches, it appeared, attended the rooms in the hopes the owners would eventually care. In his ministrations, he cleaned every single piece of armament, from chain mail and armor to the smallest dagger. Much of it had been in residence for centuries.

What the Dukes of Summerton lacked in affection for their ancestral home, the servants made up for tenfold. They were proud of this old pile of ruin. They were proud of their dukes.

A real shame neither lived up to inspection.

He trudged toward the west entrance, stopping when the others broke off and headed for the tradesmens' and servants' access. He wanted to follow them, to sit and commiserate, but hesitated, weighing their embarrassment against his need. There was another way he could join them. He'd take a couple bottles of whiskey. Men could always bond when whiskey was involved.

He stepped into the mudroom of the west entrance, surprised to see a candle, melted nearly to the base, waiting for him.

He kicked off his muddy boots and shrugged out of his waxed jacket, only then realizing he was still dressed for dinner. The trousers were ruined, of course. No doubt his valet would be hard pressed to save the rest.

An expense he would have swatted away six months ago. Now it felt like another hole in a leaking vessel. He shook his head free of such thoughts, leaving them for another time, and headed for the study to find some fine whiskey to take down to the other men, in the kitchens.

Hitches met him as he rounded the sweep of stairs bordering either side of the great hall.

"Your grace." In those two words, the butler conveyed welcome, regret, and an offer of service.

"You should be in bed," he scolded, patting Hitches on the shoulder as he walked past.

"We all have been waiting, sir."

Stunned, Summerton looked back. "All?"

"Yes, sir. Her grace, of course, and Lady Eleanor and most of the staff. May I say, for all of us, that we are much relieved to see you returned safe and sound."

"Well..." They'd been worried. For him? "Thank you, Hitches. I give you all leave to sleep until noon."

He wanted a meal, he wanted a bath, and he wanted to be looked after. But that could come later. They'd waited up all night to see he returned safely and deserved the gratitude of sacrifice.

"Men will be walking the perimeter of the Hall, sir, and we've a footman to stand outside the door of the ladies' chambers. There will be one outside your door as well."

"I will be fine, Hitches, but thank you for thinking of the ladies. There are a number of men in the kitchens, or I presume they are in the kitchens. They will be hungry."

"Of course, your grace. Cook has put food out for those returning. Her grace suggested yours be put in the study, where you would feel most comfortable. She is there with Lady Eleanor."

Her grace? Not yet, by her thinking, but it appeared she was willing to play the part. At the moment, that was enough.

"Thank you, Hitches, and will you see that a bottle or two is opened for the men in the kitchens? And have a couple drams yourself."

"Thank you, your grace."

Summerton, already walking off, waved a hand up to his tireless retainer.

A footman stood in the doorway to the study. Summerton acknowledged him with a nod and stepped into the room to find the two women in his life curled up in their respective chairs, lap rugs thrown over them, sound asleep. He glanced at his aunt, his mother's sister.

From what he'd heard, his mother hadn't been anything like her older sister. Eleanor had been a tomboy, fascinated by the natural sciences, as likely to catch a toad as her young nephew, and just as keen to dissect it—precisely the sort of thing that would have sent his mother running. How he wished those stories were his memories and not someone else's.

At least he'd had Eleanor to step in from time to time, when she wasn't wrapped up in one of her magistrate husband's investigations.

Caroline had not been so lucky. She didn't have an Aunt Eleanor.

So many things he'd taken for granted.

A delicate little snuffle reminded him that she was there, too. Strong, intelligent Caroline, curled up into a restless ball, like a sleeping kitten having a bad dream. Her brow was furrowed, her eyes moving about under closed lids.

"She's been very worried," Eleanor whispered.

"You're awake?" Summerton asked. Of course she was awake.

"Just." She sat up slowly, stretching out kinks. "You're better off not waking her. I think this is the first she's closed her eyes. She's been worried sick."

"We were fine," Summerton told her. "Nothing to worry about. Wish there had been. I don't like to think this madmen is out there somewhere..."

"Do you think it could be her Jeremy?"

"Her Jeremy?" He didn't like the sound of that. He didn't like it one bit. "Jeremy was found, badly beaten, a knife in his arm. It wasn't him," he snapped. "And where's this food Hitches promised...ah, I see it."

He headed toward the table by the window. "I'm famished. And if you're hungry, you should eat now. I've given the servants leave to sleep until noon."

Lady Eleanor rose slowly, obviously uncomfortable with the awkward rest on a straight-backed settee. "I've nibbled, no need to worry. I very much doubt I will rise before noon myself." She headed toward the door. "Summerton?"

"Yes?"

"Caroline arranged to see the servants' quarters on the morrow. If you can't manage the expense of doing anything about them, I would distract her. She's already committed you to the cottages."

He nodded, waved the suggestion aside. "There's a footman out there. Have him go with you. I'll watch over Caroline." He put a bit of pork pie in his mouth.

"Are you aware that most of the servants are now in the east wing? They've turned two of the guest rooms into dormitories. One for men, one for women.

"Have they?" he asked, frowning.

"And so they should, Summerton. The servants' rooms are not livable."

"I didn't know." He sighed heavily and put his plate down, too tired to eat. "I really didn't know."

"Will you explain to her why you were unaware?" his aunt asked.

"It sounds too pathetic."

"Well, it is not!" Lady Eleanor raised her voice. Caroline stirred, but didn't wake. They both watched her.

"Summerton, you have been working hard for all of England. You had every reason to believe your father was properly overseeing the properties. He never gave you a reason to doubt it."

"I think that's what killed him. He'd reached the edge of oblivion. By then, I don't think he dared say anything."

"Is it too late?" Eleanor asked.

He shook his head. "That depends," he admitted, looking back at Caroline. She wasn't the only figure in the equation. If he didn't do a better job than his predecessors, there was no hope, no matter how much cash he found for the coffers. And of course, they couldn't afford a bad year for crops or an animal virus or any other unexpected setbacks. No working funds meant no reserves. Anything could topple them.

Gloomy thought on top of a horrendous evening.

Lady Eleanor placed her hand on his arm, jerking him out of his thoughts.

"I thought you were going to your room," he told her.

"If you had been a gadabout," she told him, "if you'd been wasting your legacy drunkenly frequenting gaming tables or keeping a dozen mistresses—" she swatted his arm when he raised his eyebrows, "—I'm not a fool, Summerton, nor are you. For a man who isn't employed, you work very hard. I'm no stranger to politics. I'm aware of your power, your influence. Even Lady Holland speaks of you, though she considers you her nemesis."

He snorted. "Unlike her, I don't consider Napoleon a hero."

"No, you wouldn't—" she patted his arm and picked up his plate, "—nor would most English men." She put a goodly-sized wedge of cheese on it, with a thick slice of bread and a spoonful of mustard pickle.

"Here," she thrust it at him. "You are too tired to discuss this now, but if you don't, I will. She needs to know that you know better than to let your affairs get to this state, and you need her respect."

He held the plate without really registering that it was in his hands. "Did you know, Aunt? Did you have any idea?"

She sniffed and lifted her chin. "I think the only ones who knew were your father, his man of affairs, and the people of Summerton. And all were too proud of the duke's consequence to reveal the truth of it to anyone."

"It doesn't appear that bad from the outside."

"No, it does not," Lady Eleanor agreed. "One would not dare to question the duke's consequences by the looks of things."

"I should have."

"No, Summerton, you had no reason." She patted him again, and this time she did leave.

He stood, plate in hand, exhausted beyond thought. Then the fire sparked and settled, carrying his attention back to life and the young woman curled up in the wingback chair.

He added a large slice of ham to his plate, poured himself a glass of whiskey, and took both plate and drink over to the settee across from Caroline. He set the glass on the floor by his feet and tucked into his meal, watching Caroline as he ate.

She had saved his life.

She could have screamed, run away, or gone into hysterics, but no. Not Caroline. She had pulled him to the ground, risking herself.

She had saved his life.

And she wanted hers free of him. Had risked running away, into the night, to reach that end.

And he wanted her wealth to set him free of his burdens.

Except that wasn't all together true any more. He knew that. And he thought, just maybe, that she didn't want to be so free of him any more. She had enjoyed his kiss. He knew that.

Christ, what if the killer wanted her? What if he'd seen her kiss him? Had it sent him into a jealous rage?

"Summerton?" Caroline sat up quickly, still half asleep. "You've returned."

He set his empty plate aside, picked up his drink. "Yes."

"Did you find him? The one who..."

"No, but we did find your friend Jeremy." He liked the sound of that better. *Your friend Jeremy.*

"Really?" She sat up very straight, tucking adorable unruly curls back into a coiffure arranged a lifetime ago. "He wasn't involved. I'm sure he couldn't have been."

"No, he was concussed and found with a stab wound." He'd not burden her by admitting the dagger was still in his body when they found him. "He's being looked after by one of the tenants' wives. You'll be able to speak to him tomorrow, or rather, later today."

If they opened the drapes, daylight would soon fill the room, in a rainy gray sort of way.

"I'm pleased you are safe."

He smiled. "Oddly enough, so am I."

"You were so angry!"

"Was I?" he asked. "How did you know?"

She chuckled. "Ah, well, you are not as obvious as my father, but I'm learning. You became very focused and abrupt. You fueled your anger into action."

"I'd like to think I take action even when I'm not angry," he teased, leaning back, resting his drink on his crossed knee.

"You're a man of action, but when you are angry, it's swift and fierce. The way you marched me into the stables, no hesitation, no room for question. I was impressed. But that is not important now. Tell me what happened. Did you learn anything?"

"Wait, I want to hear more about how much I impressed you. I rather like that bit."

She tossed a small pillow at him. He caught it midair with his free hand.

"I was impressed as well, my dear," he told her. "How did you know he was going to throw that dagger?"

She leaned back, the fire light illuminating one side of her face as she looked at him, her lips pursed. *Those lips.* He licked the taste of whisky from his own.

"I didn't really know it was a dagger or a knife or anything, for certain. I had no idea what was in his hand. There was just a flicker of something. I couldn't have told you what. It alarmed me. Instincts, I suppose. I just went with my instincts. If I'd stopped to think about how foolish I would look if it proved to be nothing more than a stable boy with a harness or some such, well..." She lifted her head and shrugged.

"Remind me to trust your instincts."

"They are rather good."

"And did you see the culprit?"

"No, that's the worst of it. Just a shift of shadows and then a glint from his weapon. That was all."

"Were you hurt?"

"No, not really," she told him, but he knew it was a lie. She had favored her arm afterward. He'd noticed, but he'd wanted to go off and catch the killer.

She still favored her arm, kept it very still whenever she moved.

"Your arm?"

"It's fine." She rose, going to the table, cutting a small piece of the pork pie. "My whole body is sore from sleeping in that chair." She leaned against the table. "Now that you've returned home safe, I'll go have some sleep." She popped the piece into her mouth.

He set down his drink and joined her at the table, wishing he knew if it was wariness or shyness that had her eyes shifting away, her hands fluttering as if she did not know where to put them. He made that decision for her, taking her hands in his.

Before he could pull her to him to rekindle a kiss yet to be finished, she nearly toppled them both again by flinging herself into his arms, burying her head in his shoulder, wrapping her arms around his waist, and holding him in a ferocious grip. He hesitated, stunned, before wrapping his arms around her, returning, matching, her fierce hold.

"I was so worried," she said into his chest.

She welcomed him. He hadn't known that this—not the food, not the whisky—was the sustenance he craved. She needed him safe.

Thank you, God.

He smoothed her back. "I'm glad," he whispered, and nuzzled her neck, drinking in the sweet scent of a sleepy woman.

She swatted him and pulled back, laughing. "That tickles." Their eyes met, hers smiling and teary, as her laughter turned to a whisper. "You shouldn't be glad I worried."

He didn't have the fight to argue or tease. He didn't have the fight to keep from doing what he so desperately wanted to do. "Kiss me, Caroline," he said against her lips. "Kiss me and know that I am only alive because of you."

She hiccupped a sob, tears threatening to spill, and stood on her tiptoes to offer him her lips, eyes squeezed shut. His courageous, impulsive, brave Caroline, offering the kiss of a shy schoolgirl. He bit back a chuckle, bracketed her face in his hands and nudged her nose with his until she opened her eyes.

"Cara."

She chuckled, her shove insincere. "Caroline, your grace. You should, at the least, get my name correct."

"Cara," he whispered into her ear, "When we go to Italy, you will understand."

She shivered. A good sign?

"Look at me, Cara, my love."

He kissed each of her lips, he kissed the corners of her mouth, he kissed the tip of her nose before brushing her lips with his. "You." He kissed her lips once. "Were meant." He kissed them again. "For me." This time, in small increments, he revealed his hunger, his need, mouth to mouth, his hands holding her face to his.

She started to slide her hands up, around his neck, but stopped abruptly and pulled her right arm back with a small moan.

"Oh my Cara, you are hurt." He let go of her face and reached down to lift her into his arms. "Let me hold you." He meant to say, "instead of you holding me," but he was kissing her again as he carried her to sit on his lap on the chair she'd abandoned. The safest place. He'd not ravage her, as he wanted to do, in the chair.

They sat, him cradling her in his lap, her head on his chest. More comfort than he'd ever imagined, experienced. He'd just hold her, keep her close, keep her safe, for a moment. Then he would let her go.

He had to let her go.

After all, it was what she wanted, and she'd saved his life. He owed her that much.

HE WAS ASLEEP. ONE moment he was holding her close and the next he was asleep.

The chair was not a comfortable place to rest, as she well knew, but how to move him? Even if her arm had not been injured, she never would have been able to carry him as he'd carried her.

She slipped off his lap, considering her dilemma. No point in trying to rouse him. He was beyond waking. She went about the room, doing all those little things one did before shutting a room for the night. She banked the fire, and then, before blowing out the candles, opened one drape to a soft gray morning. Once the candles were extinguished, she stood before her sleeping husband.

Yes, her husband, if he still wanted her. Summerton had enough problems without her disrupting the balance of his life.

He'd taken her breath away, quite literally, the very first time she saw him.

She'd been a sullen and moody girl of thirteen, visiting her only friend from school for the winter holidays. Roz's mother had taken them for cups of hot chocolate at a fashionable confectioner in London. Spotting the future duke stepping out of a crested carriage outside the shop, she'd teased the girls, who'd been madly falling for every handsome young gent who entered the store. "That's the heir to the Duke of Summerton, and he's unattached."

Of all her crushes that winter, he was the only one Caroline had not forgotten. He'd been so handsome and regal. And remote.

She understood remote. Neither common nor gentry, she didn't quite fit into any society. Not really. This man, despite the buzz of friends about him, had mastered the art of being a part, while remaining separate.

After that day, Caroline scoured every bit of gossip news for any hint of him. She studied the streets in case he might be walking; attended the theater and walked around museums, going to every public place she thought he might be. Her infatuation deepened with each sighting, held strong through the years.

Budding dreams bloomed, blossomed. He'd stolen her heart.

On the shelf at twenty, nearly twenty one and he'd finally noticed her...

And her heart withered.

It was at the Pendletons' ball. Caroline had missed the announcement that he was entering, but Roz hadn't. "He's here!" she whispered. "And he's a duke now."

Caroline's heart tripped, quickening as she watched him step down into the ballroom.

His chestnut hair, a tad too long, revealed a natural wave, a hint of disarray. Everyone else suddenly seemed such fools for their meticulous grooming—from the precise folds of their cravats to the perfect little curls on their foreheads. She was no different. She dared not break a rule, lest she risk loosing those censorious tongues that loved to wag. Daughter of trade, she'd felt that sting far too often to feed it.

No one thought anything of her watching him, for they all did. Men bowed, women curtseyed, earning slight nods for their efforts.

She thought him bored in this place where others sought to relieve boredom. He had the right of it, a dull distraction, except for the dancing, of course. One needed a ballroom for that. She did so love to dance.

He represented the finest of class, and obviously the most arrogant. Born to it. She turned her back on him, once she'd calmed her breathing. "Just another man," she told Roz, a baron's daughter who lived in books, proudly wore spectacles, and cared little for the art of fashionable attire or ballrooms. She wouldn't have been there, except Roz's betrothed, the scholarly second son of an earl, had been pressed to attend. He'd escorted the two women.

They stood toward the back of the ballroom near a column, hidden by a mass of ostrich feathers in a vase on a plinth. Roz's intended was in deep discussion with another fellow only a few feet away.

Neither young woman cared to be seen. Roz preferred quiet gatherings and Caroline's toes had been badly trod upon and needed to recover.

And, as neither anticipated being noticed there at the back of the ball, behind the tall feathers, they were startled when Lady Pendleton and the duke came up beside them.

"Your grace, have you met Miss Caroline Howlett?" Lady Pendleton asked, without so much as a hello or a good evening.

"A pleasure." The duke reached for Caroline's hand, which she'd yet to extend, caught as she was by the clear blue of his eyes, framed by dark lashes. His gaze pierced deep inside of her.

"Your grace?" She recovered quickly enough, she hoped. She offered her hand, and dipped into a curtsy as he bent over it.

Rather than meet those beautiful eyes when he straightened, she swiveled and introduced her friend.

"Your grace, may I present Miss Rosalynn Morris?" Caroline asked, pouring as much arrogance into the words as Lady Pendleton had used while introducing her.

He bowed again, and Roz greeted him in return. Caroline hoped they'd move off quickly, so she could breathe again, but he asked, "Would you care to dance, Miss Howlett?"

She couldn't. Her palms turned so damp with the mere thought, she'd feared it would seep through her gloves. "I'm afraid this dance is promised to another."

One of Lord Howard's friends had asked her.

"Not a problem, my dear," Lady Pendleton trilled. "I will let the gentleman know the duke desires this dance."

His first dance of the evening. He'd singled her out of a ballroom full of beautiful women, finding her behind a wall of feathers, encouraging an introduction. Worse yet, he had rudely insisted on dancing with her despite the fact that she already had a partner.

He'd sought her out for a reason.

Another aristocrat with empty pockets to let.

Let him suffer her sweat-dampened gloves.

"Of course," she murmured with a smile.

She hated him for that.

Now here she was, watching him sleep, imagining life as his wife, knowing full well he hadn't a farthing to his name.

Even if he didn't know it, he could use her help as much as her money. His tenants would benefit under her influence. Times were changing.

What had her uncle said? "They need new blood, Caroline, you're just the girl to give it to 'em."

CHAPTER 12 ~ Past into Present

Loathe to leave Summerton there, sprawled in a chair she'd found too small to sleep in, Caroline went in search of a footman. Hitches had them posted outside every occupied room.

She opened the door quietly and peeked out, but instead of a strong footman she saw Jeremy moving down the hall toward the foyer, his head swathed in bandages, a sling holding his arm to his chest.

"Caro?" He stepped closer. "I've been looking for you."

"Where's the footman?" she asked.

He moved past her and closed the door behind him, moving easily into the room until he realized they were not alone. "Is that him?" He jerked his head toward Summerton, then swayed, grabbing his bandaged head.

"You've been hurt." She steadied him, tried to get him to a chair. "Jeremy, sit down. You shouldn't be out and about." But instead of going further into the room with her, he grabbed her hand and pulled her outside the chamber.

"You shouldn't wake him." He looked up and down the hallway. "He's put a watch on the Hall. There are men prowling all over."

"Of course he has. There's a murderer out there, Jeremy. It's dangerous. Look at you! You're lucky to be alive!"

"Aye, aye," he soothed, his gaze shifting about, watching for any guards.

"Summerton knows about you. You're all sorted. You are our guest now; you don't have to hide."

"Our?" he asked. "Does that mean you've forgotten about the mills?" He scowled, swore under his breath, pulling her toward the back of the house.

"Stop." Caroline pulled free. "I won't let the mills down, Jeremy." She had an idea coming, just wisps of thoughts, nothing firm yet, but she was beginning to believe she could stay without abandoning her father's affairs. "Come, help me get Summerton up to his chambers and then we'll find you a room for the night."

"It isn't night anymore," he said gruffly. "Leave him in his chair." He pulled her along the corridor. "And don't worry about me. I've got a place to stay. *We've* got a place to stay."

"With who?" she asked.

"You'll see. A helpful lass." He smiled that crooked smile of his. "She's sweet." He held Caroline's hand now, smoothed a wayward strand of hair off her forehead. "We need to talk, lass, and I don't want anyone listening."

They'd been friends the whole of their lives, but something was off, different now. "We can use the blue saloon."

"Not here." He shook his head. "We need to go somewhere else, get you out of here. That was the plan, Caroline. We talked about this."

"Yes, Jeremy, but quite a bit has happened, and I can't leave yet."

"You think it would be better to leave later?" he asked. "Why?"

"I'm free to go when I want," she hedged, "but we do need to talk first. Follow me."

She took the lead this time and guided him down the hallway into the grand entrance hall.

"Uppity place, eh?"

"It's an old family." She did not want to be critical. "There is value in that, Jeremy. Value in a family strong enough to survive countless generations intact."

He snorted. "Easy when you have their kind of power."

New blood, she offered new blood.

She guided him into the blue saloon, which was not so overly large as the drawing rooms. And the seating arrangements were more comfortable.

More important, she could see the Marble Hall from there, so she would know if Summerton went up the stairs.

She had no doubt he would check on her first thing when he awoke. He'd expect to find her upstairs. She took the chair facing the main stairway, to waylay him and avoid causing any alarm.

Jeremy hovered just inside the doorway, blocking her view. "This place is big enough to be a mill all its own."

"The mills are in better nick than this place, believe me. Now sit," she patted the chair at a right angle to hers, "before you fall over. You shouldn't be up and about."

"Had to get to you," Jeremy explained, sitting down on the very edge of a chair, holding his head in his hand.

"I'm glad you did. I need you to go back to the mills to do whatever you can, until I can join you."

"Why not come now?"

"We are going away. It's important I follow through on this," she explained. "By the time we get back, I will have everything worked out so I can help."

"You can't go." He grabbed her hand. "You're in danger, don't you see? You have to know that!"

"I will be fine"

"Not here. You are not safe as long as you are here." He looked up then, his eyes filled with tears. "I think he means to do you in when you are here."

"That's ridiculous." She sagged back in her chair, winded by his accusation, as if he'd actually struck her. "Whatever gave you that idea?"

"He married you for the money, didn't he? He didn't care, you told me so yourself."

"That doesn't mean he's cruel, Jeremy."

"Then who was it that murdered little Alice?"

It wasn't Summerton; she *knew* it wasn't Summerton. He'd been with her when Alice had been murdered. Hadn't he?

He'd been a victim, too, that very night. "Someone tried to kill him, Jeremy." She stood. "They are after him, too." Her own words sliced into her. She had left him alone in the study, vulnerable in his deep sleep.

"Pshaw! That was you they wanted."

"No!" She needed to get back to Summerton. "No, Jeremy, you have it wrong, you needn't worry."

He rose as well, and latched onto her arm to hold her back. "Your uncle is that worried," he told her. "He has someone watching you, too. I saw him the very first night you was here. I tried to catch up with him, but he slips through those woods like no one else."

"Biggs is here?" she asked, thinking of her uncle's guard. All of them, her father, her uncle, even Caroline, had guards in Manchester for fear of kidnappers and Luddites. Like his name, Biggs was monstrously big and dangerous, if you were on his wrong side.

Was she on his wrong side?

"Come, Jeremy, we have to get back to the study!"

"No!" he said, "You come with me. I'll keep you safe."

But she pulled free, already out the door and down the hallway before he caught up to her again.

"No," he snarled, "you're not safe with him."

"He's not safe right now!" Caroline argued. "He's not safe." She pulled free and ran to the study.

It was empty.

She flung the drapes open, checked all the doors. Nothing was ajar. She spun around, ensuring there was only one door into the room. Unlike the library, which featured doors at either end of two levels, the study only had one door from the inside.

Except for the hidden staircase. She didn't dare look at it with someone watching, though she wanted to, desperately.

"Come with me," Jeremy pleaded. "Come away from this place. It's dangerous."

"No, Jeremy." If Summerton were safe, he'd be looking for her. She knew he would be, she just knew it. Just as she knew the failing estate was not due to his negligence. He looked out for his own.

She was one of his own now.

He would take that seriously.

"You can't stay here." A commotion rang through the hall. Jeremy grabbed her arm, pulling her toward the terrace doors she'd just checked.

"Caroline! Where is she? Find her!" Summerton's bellow was answered by shouts and cries from the men on guard.

"Now!" Jeremy gritted out, as the sound of slamming doors and running carried all the way to the study. "Crikey! We'll never get out of here alive."

Caroline dug in her feet, "You are allowed to be here, Jeremy, Summerton knows you are around."

"No, you don't understand!" he snapped, shoving her away. "Fine, you stay here. I'm going." With his good shoulder, he pushed through the double doors to the outside.

"Go to the mills, watch them for me."

But he was running too hard to hear. She watched as he crossed the gardens, dodging this way and that, apparently seeking the cover of shadows.

"There you are," Summerton said from the doorway, fighting for breath. "I've found her," he croaked, seconding it with a louder call. "I've found her."

She didn't turn, but continued to watch her old friend run into the woods. "He is worried for me," she explained, as Summerton came up beside her. "Jeremy. He thinks I'm in danger, when it appears you are the one who is."

"*I* was worried for you," he ground out.

She smiled at him, despite the fury radiating from him, and touched his cheek. "I was about to raise the alarm when I couldn't find you here."

"Why didn't you?"

"You beat me to it."

Neither said a word.

"Is everything in order, your grace?" Hitches asked from the doorway.

"Yes, Hitches, sorry to have disrupted everyone."

"Quite understandable, sir." Hitches bowed. "These are unruly times." He left them.

"This could have been avoided," Summerton said.

He continued to look at the empty doorway, his profile as aristocratic as a marble bust despite the unkempt shadow of his beard and his tousled hair. His clothes weren't much better, but his bearing made them look artful rather than slovenly.

She couldn't tell what he was thinking, but he stayed that way—hands in his pockets, gaze beyond the doorway. She sighed and looked outside to ensure Jeremy had not run afoul of the hired guards. He'd been able to get past them twice. They obviously needed more training.

"You were alone with him," Summerton finally accused.

That got her attention. He was finally looking at her, his face twisted into a scowl. "Yes, I was alone with him, as I have been any number of times. We grew up together."

A muscle worked at his jaw, clamping his teeth together, no doubt.

"We went to the blue saloon so we wouldn't disturb you." She pushed away from the doorway. "Foolish me, I thought I could catch you going up the stairs before you could reach my empty chambers."

He turned away.

"But, of course, you took the hidden stairway. I'm sorry to have alarmed you. I really didn't think you would stir. You certainly didn't when I tried to rouse you."

Suddenly he smiled, but it wasn't a warm and friendly smile. It smoldered, kicking up his lips on one side, as his eyelids lowered halfway. He chuckled. "I don't dare say what I'm thinking."

She shoved at him. "You're teasing me."

"That I am." He eased, looking a bit chagrined as he ran his hands down his face. "I'm exhausted."

"You should go to bed, or would you rather I ring for coffee?" she asked.

He groaned. "I told the staff to sleep until noon."

Caroline followed him to the chairs by the now-cold fireplace. "I think that's been laid to rest."

"Good God! Poor Hitches was caught out in his dressing gown for the second time in as many days. I really should have searched a bit harder on my own."

"I'm grateful you didn't. If something had been wrong..."

He pulled her up against his chest. "Nothing will happen to you, do you understand? I won't let it."

"Or to you. Do you promise that as well?"

"Anything, if it pleases you."

They stood like that, clasped in each other's arms, holding each other up as much as embracing.

"Come on, you. Either go to bed or I will make you coffee myself." She smiled up at him.

His brow quirked. "You know how to make coffee?" Keeping her tucked against his side, he led the way out of the study.

"I can do all manner of things, your grace."

He chuckled. "And can you tuck a poor, exhausted man into bed?"

She didn't trust that smile. "If he's old and infirm."

"I feel very old," he warbled, "and infirm."

"You're nowhere near old enough," she started to tease, but the bells rang, a panicked clamor. Bells rung for fire, emergency, no other time.

"What the bloody hell is happening now?"

"Jeremy! It could be Jeremy!"

Together, they ran for the front drive, others pouring out of doorways, looking out windows.

"Here, this way," Summerton grabbed her hand and led the way to the stables. They rounded the corner of the hall to find people rushing about. It took a moment for them to spot the source of the chaos.

A small entourage moved up the path and past the dairy, four men carrying a cloak-covered body on a litter. A small feminine arm dangled down. Lifeless.

Behind the body, two lads were being hauled along by their collars, their efforts to escape futile. They were small lads, outsized and outnumbered.

"Who have you got there?" Summerton asked, when they reached him.

"Young Lucy, from the Inn, your grace," one man called out. "Found in the cemetery. Someone broke into the tombs. She was there, laying atop one of them marble coffins. These two were there as well."

"Sarcophagus," Summerton murmured, lifting the cape to get a look at the victim. Caroline looked around his shoulder.

"Oh, Summerton," she whispered. "I know her."

His head snapped around. "How?" He pulled her away. "She's a maid at the inn. How would you know her?"

Everyone hovered, too close. "She's the one who fell against me."

Before she could finish, Lady Eleanor pushed through the huddle around the body.

"Summerton?" she asked. "There's been another murder?"

"Yes, a girl from the inn. She accosted Caroline." That earned him one of his aunt's uncanny looks.

"She didn't," Caroline defended. But she had passed her a note. She would have to tell him, but not here, in front of everyone.

"Ah," Eleanor nodded. "I see. Perhaps we should discuss this inside?"

"Yes, Aunt, that sounds reasonable." He faced the growing crowd. "Put her in the ice house." Then, he turned toward one of the groomsmen. "Surely, Sir Michael is still here? He should be summoned."

Caroline glanced over at the captured lads. "What do you mean to do with them?"

"Put them in the stable." Summerton instructed.

"Are you certain?" Lady Eleanor asked, as she lifted the chin of one of the lads and looked into his eyes. Speaking almost to herself, she added, "I don't think the stables are secure." She moved away with a shake of her head. "Why not put these two in the cellars?"

"Do you think so?" the duke asked.

"Yes, quite." Eleanor smiled sweetly.

Caroline bit back a laugh. She'd once had a cat with just that smile. What had Eleanor seen in these lads to inspire her to make such a suggestion? They were small. Perhaps too small to be any danger to anyone. No heft to them at all.

"And send them some food, Summerton. No doubt they are hungry."

Summerton snorted. "I believe we all need to be fed." He headed back to the Hall. Halfway there, he realized she and Eleanor had failed to follow. "Come," he ordered, reminding her of the man who'd courted her. The one who'd expected the world to play out according to his design. Except now she knew it for what it was: focus, the recognition that a job needed to be done no matter how tired he was.

"We can question them after breakfast," he suggested.

"Of course," she said, joining him.

"I'll just have a quick peek at the body before I join you," Eleanor explained.

"Is that necessary?" Caroline could deal with all manner of wounds, but a dead body in a dark ice house? She shivered.

Summerton took her arm. "For some bizarre reason, Lady Eleanor thrills at such tasks. You may shudder, but she will delight."

"Ah," she remembered now, "the magistrate father and late husband. You told me she helped, but surely they didn't have her inspect the bodies."

"She has a talent for finding clues, even on the deceased."

Caroline blinked and then watched, with a new level of respect, as the older lady headed toward the ice house.

"Do you need anything, Lady Eleanor?" Caroline called after her.

Eleanor stopped, "Actually, yes," she said, turning around. "Have Jenny bring my box down. She'll know what you are asking for, and you," she signaled a passing footman, "what's your name?"

"Tom."

"Are you all called Tom?" She shook her head. "Come with us, then, Tom."

"Us?" Summerton asked.

"That would be me." Sir Michael hurried up to them, waving as he headed toward Eleanor. "Mustn't keep her waiting. Not a pleasant task, if I say so myself, but needs must be done."

Summerton put his arm around Caroline, "We shall go inside," he told the others, and led her back into the Hall, his hand gently massaging her shoulder.

A footman scrambled to open the door into the mud room, and Summerton released Caroline long enough to allow her to enter ahead of him, following as she passed through another doorway.

Once they were both over the narrow threshold, he resumed the intimacy. The weight of his hand buoyed her, easing the chill that had saturated her bones the moment she recognized the maid.

She shivered again and he pulled her close, sending a new sort of ripple through her—all hot and liquid and just as confusing.

She eased away, pulling her shawl up, high against her neck, across her shoulders. "Thank you, but I'm fine. I can walk on my own." It was a lie. She wanted him to argue, wanted him to put his arm across her shoulders once more. To pull her even closer.

"Of course. I will escort you to your rooms." His tone was so cold, she shivered.

No doubt, she offended him. "Are you going to yours?"

"Caroline, we've now had two murders, each connected to you in some way. You are not to be alone." He gestured toward the staircase they'd reached. "Shall we?"

He merely meant to lead her to her chambers.

Private rooms.

Her bed.

He would be a gentleman, leave her there.

She wasn't at all certain she wanted him to.

CHAPTER 13 ~ Ancient Halls

"I say, Lady Eleanor, are you certain you want to go attend that body?" Sir Michael held a large white handkerchief against his nose as they neared the ice house. He likely wouldn't need it, but Sir Michael had never been keen on decay of any sort, let alone the scent of it.

"I believe there is mint around the edge of the building."

"What good will that do?" he asked.

"Really, Sir Michael, you are a magistrate. Surely you've learned the tricks to viewing a dead body."

He shuddered. "Nasty business, if they've been left too long."

"Precisely." She picked a few sprigs of mint, unleashing the sweet scent. "This one could not have been left too long if she is local, and Caroline knew her. But just in case, wrap these in your handkerchief before holding it to your nose."

"What of you?"

"I really don't think it will be a problem, and if it is, I need to know what I'm smelling." She bruised some leaves, reached up and rubbed the essence around his nostrils. "I used to do this for Eddie," meaning her late husband, Sir Edward Francis. "It's good and strong, should help."

"Hm." Sir Michael took a deep sniff. "Willing to try anything."

Eleanor smiled and took a deep breath as she crossed the threshold. "She's fairly fresh."

“That’s a relief.” Sir Michael stayed near the door as she went up to the body and lifted the blanket that covered it.

“Naked? I wonder if she was violated or if this is the result of a tryst gone wrong.” Without looking up, she asked, “Wasn’t the other girl dressed in any number of layers?”

“Yes.” Sir Michael said, “The doctor didn’t think she’d been violated, though she wasn’t...”

“Unsullied?” She raised an eyebrow.

“Precisely.”

Eleanor moved to the far side of the body. “Help me here—” she nodded to Sir Michael, “—hold the blanket.” He took it, shielding the body from anyone’s gaze but Eleanor’s. “I need light,” she told Tom, who had followed them as far as the door.

As he ran for a lantern, she tried to lift one of the body’s arms. “Rigid,” she murmured.

“Ah.”

“My guess is that she died within the past day, but she was found in the crypt, am I correct?”

“Yes,” Sir Michael allowed.

“The weather has been cool and the vault is always chilly, so it may have been...wait!”

“What?” Sir Michael looked at her from across the blanket top.

Eleanor pried a thread caught in the girl’s broken fingernail. She moved down to the feet and studied the toes. “Toenails nicely trimmed, so no doubt she cared for her fingernails as well.”

“Her fingernails are broken?”

“Ragged.” She looked up, smiling, certain the girl had fought and left them a clue.

Tom was back with his lantern in hand, brightening the room.

“You,” she instructed the young man, “bring that light around here, but avert your eyes. The girl’s allowed some decency,” Eleanor ordered as she quickly moved back to the face. Tom kept his back to the corpse, holding the lantern out between himself and Eleanor.

"Splendid!" She adjusted his arm. "Right there."

"What are you doing?" Sir Michael had turned pale.

"Perhaps you'd do better not watch," Eleanor looked up from examining the girl's nostrils. "Poor gal, this nose has been broken a few times. None recent. I think there are fly eggs in there, but need..."

"Here you are, m'lady," Jenny stood in the open doorway, a large box in her arms. "Do you want the magnifier?"

"You are a saint. Yes, please, and come around here. You can help me."

Jenny came around to the far side of the body, put the box down on the end of the table, and opened it to reveal the sort of apparatus a scientist would use.

"So young and pretty," she murmured, as she handed over a magnifying glass. "Shame, isn't it, m'lady?"

"WERE YOU AWARE THAT Caroline knows how to prepare coffee?" Summerton asked his aunt and Sir Michael, as the two walked into the family dining room, refreshed and dressed for the day.

He understood their delay. He felt much better now that he had bathed, shaved, and tucked in a full breakfast, with numerous cups of coffee.

"Coffee? She makes coffee?" Sir Michael asked, lifting a chafing lid to consider the dishes on the sideboard. "You are quite a remarkable young lady."

"Preparing coffee is not a remarkable feat," she demurred.

"Oh, I don't know." Summerton shook his head and reached forward for his cup. "We will decide that when you make it for us," he teased. "But that will have to wait. I suppose we must descend into the depths of the cellars."

"Or we could have them brought up here," his aunt offered. "I don't see why we must discomfort ourselves for their sakes."

Her suggestion had merit, even though Summerton was fairly certain it had more to do with the young lads' comfort than a desire to save him a trip to the cellars. He recognized that look of Eleanor's—her attempt to look humble as she put thoughts in a person's head. She was rather good at that, but why?

"You don't think they did it, killed the girl," he said, "but they were in the crypt with her."

"They don't look to have the size or the strength or—for that matter—the motive."

"You have deduced this from looking at the body?" he said, his tone skeptical. "There are two of them."

"Yes." She touched her neck. "There was considerable bruising. You can clearly see four finger marks. I do not think a small lad could do that. What about your friend, Caroline?"

"My friend?"

"You might as well tell us, Caroline. What occurred when you spoke with Jeremy last night?"

"Oh, dear," She put down her serviette, folded it, and creased the folds. "I don't quite know where to begin without making Jeremy look terribly guilty."

"Is he?" Eleanor asked.

Caroline abandoned her inspection of the table linen to look up at them. "No," she shook her head. "No, I don't believe so, but he is very worried about me. He is aware of some danger out there."

"I would think so," said Sir Michael.

"Yes, well, that is rather obvious," she agreed.

"But you don't think him responsible," Summerton prodded. "He was injured himself."

Caroline hesitated, before adding, "The girl, Lucy—when she fell against me, she gave me a note from Jeremy."

All of the ease he'd begun to feel slipped away, replaced by a bitter cold. "You didn't think to mention this before?"

"I didn't even read it until just before dinner and then..."

"Yes, so," Eleanor nodded. "That's why you had to go to the stables. He told you to meet him there."

"At the kennels," Caroline clarified. "I had no idea anything would happen. Truly, Summerton, you have to believe me. I thought there was no danger."

That was the second time she'd said that to him today. He did believe her. It was Jeremy he doubted. "Why is he here, Caroline?"

"Because he is in charge of the mills. If we can get those working properly, they can shore up everything else."

Yes, she'd mentioned as much earlier. She depended on Jeremy.

But even as he mulled this over, his aunt surprised him by asking. "Are there many deaths at a mill, my dear?" The comment startled both himself and Caroline, though Michael merely nodded, as if Lady Eleanor was asking what he himself was wondering.

"It is a dangerous place, Lady Eleanor. Machinery goes awry, clothes get caught in gears, fights happen between workmen."

"I see." Eleanor speared a bite of ham. "What a disagreeable place."

"No," Caroline countered. "It can be rough, but the people work hard for very little. It is the responsibility of owners to see to it that they have a fair chance to live decently after putting in such hard labor."

"Hmmm," Sir Michael murmured, "it looks like you've married a Whig, Summerton."

Not a topic he cared to discuss. "About those lads," Summerton rose. "Let them cool their heels a while longer. We still haven't discussed what the newspapermen had to say"

"No help for it, they don't know the source. We are waiting for their editors to release the information. They'll run off before that information comes to us."

"Ha!" Eleanor scoffed. "They have more news here, with the murders, than they would have following the ton around in town."

Caroline stood. "They can't do us any harm, and their patronage should help the village tremendously."

"What of the murder of Lucy?" Summerton asked. "Did you consider any of them suspect?"

"No," Sir Michael responded. "We were still questioning them at that point."

"You can know that?" Summerton asked.

Lady Eleanor signaled a footman for another cup of tea. "Yes, it has to do with the stiffness of the body. The physician has been there and he agrees. Besides," she waved away other thoughts, "these murders are connected. They're all about Caroline."

"What? Me? I've done nothing..."

"I'm certain of it." Eleanor cut her off.

Caroline blinked.

"Someone is trying to get to you. That's why I wonder about your Jeremy," his aunt amended, as she prepared to rise.

"Of course, Jeremy and the notes. He knew the dead girl as well. What else aren't you telling us?" Summerton asked rather baldly, the sting of her secrecy still smarting. "Do you have another date with your friend?"

"No," she stammered, "not at all. I don't know where he is."

"He will surface," Eleanor said, "but I think you should be there when we question the lads in the cellar. You could be of use."

"Me?" Caroline cried, as Summerton questioned, "Her?"

Sir Michael nodded. "I see, Lady Eleanor, you have your suspicions."

"Yes, I do. Not about who is guilty but there are other...things." She looked up at Caroline. "You will come with us, won't you? The sooner the better."

She would override his other plans. He wasn't quite ready for that. He wanted some time alone with Caroline, the men in the cellar be damned.

"You don't think they are guilty, so why are you holding them?" he asked.

"They were found with the body," his aunt answered. "We have the right."

He just looked at her. She continued. "If you must know, I think they may be in danger for being found there. If I were the killer, I'd suspect they'd seen something. They are safer in the cellar than anywhere else."

He hadn't thought of that. "I see." He drummed the table, caught Caroline watching his fingers, and stopped. "Do you think they saw something?"

"Of course not. If they had, they would have spoken up, to save themselves from being locked up."

That decided it. He'd gained ground with Caroline. They were coming together. He did not want to lose that momentum. "As you don't think they did it, and they are secure, let them wait." He stood. "I thought it time Caroline see the whole of St. Martins."

"You are too stubborn, Summerton," Eleanor grumbled. "Very well, I will have a rest. Send a message when you are ready to speak with the...the—" she faltered, which was very unlike her, "—the prisoners."

"We will," Summerton promised, pulling Caroline's chair out for her.

They left the dining room for the side hallway, passed through the rose room with its high ceilings and landscape painting, and then walked through another hallway. He stopped before a door he hadn't crossed since youth. On this side, it matched the wood paneling that lined the wall. He wondered if the other side remained in good stead. Despite assurances it hadn't rotted, he couldn't help but worry.

"When I was a boy, this was my favorite part of St. Martins." Anticipation reigning, he pulled a key from his pocket. "I'm ashamed to say, I haven't been in here since, but Hitches promised me it has been well kept. Just don't take the stairs."

"Why ever not?" she asked, as if they would walk into an everyday space of no consequence.

It held every consequence to him. He almost hated to step inside, and have today's reality wipe away all the memories of playing soldiers and knights with his older brothers. Perhaps that was why he'd not returned.

"Rotted wood, most probably," he explained, turning the huge, iron key in the lock. "My father would bring us down here..."

"Wait." She put a hand on his arm, stopping him from opening the door. "Us?"

He looked at her hand, feeling the disconnect. He'd brought her into the heart of his family, only to find himself getting lost there. "Brothers. I had two brothers. One, Stephen, drowned in the lake. Our nurse was flirting with a footman." He turned the handle. "My other brother, William, died of an inflammation of the brain."

"I'm so sorry."

"It was a long time ago."

"And your mother?"

He'd been focused on his hand, turning the key, holding the door latch, but turned to her then. "My mother died giving birth to me. You lost your mother when you were three."

They watched each other, as if they could see straight inside, to a kinship of sorrows. Then she blinked, eyes widening.

"What?" he asked, urgent now. She looked on the verge of panic, but he didn't know why.

"My mother..." she looked away, down, shook her head. "There was a coach robbery, and the highwayman strangled her." Fierce, she met his gaze again. "Highwaymen don't strangle."

Agitated, she stepped away, paced. "Oh, Summerton, what a fool I have been not to think of that."

He took her shoulders, held them. "It couldn't be the same person. That was almost twenty years ago. He would be too old to be skulking around our woods."

She was breathing too fast. He urged her over to a chair, sat her down, chafed her hands. He didn't know what else to do.

"We will tell Eleanor and Sir Michael, but they will agree with what I just said. That highwayman would have no reason to follow you here."

"What if it wasn't a highwayman, what if someone has cursed my family?"

"Then he would have killed you by now," he snapped out before thinking. Good God, he should have held his tongue.

The key still protruded from the lock. "Come on, let's go in there. Step away from everything."

"It's magical to you." She didn't ask; she knew.

"The way a doll's tea set would be to a girl."

She snorted. "Very few dolls in my growing years. I played in the mill, with my father."

He hadn't thought.

"Well, we played with wooden swords and shields we'd made ourselves. Inspired by this room, family stories of knights defending the place." He held out his hand, and she took it. "This part of St. Martins is so old the corners are square."

"That means it's old?" she asked.

"Oh, yes," he informed her, as he pushed down on the lever, unlatching the lock, "Easier to scale square corners. They soon abandoned that design for rounded towers."

Immediately, upon opening it, he noted the old wood paneling on the far side of the door. Worm holes, but waxed nonetheless. He was at once proud and excited and wary.

Ridiculous for him, Duke of Summerton, Earl of St. Martins, to fear showing his ancestral home to his bride.

It wasn't that bad. Not yet. But it would be. Bringing it back to snuff would be a huge expense. He determined to do just that, or if that proved impossible, he would completely demolish what was beyond repair and rebuild it.

He led Caroline along a cold stone passage, past an ornately paneled curtain wall, and into the only surviving structure of the original St. Martins Hall. The great hall, where knights had gathered to plan attacks, great men to negotiate peace, and the entire household to wait out a siege.

The peaked leaded glass windows opposite them filled a wall the height and width of the room, their stained glass mosaic telling a story of battles, losses, and heroics.

"This part of the Hall was built by Henry St. Martin," he explained, "though these windows are newer. That wall was destroyed in a siege in—" of course, she wouldn't be interested in battles and defenses and power struggles that began and ended hundreds of years ago, "—during an ongoing skirmish. We managed to hold our own, but it was a close call."

He wished she would say something, *anything*. Give him a clue that would help interpret her frown. She looked up from the windows to the high arched ceiling and intricate wooden hammer-beam trusses that held it up.

At least, he hoped they held it up. The rot couldn't be seen from here, any more than he could see her thoughts written on the bare stone walls that had once been plastered white and graced by exquisite tapestries. He knew of the tapestries, threaded through with precious metals, but they'd been painstakingly stored. He had never actually seen them.

If this marriage didn't work, perhaps he could sell them.

Without the rest of her money, particularly given the stigma a failed marriage would paint on both of them, he'd have no way of reclaiming these walls. And they did need reclaiming. No mistaking the streaks, damp from a roof that had been leaking since he was a boy.

Without a word, she crossed the stone floor, stepped onto a Persian carpet lugged back from some crusade by an ancestor who had, surely, believed his descendants would treasure and care for the piece.

She stopped by the large carved host chair at the head of an oak table as thick as the length of her palm, long enough to seat ten people on each side, yet so narrow guests knees might touch in the middle.

The table gleamed.

Hitches, of course. He'd known, without being told, the new duchess would be shown the rest of the house. The butler had obviously removed the dust covers and hired a troop of maids to sweep and clean.

An expense the estate could ill afford.

He was grateful, no matter the cost. Not so much as a cobweb drooped from the stone buttresses above. Sweet oil so lavishly rubbed into the furniture, it scented the great space. No doubt Hitches had overseen the application on a regular basis to keep the ancient wood from disintegrating.

Mere months ago, he'd brushed away thoughts of cost, accepted his life of ease. Now he measured every action, every goal, by its weight in silver or copper or gold, or any damn thing he could use to pay for it.

Disheartening.

She stood inside the massive fireplace, looking up into the dark throat of the chimney.

"That was added later. The original hearth was in the center, where the table is now."

"Modernization," she murmured with a laugh.

"Exactly. That," he pointed to the oversized hearth she stood in, "is a perfect example of why they tore down the rest of the original hall. Drafts from these huge open fireplaces couldn't warm a bear in the summer. Impossible to keep heated."

He never should have shown her in here. The east wing was worse, with its buckling floors and pocked wall fabric. He should have secured her hand before bringing her to either part of the Hall.

Honesty was overrated.

"This is the real thing, isn't it?" She'd just noticed the gallery above. "Where are the stairs?"

"Beyond the wall there, but—" He'd already told her not to take them. The wood floors, supports, and stairs would be rotted with damp. No telling which step would hold and which would fall away with the slightest pressure.

"Summerton." His Aunt Eleanor and Sir Michael stood by the curtain wall. "I really think we need to question those lads now."

"I see," he responded, though he didn't at all. In truth, he didn't care.

"Cara?" He put out his hand. "Shall we go?"

She looked over her shoulder, eyes fixed on that dangerous staircase. Was that longing in her gaze? "It's not going anywhere." He hoped.

"Oh." She sounded deflated, like a child who had to give up a toy, but she took his hand.

This ruin might just win her over in a way he couldn't.

Deflating to find yourself in competition with a crumbling bit of stone.

CHAPTER 14 ~ Prisoners of All Sorts

The place was immense, full of twists and turns, impossibly wide hallways, and sweeping stairways leading to elegant galleries. There were narrow stairs and warrens of working spaces for the servants, below stairs. The house would require a massive number of servants, if it were working at its best, which it was not. Not now, not yet.

And there were troubles. The housekeeper gave her an evil eye when they passed through, on their way into the bowels of the Hall. The woman was probably still upset about Caroline's request to tour the servants' sleeping quarters. Well, she was in luck. Caroline's day had been realigned.

Just as well. She shouldn't get involved. She'd been a fool to imagine herself a partner to Summerton. Weak to fall in love with him. Did he really imagine she could help him restore this massive place? One of many homes belonging to the Duke of Summerton. What qualifications did she have to be the mistress of such an undertaking? Ancient halls, priceless art, and history. The history of it all! No wonder the aristocracy were so protective of their lot.

Her heart beat with nerves. She knew nothing about great homes. It would take an artist to see to the renovations and the tasks. Good grief, she'd not know how to scrutinize Mrs. Beechum's order of things. She was not up to the role, thank you very much. She was not born to it, and it was too late to start training now.

Traversing the original keep to the deep belly of the place, through hallways paneled in dark wood and smelling of linseed, they'd seen everything from stark castle stone to rooms dressed in silk and overseen by cherubs dancing along the cornices.

Fascination drew her in, moth to flame.

It would burn her up to nothing. An overwhelming and hungry beast, the Hall required more than money; it needed expert care.

Expansive and varied as her father's enterprises were, she understood their structure, their needs. She'd been raised within the belly of business...which was a far cry from the hodgepodge of bygone ages lovingly crafted and furnished with treasures acquired over the centuries.

What did she know of such things?

Murder, she must think of murder. They were headed into the cellars to speak with the newspaper lads.

Ah, yes, she could hear the prisoners. They could not be far now in this dank, cold place. Once below ground, they'd gone from the bustling activity of the kitchens, the servants' dining area, and further, into storage areas, and now the cellars.

She listened to the chatter as they made their approach.

"Would you stop bouncing on your toes! I'm about dicked in the nob with all your wiggling and talking. We need to think!" one complained, his a voice so young it hadn't cracked yet.

Surely a frightened child wouldn't be up to murdering, twice?

"Your grace!" A footman ran to catch-up to them from behind. "Your grace!" he panted, catching his breath. "A messenger has come, and he says it's urgent. Hitches said you would want to see him at once."

They all stopped. The lads in the cellar, alerted to their presence, tried to sneak glances at them from between iron bars designed to keep tipplers out.

Summerton looked at the cellars and then back at the footman.

"I will be there shortly," he offered.

The footman held his ground. "Hitches said this was most important, your grace."

"You go ahead, Summerton." Eleanor patted his arm. "And Sir Michael, you join him."

"But we need..."

"No, you don't. I will tell you exactly what happens. Trust me."

"This can wait until I meet with Hitches," Summerton said.

"Trust me, Summerton," Eleanor told him.

"We have the footmen to keep us safe," Caroline added.

Summerton had his eye on the two footman. One led them down into the underbelly of the Hall, another followed, each carrying a lantern. Despite the side torches spaced along the walls, the extra light was needed. The cellars were abysmally dark.

"Go." Eleanor waved them off and took Caroline's hand. "No sense dallying down here."

"Fine," Summerton said to their backs. "Come along, Sir Michael. Let us see what is so bloody important."

"Language," Eleanor scolded, without bothering to turn around. Caroline did look back. Summerton had turned, too, his scowl transforming to chagrin when he caught Caroline's eye. He dipped his head and went off, hurrying to catch up with Sir Michael.

She and Eleanor reached the barred wall of the beer cellar. Huge kegs filled the room, dwarfing the lads, who looked even smaller by comparison. Dim light came from torches that bracketed the hall on either side of the low curved entrance. The lads ignored the comfort of two stools to stand back, in shadow.

Eleanor studied the boys. "What do you see, my dear?" she asked, startling Caroline.

What was she supposed to see? "Two young and slight lads, nimble but not strong, I would guess."

"No sign of beards yet, would you say?"

Ah, yes, she'd notice their youthfulness. "Their voices haven't even changed yet."

"Exactly," Eleanor exclaimed, as she put a key Hitches had given her into the lock. "You," she signaled the footmen, "Make sure they don't rush past us when we go in."

"We didn' do nothin', I promise we didn' do nothin'. We shouldn' be in here, and they took my..." One of the lads started to protest.

"Shush! For the love of goodness, will you keep yourself quiet!" the other hissed, grabbing the arm of the talkative one to pull him back.

"They need to know, we have to get outta' here," the first boy argued. "I don't like dark places." The comment earned him an elbow in the ribs. "Ouch, why'd you do that?"

"Just be quiet!" the second one ordered.

Watching this little tableau, Caroline asked, "Surely one of the footmen will come in with us?"

"No, I don't think so," Eleanor answered. "The lads have been searched for weapons."

"But..."

Eleanor stopped what she was doing. "Come, child, you never struck me as cowardly or foolish. Think. Think of what we are looking at." And with that, she stepped into the cellar, pulling Caroline with her.

"Here," she said, as she passed the key through the bars to one of the footmen. "Lock it and then go down the passage. We wish to speak to the lads in private."

CHAPTER 15 ~ News from Manchester

A well-rounded, diminutive gentleman stood in the study, pressing his back against the corner he occupied. His eyes widened when Summerton and Sir Michael walked in, and he rubbed his watch case as though he hoped a genie might appear to save him.

From what? He hadn't been summoned, so he was there of his own volition. By dress, he was a gentleman, and should have been comfortable in a room designed for business. He'd certainly ridden hard enough to get here, judging by his mud-stained boots and creased buckskins. Multiple layers of dust clung to an immaculately tailored tailcoat. Though his collar was still high, his cravat had fallen.

"You have something important to tell me?" Summerton asked, without so much as a hello.

The man jerked around, as though struck. The duke moved around his desk and gestured for the visitor and Sir Michael to sit in front of it. The little fellow didn't move, his gaze darting between Sir Michael and Summerton.

Sir Michael continued to stand as well, his scowl confirming Summerton's own judgement that something was not quite right.

"Well?" Summerton snapped.

"I have a message for you." The man produced a letter, handed it over. "It's from Robert Howlett, your grace. He wanted to come himself, but it is impossible for him to break away at the moment. So he sent me."

"And this has you fearful?" Summerton took the letter. "Please sit," he told the messenger, as he settled into the chair behind his desk, opening the envelope, damp, he presumed, with the man's sweat.

Peeved as he was to be distracted with this business, his good manners rallied. "You've ridden hard to get here. Michael, would you ring for Hitches? Let's get this man some refreshments."

He ignored the murmur of voices, the coming and going of his butler, who must have been directly outside the door with a tray ready. Instead, he focused on the words on the page.

You may know by now that Caroline was not eager to be wed.

Summerton snorted. Not eager? Adamantly against it, more like. No wonder this fellow was nervous, having to acknowledge a tainted deal.

He continued to read.

Breaking her trust was necessary. There is much she does not know and much she would not readily believe. Her faith is in her father's manager, young Jeremy. Before he died, my brother began to suspect deceit, but it was a delicate situation. The lad had been given a great deal of authority before he proved treacherous.

Occupied by society, Caroline knew none of this, and I very much doubted she would believe any of it. In fact, due to my clumsy attempts to manipulate her, she will place me as the villain in the piece.

If Jeremy reaches her, he will use her badly. He means to gain control of the Howlett Mills, to make them his own. She is his only means of doing so. You must not allow this to happen.

Worse, you must not let her know of the danger. She is spirited enough to try to solve the problem, which will only make her more vulnerable.

You were chosen, from a number of possible suitors, precisely because you were judged to have the superior power to keep her safe. I leave this to you now.

Take Caroline on your wedding journey. As you know, her dowry is held in trust until you do so. I urge you to follow through immediately. Once you are out of the country, he won't be able to reach her. Until then, be watchful and keep her close.

I must stress, Do Not Allow Jeremy Near Her. She believes he means best and will refute any words against him. He is an evil creature, ruthless and dangerous.

Robert Howlett

After three readings, Summerton looked up at the messenger, who had barely touched the triangle sandwiches on the small table beside him. Even with the beer mug tilted to his mouth, his eyes scanned the room as if monsters might break free of the drapes at any moment. Placing the mug down, he twisted around to look behind himself.

"Stop!" Summerton ordered. "You'll snap your neck. I can see well enough behind you. There is nothing there but furniture, books, and a globe. Would you like us to lock the door?"

"No." The man pulled himself together, straightening his coat front, patting his cravat. "Of course I am safe. We are safe. I checked the French doors myself." Panic tinged his chuckle. "No need to fret." He took a calming breath, but it hitched halfway in.

Sir Michael ignored him, watching Summerton instead.

"What is it?" he asked.

"I'm not certain," Summerton admitted, handing the letter over.

Who to trust? Caroline's faith in Jeremy or Robert Howlett's poorly demonstrated concern for his niece? What man pretends to euthanize pets or sack employees as a means of control? Whether cruelly creative or eccentrically brilliant, the plan had worked...but at a price. Caroline held no love for her uncle.

Greed had created this scenario. Everything revolved around her father's businesses. Who owned them, and who wanted to own them.

"What do you know of this?" he asked the messenger, realizing he didn't even know his name. "And who are you?"

"Mr. Little, sir." The man set down the petit four he'd been about to taste, "And one thing I know for certain, it's dangerous here. We have a man on the grounds who's confirmed as much."

"What?" Sir Michael, who was now sitting beside the man, turned to look at him. "You have your own man on the grounds? And you didn't think to tell me, the magistrate? Or his grace?"

"We never thought Jeremy would find her here, but we wanted to be sure. We made certain to keep it quiet that she was due to visit St. Martins before leaving the country."

"Well, I never," Sir Michael groused.

"It's all right, Sir Michael," Summerton soothed. "He's telling the truth. Caroline thought we meant to leave from London. She had no idea we were coming here."

"Well, that's a damn sticky way of planning a wedding," Sir Michael argued, but he sat back.

Mr. Little tried to explain. "At that point, we didn't know Jeremy's involvement, not for certain. So we didn't dare risk anyone finding out. Thought it best to keep her uninformed."

Summerton drummed his fingers on the desk. "I thought Jeremy managed the mills."

"He did, sir, but he is no longer employed by the mills."

"He was at my wedding." Summerton stood, the man's agitation catching. "Surely, he must have only just been released."

The man took a deep breath, either in preparation for a deep lie—or perhaps an embarrassing truth? Summerton waited, fingertips on the desktop, as he looked down at the fellow.

"Mr. Little, we have other affairs to attend to. If you would get to the point."

"It was my error, you see." Little admitted. "We knew there was a problem with money. It started shortly after Mr. Howlett, Mr. Robert Howlett's brother, passed away. We couldn't find the source."

"I see."

"Jeremy, who in his capacity to oversee the mills can also access all the accounts, found minor ways of draining funds into an account for himself. That was the problem. There were thousands of small leaks rather than one large one." Little adjusted his cravat. "I discovered the source right about the time you were getting married. It was Jeremy. The alarm wouldn't have reached London until after you arrived here."

"You are certain it is him?" Summerton pressed.

"We were, your grace, but we feel even more certain given everything that has happened."

"What the blazes do you mean by that?" Michael asked. "Do you think him the murderer?"

"Jeremy never liked things out of his control. Your marriage, Caroline being kept away from the mills and from his influence...it has flung everything beyond his reach. Apparently it's turned him quite wild."

"Quite wild? Does he even know he's been found out?" Summerton asked.

"We don't know. We haven't been able to find him."

"He's been here in hiding, in contact with Caroline."

"You know that?"

"Yes." Summerton wasn't about to tell him that they'd had Jeremy in their grip, only to lose him. Or that Caroline had been alone with him.

"Well, you see..." Little drew out the words.

Summerton fought for restraint as he waited for the man to speak.

"You see, Jeremy did not take a small portion when he left for the wedding, but a crippling amount."

"And you know, beyond a doubt, he was the one who took it?" Michael asked.

"Oh, yes, sir," Little answered. "He did it with the help of young Suzy, who thought she was going with him."

"And she told you this?" Summerton snapped.

"Not exactly." Little stuck a finger between his collar and throat, his face gone crimson.

Summerton came around the desk, towering over the man, who leaned so far back he nearly toppled the chair. Summerton reached out to keep it from doing just that. Little squeaked with fear.

Sir Michael stood. "Come now, Summerton, you're frightening the poor man."

Summerton backed up. "Fine." He leaned against the desk, half a step from his target. "You'd best stop playing riddles, Mr. Little. Did she or did she not tell you?"

"Her diary did."

"Diary?" A squirm of unease crawled through Summerton.

"She is dead, I'm afraid, but it seems she kept a diary. Who would have known that a sweet little mill girl would know how to write, let alone have the resources to keep a diary. But she was raised in..."

"She's dead?" Summerton cut him off. "And you think Jeremy is responsible? Yet you failed to let us know until now?"

The small man sat upright. "You, your grace, were supposed to be out of the country by this time! It was part of the marriage agreement."

Summerton sagged against the desk. Yes, it was part of the marriage agreement, and they'd planned to leave immediately, except his bride had tried to run away and two murders had rocked the household.

"I don't mean to be insolent, but leaving would solve all your problems."

Except for wooing his bride with the one thing she appeared to appreciate—St. Martins.

He relented. "You've come a long way. Hitches will see you are settled for the night. Refresh yourself. We'll speak of this over dinner."

"But I can't stay..." Little tried to argue.

"You will stay," Summerton commanded, adding, "Keep in mind, we dine early in the country. Hitches will tell you when to expect the gong." He left the room, determined to reach Caroline in the deep, dark belly of the house.

Sir Michael stood. "Do as he says," he ordered, heading after Summerton. "He won't take kindly to your ignoring him."

THE BEER CELLAR WAS tidy. Besides the stools, a table, cots, and a single lantern were supplied for the lads. Caroline ignored the bucket placed in the shadows along the back wall and kept her place near the barred door.

Eleanor was not so shy. She removed her gloves and sat on one of the stools, neatly placing her gloves on her lap. The lads hovered against the long row of kegs, shifting on their feet. They wore soft shoes. One bounced up and down on his toes.

The other boy complained about the bouncing. Instead of bouncing, that one bit his lips tight. Both looked wary, if not outright terrified.

No, these were certainly not killers. Caroline relaxed, but she didn't say anything. Eleanor saw something in these two that she'd yet to reveal. Caroline would let her get on with it.

"Well," the older woman said. "Why don't you tell us who you are, why you are here, and why, for goodness sake, you are dressed as boys?"

Everyone gasped, except Eleanor.

Of course! Caroline should have seen it herself. Almost laughed when one of them tried to deny it.

"We *are* boys," one of the girls said, even as the other gushed, "How did you know?"

"Obvious," Caroline said to support Eleanor. "The pitch of your voices and lack of whiskers imply very young boys. Though small, you are too tall to be lads, and your features are too mature."

"I knew you would see it, my dear," Eleanor told her, turning back to the girls. "But why did you do such a thing? What would compel you?"

Caroline snorted, "That is easy to understand. It's a man's world. Very hard for a woman to make her way on her own." She had tried the same hoax only two nights ago. "But how did it come about?"

The smaller girl pulled free. "It was my cousin's idea, you see. That we write news. The governor said he'd buy our articles if we got them, but he wouldn't stick his neck out for us."

"You're reporters?" Eleanor smiled. "I see."

"In a manner of speaking." The older one stepped forward. "I'm Bevieann, and this is my cousin, Liz. Bevieann Ross and Liz Evans. I write articles, Liz illustrates."

"But you don't have any of the accoutrements needed." Eleanor gestured to the empty desk.

Liz lamented. "That crowd of louts grabbed us and left our things behind. No doubt they've gone through and stolen everything. All my pictures! Really, as if we'd done something wrong."

"You were found with a dead body," Eleanor reminded her. "A girl was murdered."

"We didn't do it," Bevieann snapped.

"No," Eleanor agreed. "I never thought you had, but you weren't safe out there and I had hopes you might have information."

"We just wanted a story, that's all. I just wanted to draw her. I didn't hurt her," Liz said.

"But you saw the body," Caroline said.

The two exchanged a long look.

"We need to know what you saw," Eleanor explained.

"There wasn't much to see," Bevieann said, "other than the strangled girl, o'course, but I did take notes and Liz took sketches."

"And how good is your eye? Either of you?"

"Liz's very talented. She doesn't miss much, but she knows when to leave things out," Bevieann said.

"And Bevieann's stories are printed so often because she gets bits everyone else misses. She's the best," her cousin said.

"Good!" Eleanor rose. "Let's go look at where the body was left. We'll see if we can find your notes and drawings."

"Do you think they might still be there?" Liz asked.

"We can only hope," Caroline answered.

"And if they aren't, perhaps you can remember how the area looked when you found the girl," Eleanor suggested. "Then we will bring you back to the Hall and you can write and draw from memory."

The young ladies exchanged glances. Bevieann nodded, but Liz looked doubtful. "Go on, then. Tell them."

"What?" Caroline asked.

"It's just, the girl had a secret sweetheart. We saw them together. Walking in the woods, before she was murdered. He was posh."

"Posh?" Eleanor asked.

"Nice clothes, you know. But his words didn't match his clothes. You know, posh like."

"Interesting," Eleanor admitted.

That sounded too much like Jeremy, and Jeremy had a lady friend. He'd told her so. Only he'd been leaving to go to her, hadn't he? This girl would have been murdered by then.

She shook her head. It wasn't making sense.

"Just because she was sweet on someone, doesn't mean he killed her," she argued.

"Possibly not." Eleanor nodded. "But he might know who did."

CHAPTER 16 ~ The Crypt

Chilling fingers of fog clung to Caroline's shoulders. She wrapped her shawl tighter, protection against the cold, against an insidious fear. It didn't ease, even with all the able-bodied men around her, or bright torches fighting the gloom.

She jumped at every sound, noise distorted by the weight of the mist. An animal scurrying in the underbrush ticked up her heartbeat. The eerie hoot of an owl rippled down her back. All so far, yet so near.

She wished Summerton wouldn't take such a prominent place at the front of their little entourage, not after what happened last night. Or Lady Eleanor, who hurried along beside him, eager and intense.

Once they'd informed Summerton and Sir Michael about the female reporters, and had, in turn, been told about Mr. Little's visit, Eleanor insisted they go to the crypt. She'd been chomping at the bit ever since she'd spoken with Bevieann and Liz.

There was no discernible path in the fog. They walked through wet spring grass, wild and tenacious undergrowth. Dew saturated her boots, and the hem of her skirts. The musty scent of earth and churned debris, from two seasons before, made it feel more like autumn than spring.

How easy it would be for an assassin to hide behind the fog, in the tumble of young trees taking over the landscape.

The duke had begged her to stay behind at the Hall. Caroline had refused. She'd rather be there with him than fretting and worrying.

Sir Michael had joined them for this adventure to the crypt, and, of course, Liz and Bevieann were also there.

"Who's out there?" The call surrounded them, muted by the dense air.

"The duke," one of the guards bellowed.

Like a specter, a young man stepped out of the fog. His lantern barely cast a glow against the mist, but in its weak light, his eyes were wide, fearful. Behind him, an iron arch crowned an ornate gate. Purely decorative, for anyone could cross the stone wall on either side of it.

Eleanor stepped up to the gate. "Thank you, Summerton, for the guard," she told him, as she walked under the arch. "It wouldn't do for this to be disturbed."

Summerton stood aside, letting the others precede him in. "No one cared to, Aunt. Why you do is beyond me, but here we are."

"Yes." She looked about, distracted. "Yes," she murmured to herself.

Caroline wondered what drew her attention other than the overgrown grass, weeds, and young wildflowers crowding the headstones. She saw nothing of note.

"No!" Eleanor snapped, having noticed everyone crowding in on both sides of the cemetery path, still discernible despite obvious neglect. "Wait just a moment, please. Stay where you are." Again, she investigated the ground.

"What is it?" Sir Michael asked.

Rather than offering a response, she tapped a bent knuckle against her lips, all her focus on the ground beside the path.

"If you tell us what to do, Lady Eleanor, we could help," Caroline said. "But the only things I see right now are trampled grass and broken lilies of the valley."

"Where?" Eleanor demanded, hurrying over to Caroline. "Ah! I see." She turned to one of the guards. "Bring that torch over here, will you?"

And then Caroline saw the obvious. Someone—or someones—had trampled a route from further down the wall to the pea-graveled path.

"They went back and forth this way," Eleanor explained. "The gate must have been locked."

"We keep it locked," Summerton confirmed, "though Lord knows why."

"Animals," Sir Michael ventured. "Keeps them out."

"Did you walk this way?" Eleanor asked the newspaper women.

"No, ma'am." Liz pointed beyond the orb of light, in the opposite direction. "We came from there."

Eleanor led the way. The path ended at the door of a large stone edifice, covered in carvings and statuary of cherubim and angels. It seemed to sprout from a mound of earth. The aboveground part was tall and ornate.

"Scary, isn't it?" Liz whispered from beside Caroline. "Can you imagine, someone lived in there?"

"What?" Eleanor turned. "Did you say someone lived in there?"

Liz bounced up on her toes, looking from Bevieann to Eleanor, a sure sign she was nervous. Bevieann didn't say a word, just watched her cousin with a resigned sigh. Liz must have taken that as a nod of acceptance, for she elaborated.

"Seemed so. There were clothes and a palette, though the blankets were thin. Candles burnt to nubs, and a tinder box. Must have been really cold in there because it's a chilly place and..."

"This is our family crypt." Summerton confirmed.

"Yes," Eleanor agreed. "Where the body was found." She turned back to Liz. "Any sign the person had been there recently?"

Bevieann chimed in this time. "He had a plate and a beer jar. I thought the girl might have brought it from the inn."

"So you knew the girl?" Summerton asked.

"Well, yes," Liz answered. "We stayed at the inn. And she worked there and the plate looked like it was from there and..."

"Yes," Eleanor quieted her, already moving on. "Is this normally locked, Summerton?"

"It was unlocked for Father's internment. I couldn't tell you if it was locked afterward. Too many other issues to worry about disturbing the resting place of those past disturbing."

"I dare say." An eerie creak shuddered through the night as Eleanor opened the door. "Sir Michael, will you take one of the lanterns and join me? The rest of you wait where you are. We do not want to disturb the evidence."

The two stepped through the ornate doorway and down into the dark of the crypt. Eleanor broke their stillness, returning to the entrance moments later.

"Summerton, bring a torch, will you?" She asked. "There's a bracket to hold it. The lantern isn't strong enough."

The duke touched Caroline's shoulder as he passed her, leaning close to whisper in her ear. "You'll be fine. Just stay close to the guards. We won't be long."

She watched as he gathered the torch and stepped down into his family's vault, leaving her behind, feeling rather useless. She was not used to being useless.

"May I have that lantern?" she asked one of the guards. They still had two torches, so they wouldn't be without light.

"Where are you going?" Bevieann asked.

"I want to follow the path Lady Eleanor noticed. Perhaps I can find something."

Liz frowned. "Do you want us to go with you?"

"No, I'll be fine."

One of the guards joined her. "No," she told him, "really, I'll be fine. We don't want to disturb anything more than we have to." She would stay within the stone walls. Everyone would hear her if she called.

Eleanor learned from the bent grass and broken flower stems. Caroline decided she would try to do the same thing, look further afield, for anything out of the ordinary, or for something dropped. If only the fog weren't so thick. Worse, dark had settled in. Between the two, the lantern did little to illuminate the area around her.

She reached the end of the building. Two wings spread out from the entrance, she noticed. A massive tomb, for a long line of dukes. She shook her head at the folly of imagining she could fit into such a lineage as she rounded the corner to the far side of the tomb.

A hand reached around, covered her mouth, and pulled her hard against a body much larger than hers. She fought as he pulled her further from the building, deeper into the dark.

SUMMERTON SETTLED THE torch into the cast iron bracket. He hadn't been here since his father's burial and hadn't liked it then—and that had been a bright and sunny day. This evening was anything but. He didn't care to leave Caroline out there.

"Do you see anything, Aunt?"

"Nothing here, your grace," Sir Michael grumbled. "A lot of fuss for nothing."

Eleanor looked up at him. "Really, Sir Michael," she snapped. "That there is nothing here anymore speaks volumes."

"Does it? How so?" Sir Michael asked.

Eleanor stood in the center of the main aisle, having looked into, but not entered, the four large wings. The center area was the oldest section of the tomb, built by the first St. Martin back when they were mere barons. Since then, four chambers, each with multiple burial nooks, had been added, off the sides of the central chamber.

She pointed to the first crypt, to their left.

"Is that where your father is?" she asked Summerton, waiting while he checked that all the gates were unlocked. "With your mother?"

"Yes." He opened the iron doorway leading into the chamber. "And my brothers."

"Come, Sir Michael," Eleanor demanded, "bring that lantern, I'll pay my respects."

"Now?" Both men asked.

"Yes, now. I don't know when I will be back and I want to settle myself that he is with her."

"Where else would I have put him?" Summerton asked in disbelief, as she stepped past him. She stopped, patted his cheek.

"Of course you would have put him there, but you wouldn't know the importance."

"She was his wife."

"Oh, but she was more than just a wife. She was the love of his life. They were inseparable from the time they were children." She stood before the tombs of her sister and brother-in-law. "We all worried that he would die after losing her. Oh, he mourned so." She sniffed.

"As he did after the loss of my brothers." Summerton leaned against the gate, touched by Eleanor's sorrow, the hitch in her breath.

"That's why he preferred to be alone here, Summerton," she told him, not looking away from the tombs. "I dare say it broke his heart all over again, every time he came back here."

"It was a long time ago," he reminded her.

"Yes." She nodded. "A long time to mourn."

"Lady Eleanor?" Bevieann peeked into the crypt. "Did you find my notebook?"

"Or my sketches?" Liz asked from behind her. "They should be here, that's where they found us," Liz continued with barely a breath. "We lit the candles so I could draw and Bevieann could write and..."

"No," Eleanor scooted Summerton out of the wing chamber. "No, there wasn't anything here. Perhaps you could show me how the body was found."

Liz marched up to the tomb of the first baron of St. Martins, a small rectangular box with the effigy of a knight carved on top. "She was there." Liz pointed.

"How?" Eleanor frowned, looking at the intricate design of the tomb, which was carved like a realistic armored figure. "How could she have been on there without falling off?"

"Like this," Liz splayed herself face down on the tomb, laying lengthwise.

"That would explain quite a bit." Eleanor tilted her head, studying the position.

Bevieann tugged at her cousin, who was looking between the sarcophagus and the wall. "Get off, Liz. You're laying on top of a dead body."

"Oh, I...oh, I!" Liz scrambled down. "There's a cloth..."

"Just a moment," Summerton said to Liz. "I want to know what that explains. Aunt?"

"Well—" Eleanor hesitated, "—if you really want to know, fluid, in a body, gathers at the lowest point, causing patterns of discoloration. Lucy's coloring was most unusual...but Liz, what did you find? A piece of cloth, you say?"

Summerton looked over for Caroline's reaction to the morbid conversation, expecting her to have come in with Bevieann and Liz. She wasn't there. He glanced in the chamber they'd just left, and then another. “Where’s Caroline?” he shouted, as he went to look into the other two vaults. The stunned reactions were answer enough.

They all rushed to the main door—just as Caroline filled it.

“Here,” she answered. “I’m here.”

She was disheveled, her voice shallow, breathy.

“What happened?” He would kill anyone who threatened her. “You’ve been hurt.”

“No.” She shook her head. “I tripped and dropped the lantern, but I’m fine.” She pulled away from him.

“What have you got?” Eleanor reached for two books.

Caroline looked down, as if she’d forgotten she was carrying anything. “I found them, and thought you might...”

“My sketches!” Liz cried.

“My notebook!” Bevieann snatched the books from Caroline in one swipe.

“Where’d you get those?” Summerton asked, knowing she hadn’t found them just laying about. She’d been thrown to the ground, or dragged, or...

He headed out of the crypt, set on finding whoever had hurt her.

“Stop! Jeremy! Please stop!” she shouted.

He did stop, stunned.

“Did you just call the Duke of Summerton ‘Jeremy’?” Aunt Eleanor asked.

He turned, slowly, watching the lie skitter over her face as she shook her head. “No, of course not, I...”

“But you did, which means Jeremy gave you those books, just now.”

Her mouth opened, but whatever she had meant to say was interrupted by Liz’s wail. “He’s taken the picture of the beau out!” The girl looked up. “He’s taken out the picture of him and the girl who was killed.”

“He didn’t kill her,” Caroline denied.

"Then why would he remove the picture, my dear?" Eleanor asked.

"He didn't," she tried to explain. "He'd found those, tossed aside. He saved them to give to me. He didn't kill anyone... He's heartbroken and frightened for himself, for me—" she looked at Summerton, "—for you. You must believe me, he didn't kill anyone, *couldn't* kill anyone."

Summerton knew too many men who had fooled too many women to trust 'her' Jeremy. "Your father's man, Mr. Little, thinks that's precisely what he did."

"Mr. Little is no great resource for such information," Caroline denied. "Just ask him about his son's treatment of poor, defenseless animals." She turned on her heel and headed out of the crypt.

"Your Mr. Little and dinner will be waiting," Eleanor offered. "Perhaps we should head back. We have the information we need."

Summerton held back as the others filed out, Eleanor remaining with him. "He hurt her," Summerton gritted out.

"There did not seem to be any bruises, but I'll see what her maid says before I take a stance."

"She called me Jeremy," he reminded her.

Eleanor patted his arm. "Yes, I daresay she did. I wouldn't put too much stock in that. She was worried about you, and she's been worried about him. The two worries just slid together."

"Do you really believe it could be that simple?" he asked, leading her out of the crypt as smoothly as he would have led her in to dinner.

"I do."

"Well, I don't."

Caroline waited by the gate with the footmen. As soon as they were all above ground, she led the way back to St. Martins. They were a quiet group.

CAROLINE STEPPED INTO the great hall, buoyed on a wave of fury. He thought her foolish for believing in Jeremy when he knew nothing about the man, except for what Mr. Little had told him.

Mr. Little, who had raised a beast of a son, then blamed the boy's bullying on his victims. Or so it had always seemed. The man continually disdained her and she'd been everything polite to him. Really! A small-minded little man. He should be begging her forgiveness after the tricks his son, Roger, had played. If she'd had her druthers, her father would have released him years ago. She had never understood the loyalty.

She untied the ribbons of her bonnet as the others came in behind her.

"Beg pardon, your grace, but Mr. Little has come down for dinner," Hitches said. "He's in the rose room."

Caroline shuddered, earning a scowl from Summerton, who told Hitches, "Let him know we've been delayed."

Caroline gave the duke her brightest smile. "Why don't I do that, your grace?" she offered. "It's past time I greeted our guest."

Before he could object, she crossed to the receiving room, to find Mr. Little peering through a crack in the curtains. "Mr. Little!" she called out, thrilled when he jumped, spinning around at the same time.

"Mr. Little," she said, as she stepped into the room. "You must forgive us. We've been down at the crypt, where the body was found last night. No doubt you've heard of the excitement here?"

Mr. Little scowled as he crossed the room to her. "Caroline, behave yourself. You are just going for effect."

She stopped in her tracks, stunned by his accuracy and a bit ashamed.

"You are a duchess now," he admonished, "not some hoyden." He shook his head. "I didn't go along with this wedding. Doubt either the duke or you knows what you're in for."

"I never realized you had such a low opinion of me," Caroline whispered.

"No." Little shook his head. "I've always admired you, in your place. But you are not in your place anymore. Everything you do reflects on your husband, and even more so, on the people who work for him. They take great pride in their positions. You will do well to remember that. Do not bring your side down, Caroline. Any class can be respected." Looking over her shoulder, he cut his lecture short.

She followed his gaze to see the duke, elegant as ever, his overcoat exactly where it should be, in some closet under Hitches's direction, while she stood, muddy shoes on the Aubusson carpet, her hair, no doubt, trailing down around her shoulders.

Hoyden indeed.

In your place.

She was a proud daughter of the working class. This place, these people, Summerton, St. Martins, a long line of dukes with distinguished tombs to prove it. These were not *her* places, her people. Her grave would be lost in time. Forgotten.

"Your grace." Little bowed to Summerton.

"No doubt her grace informed you that dinner will be delayed," Summerton told him. "I trust Hitches has offered you refreshments."

"Yes," Little said. "I'm fine, perfectly fine."

Except she wouldn't be acting as 'her grace' once she left. Caroline fought for steady ground. Right now, she was Summerton's duchess. She would not let him down. She would do him proud.

To prove she was an intelligent young lady, capable of conversing on affairs at hand, she asked, "And the mills, Mr. Little? Have you brought word on the mills?" It was their common ground, something they both understood and appreciated.

Little's gaze shifted from her to Summerton and back again. Obviously, she'd crossed another taboo line.

"My dear, surely you needn't worry about such things. Business—" he raised his eyebrows at Summerton, "—leads to over-excitement in a female. Not good." He shook his head. "Best to be avoided."

Summerton failed to defend her, but in all fairness, he appeared to be as angry as she felt, perhaps more so. She recognized the signs, the hard set of his jaw, the flare of his nostrils, his fingers restlessly rubbing the edge of his shirt sleeve.

Only a few short days had revealed so much about him, the differences between the two of them. Summerton could control his anger, keep a lid on it, as she went flying off, like that chafing dish lid the other morning.

She'd never liked Mr. Little, but she'd grant him his due. He had her pegged.

The duke took her arm. "If you will excuse us, we will change for dinner." He dropped his hold the minute they left the room, though he remained beside her as they walked up the stairs.

"Eleanor saw to the two newswomen. They'll sleep in the nursery."

Caroline should have seen to that. A duchess would have.

"I'm sorry, I didn't think."

"You were distracted," he offered, generous to a fault.

"They'll need a guard," she realized. "They can identify people."

"They can identify Jeremy," he reminded her.

"Yes." She wouldn't argue her cause again. Not now.

They reached the first landing and rounded the corner of the staircase.

"Did he hurt you?"

She missed a step; he helped her.

"No." She shook her head.

"You looked...disheveled, like you might have been...injured."

He frowned, intent on his own thoughts. He didn't look at her. He didn't really look at anything until they reached the floor of their respective chambers. From there, he studied the hallway, as though facing a long and difficult journey.

He took a fortifying breath before heading down the hall.

Not able to bear this silence with him, she said, "He didn't hurt me. He covered my mouth in case I screamed." She took his arm, hoping movement would help her find a way to describe what happened without putting Jeremy in a bad light. "I didn't know it was him, so I fought. That was all. It was my fault." It had made so much sense at the time, but now the explanation didn't even convince her.

"If you need time for a bath, take it. It will ease your muscles. We can hold dinner."

She sniffed back tears. He was such a gentleman, stuck with a shrew of a bride. She would do better by him. She would not embarrass him. She could be good, at least, for the length of the bridal journey.

Then he could find himself a new wife. A woman of his own kind. And she would continue to be the bad-mannered, impulsive woman that she was.

They entered their shared sitting room. She watched the proud line of his back as he crossed to his chamber door. When he hesitated, she sidestepped to her own doorway, afraid of being caught all doe-eyed and yearning.

"Caroline?" He looked over his shoulder.

"Yes." She swallowed, thinking to say it again, for he couldn't have heard her strangled whisper.

He lifted his hand as though to point out an argument, but she didn't look at his hand, she looked into his eyes.

Not angry.

No.

Hurt.

His whole world was falling apart—his finances, his legacy, even his people, and then there were the murders. All of it her fault. As Mrs. Beechum had said, it had been a peaceful place until she'd shown up.

His hand dropped. "Never mind." He closed the door firmly behind him.

CHAPTER 17 ~ Motive Anyone?

Shadows danced in the candlelight, caught on a breeze sneaking through some hidden fissure between window frame and wall. At a glance, the magnificence of St. Martins hall intimidated, but within minutes of entering it, damp drafts, warped floors and gaps, the crystal chandeliers displayed a distinctly different view.

Such was the state of ancient family monuments. St. Martins Hall should have been the heart of a productive enterprise but had not been managed properly. Caroline was her father's daughter, knew how to manipulate difficult and complex organizations. She could no more turn away from a challenge than her father had been able to. He'd raised her to thrive on the impossible.

Returning this ruin to its former glory was a daunting task, all the more tempting because of that. But it was beyond her skills, all that art and preservation and, no doubt, a hundred other special skills she knew nothing about.

She should be thinking about the Howlett holdings; a business she understood.

A place where she'd earned respect.

Not like here.

What had Summerton been thinking? There were other heiresses he could have married, some as wealthy as she. There had been no need for him to wed a commoner.

Shadows brushed his cheek, darkening an already solemn expression. She yearned to do that, to touch his face, to feel his arms around her again.

He looked up from under his brow; its crease smoothed and his lips tipped up on one side, erasing his frown. No more than a glance, but it slipped deep inside of her.

She raised her serviette to her lips and lowered her eyes to the table, avoiding him.

She'd allowed too much intimacy. They must not be intimate in any way, not so much as a touch. Not now that she'd decided she could not stay after all.

She was perfectly comfortable in her world, but a painful undercurrent of contempt ran through Summerton's level of society. She could not live with that humiliation.

Here she was, bound by the strictures of gentility. Even the likes of Mr. Little, so far below her in status, could treat her as a troublesome object and an inferior merely because she was a woman. Not only a woman, but the product of trade. In her rightful place, in the mills, she could step on a toe-rag of a man like Mr. Little and crush him.

"You really must take her out of this country, your grace." Mr. Little didn't so much as bother to look her way. "Everyone would be far safer if she were not in this place."

The man did not want to be here, that much was clear. He twitched at every sound, looked over his shoulder at every shadow. Summerton didn't help matters, having grown darkly quiet after that one heated glance.

Sir Michael, still present as matters grew ever more serious and complex, offered little more by way of conversation. After interviewing the reporter and illustrator, looking over their notes and drawings, he'd settled into observation, rather than interrogation.

Not so for Lady Eleanor. "So unsettled, Mr. Little," she asked. "Why do you believe our Caroline is responsible for these ills?"

Like a startled bird, his head whipped around, away from his nervous study of shadows behind him, where a footman stood at attention. "No, no." His voice hitched, his answer was no answer at all.

"Surely nothing could happen with Biggs here," Caroline added, not doubting for a moment that Mr. Little knew of Biggs's presence. They were both her uncle's men.

"You knew?" Summerton snapped.

She'd offended him by not speaking of it sooner. Yet his accusation proved his hypocrisy, for he must have known as well.

"Yes." She helped herself to a syllabub. "I meant to speak of it, but quite forgot."

Despite the expanse of the table, for they sat in the formal dining room, she saw Summerton's brow furrow. "Well, do tell us now."

"Why don't you? Obviously you know as much, if not more. I only know that he's been seen in the woods," Caroline challenged.

Summerton placed his wine glass back on the table. "Your uncle heard about Alice." His gaze was sharp rather than seductive. "He sent Biggs to look into the affair. Mr. Little was good enough to tell me."

"I see." But she didn't see. Jeremy had seen Biggs before anyone knew about Alice.

"Do pay attention, Mr. Little," Eleanor snapped.

"I...I am," he stuttered.

"Are you?" Lady Eleanor spooned a bite of sweet. "You act as though an assassination is imminent. Are we all in danger?"

"No, no, no, no." He shook his head. "You should be perfectly safe," he said, placing heavy emphasis on *you*. "Everyone should be perfectly safe, once the duke and duchess take their leave and depart on their journey. He won't be able to get them then."

"Mr. Little," Summerton said, but Caroline interrupted him, leaning forward.

"What do you mean, 'he' won't be able to get us? Who, exactly, is 'he'?"

Mr. Little fidgeted.

Summerton caught his bride's eye. "Caroline, you needn't..."

"Yes, I do indeed need to know." She gave *him* a steely-eyed stare this time. "Who, Mr. Little?" She sat tall. "Pray tell."

"Your grace," he addressed Summerton.

"Look at me," she ordered, surprised when he did just that. Good.

He swallowed.

"I may not shout and curse and bully, but I am my father's daughter." Her voice shook with anger.

The spark in Mr. Little's eyes did not match his agreeable nod.

Summerton must have seen it, for he added, "She is more than her father's daughter, Mr. Little. She is my wife, the Duchess of Summerton. I do not take kindly to any measure of insult. Do you understand me?"

Little swallowed again.

"Well said, Summerton." Eleanor smiled, turning to Caroline, then winked before suggesting, "My dear, are you not tired of masculine conversation?"

"I would be happy to leave once he tells me who is responsible for these murders." Caroline squared her shoulders.

Little looked at Summerton, then Sir Michael, and finally at the plate in front of Caroline. He could not meet her eyes. "Your father's manager, your grace. Your uncle has good reason to believe it is your father's manager, Jeremy."

"I see," she said, pushing back her chair. "Then we can all rest assured."

"Caroline?" Summerton asked.

"There is nothing to worry about. Jeremy would not harm us," Caroline insisted as she rose.

"You are quite right, Lady Eleanor. I have grown tired of masculine conversation," Caroline said. "Shall we retire to the blue saloon and leave them to their port?"

THE NIGHT WAS NEARLY through before Mr. Little retired. Fortunately, the rest of the party remained. They had quite a bit to discuss.

"Shall we move to the study? Hitches has seen to a fire," Summerton said.

"Superb," Eleanor exclaimed. "Imagine, having a fire at this time of year. It is truly awful weather."

"Heard the Thames froze so hard this winter they roasted a whole mutton on the ice," Sir Michael said. "Is that so, Summerton? Did they really roast an animal on the Thames?"

"That they did," he said, as he led the way to the study. "They turned the whole place into a market. People skated. Caroline," he asked the top of her bowed head, "did you go skating this winter?"

She'd been surprisingly reticent after dinner, offering no window to her thoughts.

"Yes," she answered simply. He frowned.

"Oh," Eleanor took her arm, "I used to love skating on the lake here. We had a delightful time. There would be chestnuts roasting and hot chocolate." Her sigh filled the hallway as Summerton stepped back for the ladies to precede him into the study.

"Interesting chap, Mr. Little," Sir Michael noted.

"Yes," Summerton agreed, distracted by Caroline's introversion. "He disturbed you, didn't he?" he asked her

She looked up at him with her beautiful emerald eyes, jolted from her reverie. Before she could respond, Eleanor piped in. "Of course he did. The man has been condescending all evening. You really should have spoken up sooner, Summerton."

"How was he rude earlier?" He'd walked in on something in the rose room, but not soon enough to hear.

The women exchanged amused glances.

"What did I miss?" he insisted.

"It doesn't matter." Caroline smiled as she rang for tea. "You were very gallant."

"Of course he was." His aunt took her favorite chair by the fire and sat on the edge to face Caroline. "But, my girl, why do you believe Biggs was here before—not after—Alice was murdered?"

Caroline blinked. "How did you know?"

"Biggs arrived earlier?" Summerton snapped.

Eleanor settled in her chair. "I didn't say he actually arrived earlier, but that Caroline believes he did."

"He was seen," Caroline said.

"You were told he was seen," Eleanor corrected. "That doesn't mean he was seen."

"I had a trustworthy source."

"I'm sure you did," Eleanor offered. "And your source may believe what they told you, but sometimes people confuse the order of things. The most important question for us to consider is who would have the strongest motive to kill those poor girls."

"Could it be two people?" Summerton asked.

"Possible," Sir Michael said. "We should keep our minds open. Though it appears, if those two women can be trusted, only one man was staying in the crypt," Sir Michael suggested, as he flipped his coat tails before seating himself in the chair beside Eleanor's.

Summerton looked at Caroline on the settee, opposite his aunt and the baron. Hitches had slipped into the room quietly, and the two were conferring about refreshments. He heard Caroline request tea *and* spirits. He smiled, comforted that his wife had guessed and thought to ask.

But she didn't want to be his wife. Not really. Early this morning he'd hoped she might accept that role. Tonight, despite these domestic duties, he wasn't so certain.

They suited each other more than he could have hoped. No fainting damsel, she had stood by his side, steady and strong through the past tumultuous days. There were so many things about her that impressed him, moved him. The way she acted with his tenants and her blasted menagerie of animals, her infatuation with his crumbling estate. He needed her, duchess or not.

Which meant he needed to slay her doubts. That task would be difficult when he didn't even know what they were.

Rather than sit on the settee beside her, Summerton leaned against his desk. On the outer edge of the fire and lamplight, directly opposite the seating area, between everyone else and the windows, it would give him a better vantage point to catch each one of Caroline's expressions, every reaction. He would watch.

Eleanor sighed. Everyone looked at her, expectant.

"You wish to say something, Aunt?" Summerton asked, only to be interrupted by Hitches's arrival with the maid and her tea trolley. There was a bottle of spirits on the tray.

Normally, he would ignore servants, but Eleanor remained quiet. He followed her lead. They were all eager to discuss the findings in the crypt, which Mr. Little's presence had prevented them from doing earlier.

Caroline must have noticed the hesitation as well, for she changed the subject.

"I find Mr. Little off-putting," she admitted, after assuring Hitches that she would serve. "Sugar, Sir Michael?"

"Sir Michael does not take sugar," Eleanor responded for her friend, "though I do. Two, please." She paused, waiting for the servants to leave the room, then said, "To answer your question, Summerton, I'm wondering how much of this has to do with Caroline and how much has to do with your marriage to Caroline."

"Because someone wants the mills?"

"Or Caroline."

"Me!" Caroline sloshed tea over the sides of the cup she was carrying to Summerton.

"I've been known to sip from the saucer," he teased, doing just that. He would wait for the spirits.

She looked away. A shy maiden, easy prey to the slightest flirtation. A good sign, that she reacted to his teasing. He looked to his aunt to continue, but she was frowning at Caroline.

"Caroline assured us there was no one of that nature in her life," he defended.

"I never said I thought Caroline was attached. Young men often think they know best for the objects of their affection."

"There is no one," Caroline confirmed.

"What of Jeremy? What did he say?" Eleanor asked.

Caroline studied the weave of her fingers in her lap. "He didn't know Alice, but her death worries him. He's not sure who or where is safe. The mills are his life, but he's afraid to go back there."

"He wants you to go with him?"

"Yes. But not in the way you think. My father raised him as a son, taught him everything. He trusts me as he trusted my father. He thinks we can set matters right. But it will take the two of us."

Sir Michael cleared his throat. "And your uncle—did he mention your uncle?"

"We didn't talk about that; there wasn't time. He knew we had guards, that they would come looking. He just told me what I told you and gave me the books."

"And let you go?" Eleanor murmured. "Knowing there were guards."

"He let me go. He knows I'm safer with you than out searching for cover with him."

"Or so he claims," Summerton added, not liking the image of Jeremy as some gallant knight intent on rescuing everything Caroline loved.

"If he wanted to kidnap you, that would have been a good time." Sir Michael leaned forward. "That fog would have hidden a multitude of sins."

"But it was also disorienting," Summerton argued, "which would make it dangerous, if you didn't have a place to go."

"So," Sir Michael asked, "you believe this is a build up to a kidnapping?"

"Perhaps," Eleanor said. "If Jeremy wanted Caroline—" she shook her head at her, "—I'm merely saying *if*, we mustn't rule him out yet. And personally, I would prefer it if the murderer were Jeremy. He would need to keep Caroline alive if he hoped to gain control of the mills through her influence."

"But not the duke," Sir Michael stated bluntly. "He would believe having Caroline would depend on getting rid of his grace."

"Jeremy didn't send the note."

They all stared at her.

"What?" Eleanor asked.

"Jeremy did not send the note. He didn't even know about it."

"So he says," Summerton responded.

They all studied their teas.

"Perhaps you would like something stronger?" Caroline broke the silence. Both Summerton and Sir Michael nodded. Her hands trembled as she poured two snifters of brandy.

"But why the murders?" Summerton asked. "Why take those girls' lives?"

"We've already concluded the first girl looked like Caroline. He merely grabbed the wrong one. She would have seen him, possibly recognized him, so she couldn't live. The other girl was connected to him through the note. They both knew too much."

Caroline covered her mouth, but couldn't hold back a whisper. "Which means it could not have been my uncle, because he received what he wanted from my marriage."

"Did he?" Eleanor asked over her spectacles.

"Yes." Caroline nodded. "He received a portion of my dowry."

"But if you ran away?" Sir Michael asked. "If the marriage were not secured?"

Silence. None dared speak, though they all knew what that meant. It was in their eyes. If the marriage failed, the dowry would be rescinded. If Caroline died, money meant for the dowry would revert to her uncle.

"Ah, I see. You don't think the assailant is intent on kidnapping her," Sir Michael said. No one responded.

CHAPTER 18 ~ Bridal Journey?

Summerton slept amazingly well. Who wouldn't, after two sleepless nights? Even if their whole world was falling apart and he needed more answers.

Should they leave on an extended journey or stay within the walls of St. Martins? He could regulate security here, but he would never forgive himself if more deaths occurred.

If they left for the continent, they might or might not outrace the murderer. It would be harder for a stranger to hide in a small village than in the streets of Vienna, but St. Martins was far more accessible than the Austrian capital.

The second installment of the dowry hinged on a grand tour. Dignitaries awaited his presence for the Congress. It had all seemed so important before the murders.

He couldn't leave, even if it meant forfeiting a good portion of the dowry. He was the duke; these were his lands, his people. Which was why he and his steward stood looking down at extensive plans to reinvigorate the estate.

They'd spent weeks working out details dependent on Caroline's dowry, but everything had changed. He'd be lucky if he could keep a third of the anticipated funds.

"Her grace promised the tenants new roofs."

"A shame to waste the money on that if you're going to rebuild, your grace," Tom argued. "It can wait."

"Those cottages need something now. I'm not certain how long they will have to wait for rebuilding." Summerton tapped the desk. "We need to cut back, Tom, drastically. We've already implemented the new farming techniques."

"Fat lot of good it will do us. This spring will ruin normal crops."

"It was warm in April."

"Hasn't been since."

He was beginning to understand the biblical Job. His luck seemed to worsen at every turn.

Summerton looked out the window, at the beginnings of a beautiful day, the first in weeks. "We're already committed to the changes in the crops. Weather doesn't stop that."

"Righto," Tom agreed. "Righto, and what else?"

If only he knew Caroline's mind, if she meant to stay. That possibility was one bright spark amidst all the gloom.

As if conjured by his thoughts, she knocked on the door and then stepped into the room. "Oh, I am sorry. I didn't know you were busy."

He gestured for her to come inside. "We were just finishing."

"I have a tray here. Hitches said you hadn't eaten. I thought you'd at least need coffee."

Her love of coffee. He nodded to her, telling Tom, "We'll discuss this more later. In the meantime, see to those roofs, will you?"

"Yes, sir, your grace."

A maid carried in a tray of coffee. Caroline brought him a cup, but abandoned him to look at the papers splayed across the table. She studied the columns of figures and tilted her head to better understand the drawings. He'd rather she didn't. It proved how desperately he counted on her money, and if she didn't stay, it was all a fool's dream.

Either way, it did not present him in the best of light. It proved her point; he had married her for her money. He'd failed to make it known how desperately he wanted her for himself.

He brought her a cup of the dark brew, but to his surprise, she was so absorbed in his scribbles, she barely registered her morning favorite.

"These are your plans for the estate? For St. Martins?" She took the cup, sipped, and sighed.

If she'd been any other woman, he would have assumed her interest was superficial, but she was not any other woman.

"They were. I'm revising them."

She blushed.

"Nothing you need worry about." He flushed, remembering Mr. Little's remonstrations. "Not that you wouldn't understand," he tried to backtrack. "But it is a mere draft. Very probably irrelevant."

"These are quite detailed," she said. "Well calculated."

"Again, irrelevant."

"Yes." She pivoted toward him, then away, head bent. She knew what he wouldn't say outright. *She* determined the relevancy of his work. "Well..." Finally, she met his eyes.

"I'm not faulting you."

"Of course not. But you should. You really should, but I'd prefer we not go there. Not just yet. As I said, I came because Hitches said you hadn't dined yet this morning. If you're at all hungry, the smoked haddock looks decidedly..."

"Like something I would enjoy?" He held out his hand, wanting to have that discussion now, right now, but willing to wait for her.

Hesitation was a good thing. It suggested indecision, the chance she might stay with him. A step closer than the night he had found her running away.

"Yes." She ignored his hand, wrapping her arm around his. Did she lean against him, just for a moment, or had that been an accidental brush of her body against his arm?

They walked to the dining room in silence, he distracted by his discussion with Tom. Her...well, he didn't quite know why she was quiet, but he suspected this reserve was unusual for her.

"A penny for your thoughts?" she asked, as if she had read his mind.

He looked down at her pale sprigged muslin dress, perfect attire for a debutant. He'd not given her much opportunity to prepare a trousseau. "The weather is almost as beautiful as you are." He pulled out the chair to the right of where he usually sat at the head of the table. "I'd begun to doubt we would ever find a warm day this spring."

"You are a fibber." Caroline softened her scold with a smile as she sat in the proferred chair. "That frown could not be for the sun."

She smelled of lilac and sunshine. "You've already been outdoors?"

"Yes—" her eyes sparkled, "—visiting the kennels and the stables." She craned to look at him as he pushed in the chair. "How could you tell?"

Not by the lilac, they wouldn't be in bloom, but there was a freshness to her, redolent of spring. Impossible to explain without sounding like an eager dog, sniffing away. "The color on your cheeks," he prevaricated.

"And what was the frown on yours?"

"I was thinking of our journey," he lied. That, at least, was settled. He knew what they were doing for the moment. He didn't know if it would mean forfeiting the release of the funds he'd been promised, but extraordinary times demanded extraordinary decisions.

"Oh." A footman placed another cup of coffee beside her plate and she lifted it with both hands, breathing in its scent as though she hadn't just enacted this same scenario moments ago in the study. It was like watching a child with a toy of which she never tired.

When she looked over at him, he continued. "Mr. Little just left. He assures me you must go, leave this very day. In the name of safety."

"Does he?" Apparently, her morning coffee held more appeal than Mr. Little's edicts.

He rose again as Eleanor entered the room. "Aunt, I thought you had breakfasted in your chamber."

"I did. That's not why I'm here. Have you seen Sir Michael?"

"After seeing Mr. Little out, he had more questions for George, who found Alice."

"Very good." She turned to leave, then hesitated and pivoted toward them. "This journey we are to take..."

"We were just discussing that," Caroline told her.

"You aren't actually planning to go, are you?"

Again, Caroline piped up. "Of course not, Lady Eleanor. Summerton couldn't possibly leave until this mess is sorted out."

No, he wasn't going to leave. But she could. "I've instructed your maids to prepare for your departure this afternoon. You will sail first thing tomorrow morning."

"But we couldn't possibly..." Eleanor started to argue.

He interrupted her. "I, however, will not be joining you."

Both women stared at him.

"It isn't safe here," he explained, "and Caroline has been promised a tour."

Eleanor raised her brow. "A bridal tour."

"Bridal tour, grand tour, it doesn't matter. Her father wanted her to have the opportunity. It will be far safer for her over there. And for you as well, Aunt. I'm afraid your investigations will make you a target."

"But what about you?" Caroline asked. "You are in as much, if not more, danger than we are."

"I will be fine."

"I won't go." Caroline straightened her already rigid back. He knew it meant she was digging in her heels, and it amazed him that he knew.

"You don't have a choice."

"Actually, she does." Eleanor looked over the spectacles perched low on her nose. "If I understand correctly, I am her chaperone. I do not feel up to the task."

Eleanor sat down, fine and fit and more than capable of partnering Caroline on a trip abroad. He ignored her, deciding to take a different tack.

"Caroline," he said, "if your uncle has become greedy and decided he wants to keep your dowry, he could be intent on murdering you. Especially if he believes the marriage could be annulled."

"I don't believe it. How could he know that?"

Eleanor sighed. "I'm afraid Summerton is correct. Servants talk, word gets out. Those reporters have set tongues wagging. This will not do."

"I have a solution," he informed them both. Based on her smile, his aunt already suspected where he was going and approved of his decision. "I would like to see us well and properly married before you leave. No room for annulment."

"Married?" Caroline blinked. Her eyes widened as she looked from him to his aunt.

He pushed his case. "You are safer as my wife. It's time you decided, my love. I hadn't wanted to put you through this so soon. I had hoped to give you the length of the journey to decide, but the situation here has changed everything."

She blinked again, straightened her serviette in her lap. "Actually, I thought it would be better to let people know we aren't truly married. That we won't be."

"Oh, my dear, you haven't done something foolish?" Eleanor challenged.

"No," Caroline said. "No, but I think ..."

"Then don't," Summerton ordered. "You are safer as my wife."

"And you are safer as an unattached man."

He sat back, as if served a blow. "You mean to protect me?" He couldn't grasp the concept.

"Yes."

He placed his hands behind his head and leaned back, looking up at the pretty little ceiling of the family breakfast room.

"Oh, my love, you deflate me. You totally deflate me."

"How so?" she asked in all innocence.

He didn't bother to answer, leaving it to his aunt to step in with a response.

"You've flayed his masculinity, Caroline. A man likes to think he is the protector of the family. You, as a woman, are to offer the gentler side of things, such as compassion, good taste, caring. We, of course, know better, but allow them their illusions."

He sensed her hesitation, then she said, "All the more reason he should not be wed to me. I am not a sweet, gentle woman."

"No, you have the backbone of a duchess," he snapped, wanting to reassert himself in the conversation. "You are smart and beautiful and so, so far more capable than any other ingénue I've ever met." He tried to calm himself, but desperation won out. "Marry me, Caroline, as you promised you would before the priest. Be my bride, my true wife, my helpmate. I need you."

She didn't blink this time. If she had, the tears filling her eyes would have spilled over, but her chin did tremble. He hadn't intended to make her cry.

She pushed away from the table.

"I'm afraid I cannot," she informed them. Before she could leave, he was up and out of his chair, urging her to face him squarely in this.

"Why not? We suit, Caroline. We work well together, and I...well, I thought you were coming to care for me, just as I have come to care for you."

"It's too much," she choked out. "It's all too much for me. I don't know how..."

"Don't know how to what? What don't you know?" he asked, but she pulled away and ran from the room crying. She'd come to him angry but whole, despite the bullying of her uncle, the horror of thinking her animals had been killed. She'd seen murder victims and faced the threat that she might become one. But this, his request that they stay together, had broken her.

He rather felt like crying himself. "She still needs to get away from here," he told his aunt. His eyes on the doorway, willing Caroline to return. "I need you to accompany her." He tore his gaze away. "There isn't anyone else I can trust with that."

"Yes." Eleanor put her serviette on the table, as if it were a piece of porcelain rather than a square of cloth. "I do wish you would come with us."

"I will," he promised, "I will join you as soon as we get things sorted here."

"You will be careful."

"I will." He looked back at the door. "Tell her, if she refuses to be my bride, she is not welcome to stay here."

"You don't mean that."

"No." Of course he didn't mean that. He would do anything to have her here, by his side. Anything, that was, but risk her life. "Tell her all the same."

She couldn't leave without use of his coach. He would see to it that she was safe.

CAROLINE STOOD IN THE middle of the room, in the way of Bitsy, who directed an army of maids. Pure bedlam reigned—gowns spilled out of trunks, bonnets and hats scattered about, delicate lingerie arranged in neat little stacks, and everywhere there was tissue paper for packing.

Caroline watched, unable to direct or guide the proceedings, though she should do something. Leaving might offer the greatest help, but some memory or idea was tickling on the outskirts of her mind.

It refused to surface, skirting awareness as purposefully as a sheer nightrail skirted propriety.

"Could you direct me to the nursery?" she asked. "I understand we have guests there."

A little ginger-headed maid pointed. "The stairway 'tween your chamber and Lady Eleanor's. They go up to the nursery, just at the top. One flight is all."

"Ah." Caroline looked at the door, then back at the heaps of clothes slung over chairs and trunk lids. "I wonder—" and suddenly that slippery thought set foot into awareness. "There is so much here, more than I can wear." She fretted, tapping her foot. "I believe the newswomen lost their clothes. They were stolen," she lied.

"More's the pity," another maid said.

"Yes, but it's also a shame, when I have so much." She felt invigorated. "Bitsy, let's find them a couple of my dresses, shall we?" She grabbed a satchel she'd tucked deep in a wardrobe. "We can put them in this."

"Where did you find that?" Bitsy looked at it askance. "Looks like a gypsy bag."

Caroline cocked her head and studied the old canvas holdall. "I couldn't tell you where, but it will work."

"No, yer Grace," the ginger-headed one argued. "Your fine dresses would get all mussed if they were stuffed into that."

"Roll them," Caroline said. "They will be fine, much better than the trousers those ladies have been wearing."

"Are you certain?" Bitsy bit her lip.

"I'm perfectly certain."

"If you say so." A few moments later, she handed over four rolled gowns. "If your grace could get back right quick? We have to change you into your traveling gown."

Caroline waved her hand. "I'll just wear this and—" she looked about, "—ah, yes, that bonnet." She pointed to a straw bonnet with a deep brim.

"That's all wrong, your Grace! A poke bonnet isn't for such travel, it's too deep, you'll be catching on the window and wall and that dress you're in will show every wrinkle if you don't change."

"I'll take the bonnet off when I'm riding in the carriage and this dress will not show the dust. It's such a lovely day, I want to wear something to match. I should be fine, with a shawl. Hand me that one, over there." She pointed to a pretty paisley wrap.

Bitsy scrunched her nose.

"I've barely worn this an hour and his grace is anxious for me to be on my way. There's no time to change if I want to say my goodbyes."

"If you say so, miss."

"I say so." Caroline opened the satchel and stuffed in the rolled dresses.

She held still as Bitsy put the shawl over her shoulders. "And the hat." Bitsy handed it to her. "If Lady Eleanor is looking for me, tell her I will meet her outside."

WELL BEFORE DEPARTURE, while trunks and satchels were being loaded into carriages, Caroline slipped into the duke's well-sprung traveling coach. She ignored everything and everyone around her and sat on the far side of the seat, staring out at the drive they would soon take.

She acknowledged neither Lady Eleanor nor the duke, who helped his aunt into the carriage. She ignored his comment, "You haven't far to go tonight. Two hours at the most. You will have enough daylight to enjoy a walk along the sea."

She didn't turn to see aunt and nephew exchange looks, but kept her head bowed, sniffling quietly, her legs bouncing with restlessness.

"Travel safe. You've armed guards with you the whole way."

"We will," Eleanor relented, when Caroline held her silence. "I will take care of her."

"Caroline?" he asked, waiting. "Fine!" He slapped the carriage as he backed out, then stopped and leaned in once more. "While you travel, I would ask you to reconsider your feelings."

She nodded.

"Thank you. I will join you as soon as possible."

She nodded again. He stepped down from the carriage and closed the door.

Caroline sniffed, from deep inside the poke bonnet, leaned the side of her head against the squab, as though to sleep.

"Do stop bouncing, Caroline. It is most distracting," Lady Eleanor snapped.

Caroline stilled.

It would be a long journey.

SUMMERTON WATCHED AS the post chaise, Caroline's from before they said their vows, disappeared into the distance. The Summerton carriage, older but still quite comfortable, followed. It carried the ladies' maids and luggage, with another luggage wagon following.

It certainly hadn't taken long for Caroline to remove any sign of herself from St. Martins. The plan had always been to leave on their bridal journey. The majority of Caroline's things never removed from their trunks. Packing could take days but moving a trunk to a carriage would take no time at all.

Still, he hadn't expected her to leave as she did. He had rather thought she would argue and fight.

Or find a way not to leave.

It was his own fault. If he hadn't pushed the issue of consummating their marriage, she may have done just that. Damn foolish of him. As Eleanor had pointed out that first night, only the four of them, if he included Sir Michael, knew about her hesitation. Even if others suspected, they wouldn't know—not for certain—that the marriage could be annulled by lack of consummation.

Sir Michael, who had trailed him outside, patted his shoulder. A commiserate gesture. "We'd best get back to business, if you want to catch up with them before they hit Vienna."

"I'm stymied," Summerton admitted. They had made no progress in finding the killer, and he was not sure what to do next. "I've sent a man to Manchester. Feet on the ground. He's to get a feel of what Mr. Howlett's people think. I want to know more about this Jeremy fellow."

"I'll go, as well. Leave this very afternoon," Sir Michael offered. "I'll speak with the uncle."

They would all be gone, Caroline, Eleanor, and now Sir Michael.

"Watch your back."

Summerton snorted. No value in his back. Not anymore. Or in his heart. That had just ridden away in a fancy post chaise.

CHAPTER 19 ~ The Ambassador

He called himself the ambassador, liked the jib of it. Representative abroad and all that. He stood to the side of the road, in a crowd of other men. Not allowed on the grounds of St. Martins, the newspapermen spent hours on the road, opposite the entrance—the two women weren't there, probably still locked up in the cellars of St. Martins. More's the pity.

An ambassador's role was to fit in with the society he inhabited, so he told these men he reported English news for Americans. None had heard of his paper, but then they wouldn't have. It didn't exist.

They accepted him easily enough. Allowed him to mingle, to be there when word came that the duke had ordered his traveling coaches to be readied. So they all waited, in the delightful afternoon sun, just outside the gates to St. Martins.

The thunder of hooves traveling at a quick clip—too quick if they didn't want to wear the beasts out—filled the air, followed by the creak and rumble of heavy vehicles. They stood and watched as the first came into view.

It was an expensive post chaise Caroline's father had commissioned for his daughter. All polished wood and gleaming hardware, not too fancy but stylish enough.

Fancy wouldn't make it any more secure than her mother's carriage had been. He smiled. Duke or not, Summerton would not be able to protect her. Like father, like son. Caroline didn't stand a chance.

He spat, his head turned so Caroline wouldn't see his face.

"Only ladies in those coaches," one man noted. "The duke's not with them."

"Did you see the luggage?" another asked. "Piled high. They aren't going on a short jaunt."

"To London, do you think? For the last of the season?"

"Could be," someone else muttered, as they started to scatter, off to ask questions, talk to the locals, get information.

"She's run away from him," the ambassador offered. "Frightened for her life. I wager she's leaving him."

The departures stopped. The men gaped at him.

Finally one frowned. "Do you think so?"

"He isn't going. Barely married."

The one he called Scribbs, because he was always scribbling, opened a little book, pencil in hand. "Do you know something, or are you still hanging on the reason we came in the first place? That didn't pan out. The duchess herself laughed at that."

"He's not with them. She's not using his coach."

"His seal is on the other one," Scribbs argued.

"With servants," he said. "Loaned it out, didn't he, to get the maids moved."

He didn't like the way Scribbs was looking at him. The others lapped up information like a dog to water. Scribbs studied it first to see if it was poisoned.

What an idea. Maybe that's how he'd get rid of the man. Feed him poison.

He doffed his hat at Scribbs. "Just thinking aloud," and sauntered off, wondering how to disguise the taste of poison.

"Whole thing's fishy to me," he heard Scribbs mutter behind him.

BEVIEANN ADJUSTED THE 'lad's' collar. "The servant stairs are quiet this time of day, but be careful."

"Of course," her friend said. "I'll slip out with none the wiser."

But as they got to the top of the stairs, Bevieann held out her arm, stopping them both. Someone was coming up the back stairs. They scurried into the nursery, but Bevieann remained alone in the play area while her friend took to the bedchamber.

"Miss Ryan," the duke called out, announcing his arrival.

"In here," she called out, glancing at the door to the bedchamber, opened a crack. She wanted to shut it to take away any risk, but she didn't dare.

Summerton already stood in the doorway, but he didn't venture in. Just stood, looking around. With a shake of his head, he told her, "I haven't been in these rooms since I was a child."

She smiled. "Perhaps you'll have more use for them now."

His expression doused her smile.

"I'm appalled to admit that it isn't safe here, for you or your cousin." He cleared his throat, "But I have an idea. One that will give you the chance of a story without endangering you."

"The story is here at St. Martins."

"But at what expense?"

"I will pay..."

He waived that aside. "I meant the risk to your life. We do not know the culprit's identity. We must discover him."

"You want me to investigate?"

"You strike me as resourceful and intelligent, and your cousin is an exceptional artist."

She wondered how much to tell him. He appeared honest enough. She glanced at the door, its thin sliver of dark beyond, knowing this conversation had a witness.

"What does that have to do with anything?"

"I have a proposal."

She tilted her head. "What sort of proposal?"

"I've instructed my solicitor to look into the affairs at Howlett Mills, and even wider, all of the Howlett Enterprises. He's to get a man on the ground, to ask questions, but I realized—" he hesitated, "—my aunt helped me see that oftentimes women speaking with women cover more territory with less time."

"You want me to spy."

"I want you to look into the character of her grace's uncle and the man who manages the mills. Will you consider such a task?"

"Do I have to respond immediately?"

He turned back. "I would like you to leave within the hour. I will pay all expenses, of course."

She didn't dare look behind her. "It will just be me. Liz, she's already planned to leave. Give me two hours."

"Try to make it less," he ceded. "Sir Michael is going. You can ride with him."

"Fine." Something crashed in the other room.

The duke lifted an eyebrow.

"Liz is packing," she explained.

"I see." His frown told her he *didn't* see, but he didn't press her.

The minute he was gone, she rushed to the bedroom. "What was that?"

"The chamber pot. It was empty."

Bevieann shook her head.

"I thought, if he came in, I could distract him, hit him on the head..."

"Don't be foolish." Bevieann laughed. "Now let's get you out of here."

"Just to the servants' rooms, above stairs," the girl reminded her.

"Obviously you haven't been up there or you wouldn't say 'just.'" Bevieann wrinkled her nose.

"And you have?"

Bevieann lifted her chin. "I'm a reporter. Of course I investigated. But, truth told, you are safer up there than outside these walls." She folded the blanket for the girl to take. "I'm thinking it would be best if I were to stay?"

"No!" The other one shook her head. "His idea is good. Very good. You ought to go."

"Alone?"

"You will have to."

She studied her friend, dressed in ragged trousers and a dirtied linen shirt, her hair stuffed under a cap. "Be careful when you go outside. It's dangerous out there."

"I'll be fine."

"Let me go with you."

"No," the other girl shook her head. "I will be fine. It's his grace you need to worry about. Keep your eyes open."

SOMETHING WAS WRONG, very wrong.

Eleanor did not like being away from the trouble, especially when her instincts were screaming at her to help. Normally, a quiet hour in a coach would give her just the time she needed to sort through her observations and questions. Solutions would rise to the surface, like cream in a milk pail.

But it hadn't worked. For the first time in ages, her temper had gotten the best of her. Caroline had not responded as expected. She'd refused Summerton. Ridiculous. The two were meant for each other—she knew that as well as she knew the nose on her face. Brooding about it kept her from thinking about what was important.

What was it?

The springs of the vehicle were no match for Caroline's bouncing legs.

"Really! Must you do that..." She looked over at Caroline, dressed in the pretty sprigged muslin dress she'd worn that morning. The same dress she'd worn at breakfast.

Caroline, like all women of style, changed constantly throughout the day, and would most certainly not have worn a pretty muslin dress for travel.

Yet here she was in that same dress, paired with gloves and a poke bonnet she hadn't taken off despite the stuffy confines of the carriage, for they'd closed the windows against the rain.

And she was sniffling, as if still crying.

Caroline was not the sort to cry easily, let alone for an hour straight.

"Liz Evans! What are you playing at?"

The girl whipped around, eyes a perfect match to the 'O' of her mouth. "How did you know? I told them you would know. I just knew you would figure it out, which you were bound to do eventually, once we arrived, because..." She sneezed.

"How have you managed to keep quiet all this time?" Eleanor rapped on the roof of the coach.

The coachman slid the trapdoor open.

"Turn around. Get us back to St. Martins as quickly as possible," Eleanor ordered.

"Yes, m'lady," the coachman said, and slid the hatch shut.

That was it. Caroline was stoic and still. This girl could barely hold still. Amazing how well she had done.

"She wants to find the killer. She's that worried about his grace."

"The little fool. Oh, bless her heart." She looked out at the verges on either side of the coach. "It could be miles before he finds a place to turn, and he's just as likely to get stuck in this rain. What are we to do?"

"Caroline didn't expect you to turn around."

"No." Eleanor lowered the window, ignoring the rain, and stuck her head out to see if she could help the coachman find a spot. "She wouldn't. She would take the whole thing on her own shoulders," Lady Eleanor said. "What was her plan?"

"She's going to dress like a lad, and go find Jeremy. She hopes they will be able to find the killer together."

"Impossible! What if the murderer is Jeremy?"

"She would know if it was him."

"This murderer is clever, very clever."

"She's taking her dogs."

"That's slender protection. No one will be there to help her!"

"Do you think it really could be Jeremy?"

"We don't know!" Eleanor snapped, then stilled as the coach stopped rocking. She slid the window open again, leaned out. "The coachman found a spot to turn around." She sat back.

"Do you really think she needs help? She thought it would be easier to go unnoticed this way. The killer won't suspect she's about."

"She needs help." Eleanor ignored the rain coming through the open window. "This carriage is too slow. We'll never get back in time."

Liz bounced in her seat. "If you loosen one of the horses, I could ride it back."

Eleanor stiffened. "Do you think so?"

"I'm good with horses." Liz promised.

"No doubt you are." Eleanor rapped on the trapdoor. "Why didn't I think of that? Much faster than a coach."

The coachman opened the divide once more.

"We need to send someone to St. Martins immediately!" Eleanor told him. "Can one of the outriders go?"

"Yes, m'lady, but that would make us vulnerable. The duke would never allow such a risk."

"Damn the risk! The duchess is not with us! We must get word back to the duke!" she said, sitting back, fanning herself.

"Oh, dear," she murmured, "Oh, please Lord, don't let her be killed. Please don't let her be killed."

"Do you think that might happen?" Liz asked, startling Eleanor, who had quite forgotten she was there.

"One would hope not," she said. "The girl would make a perfect duchess for my boy. I am sure of it. Once she comes to her senses."

If she lived to do so.

CHAPTER 20 ~ Danger

Too risky to stay in the nursery, especially after Summerton's visit. Caroline pulled together her little satchel and carried it up to the servants' rooms under the eaves. Cold, damp, and abandoned—with good reason. She didn't trust the floors, tested each step before she took it.

She could just see one of the young ladies from St. Ann's up here. No, wait, they'd not traipse up these stairs or fuss about provisions for the servants.

She couldn't think of any who would be worthy of Summerton.

She brushed her hands, having dirtied them on the stair rails.

"Caroline?"

Her head shot up. Her stomach plummeted, even as it threatened to return her breakfast.

"I knew you wouldn't abandon me. Saw your carriage leave, but you weren't in it, were you?"

Roger Little? But it couldn't be Mr. Little's son. He had been sent off years ago, under watch. An evil, evil man.

Yet there he stood, just above her. She'd been too busy studying the ground at her feet, careful not to tread on a rotten floor board, to notice his approach.

He hadn't changed much through the years—handsome face, light brown hair parted in the middle—though she hadn't seen him since his teens, a good ten years ago. He looked so normal, like a regular man, it was hard to imagine the cruel games he loved to concoct.

But she knew them.

Caroline took a step down from the landing where she stood.

"No, no, no," Roger moved forward. "You don't want to do that." He grabbed her arm.

"But I do." She yanked on her arm, pulling him down past her, but he caught himself on the balustrade, his lip bleeding, having hit her knuckle as he fell.

She kicked out, knowing she needed to get past him, knowing, with stunning clarity, who'd killed those girls.

You'd still be a nobody without my father, he'd shouted at her da, furious over being banned from Howlett Mills. A girl had been found, raped and beaten. *You're just taking her word for it because she's from the streets like you.*

Frantic, the boy's father had pulled him away. Mr. Little refused to believe his son would do such a thing. Impossible that Roger could be responsible for the mangled cats and tortured dogs left on the Howletts' grounds.

But he was. Roger had done all those things and more. His guilt had been proven by how abruptly the evil doings had stopped after he was shipped away.

Caroline had forgotten him. Never, not once, had she suspected to find him here at St. Martins.

More fool her.

He pouted about the blood. She took advantage, slipping past him, nearly making it to the floor below before he grabbed her hair. She refused to let him stop her. She had to get free, no matter what. Even if it meant putting him between her and the ground floor. She'd risk it, though she hadn't a clue whether there was a way out from above.

She dropped down and yanked her head forward, her hair ripping from its roots. Tears blurred her vision, but she was distantly aware of a body sprawled below her, arms raised, one hand still twisted in the ends of her hair. She reached blindly, latched onto a little finger and yanked it back, hard and fast. He screamed, releasing her hair.

Free of his grasp, she pulled away and ran for the upper floor, not daring to jump across him to get to the bottom. She heard the flick of a knife, a familiar sound, for every young man in the mills had such a device in his pocket.

Not all the streets were safe in Manchester.

His groans carried up to her, as did the sound of him rising, hindered by some injury. Breath ripped through her as she ran along the sides of the corridors, hoping, praying the boards would be stronger there than in the middle.

"You'll never be entirely free." His venomous whisper slid down her back.

Somewhere, this part of the house had to connect to the other wings, or to the staircase leading into the old hall. She didn't bother searching for a place to hide. Her harsh and panicked breathing would just give her away.

Oh Lord, why had she decided to try and fight on her own?

She needed Summerton, but Roger would kill him quicker than he would kill her. Because Summerton wouldn't know how to fight dirty.

She knew. Her father had taught her how to protect herself in the rough side of town.

Oh, Lord, let me live through this. Let Summerton live through this. Let this be the end of Roger Little.

She spun at the sound of splintering wood, closer than she'd thought. She looked behind her. Roger pulled his leg out of the hole in the rotting floorboards.

Impossible to go back.

She shouldn't have stopped. Shouldn't have risked allowing him to gain on her. The sight of his wretched smile a haunting picture she couldn't shake, even when she turned away. His eyes sparkled with the thrill of her terror, his nostrils flared in anticipation of torture. The vision spurred her on, even as it stole away any sense of hope.

SUMMERTON AND HIS STEWARD, Tom, stood before the kennels.

"Do you think it might work?" Summerton shouted to be heard over Baver's howls.

"Don't know, your grace. I've only trained dogs to go after foxes and the like. Never saw one what chases humans."

"But it's been done before, and with this breed. He found the girl."

"He picked up the scent of death. But I see what you're thinking." Tom looked doubtful. "We can try, your grace, but don't get your hopes up. Have you got anything to use for scent?"

Summerton looked down at Baver, wondering what Caroline thought to do with her animals. If she left, when she left. A shiver of unease slipped down his back. He shook it off. She was safe, away from this place.

"Something was found behind the first baron's tomb. One of the newspaper women noticed it, but there was a distraction, so we all forgot."

"I looked this morning, and it's still there. Didn't know if I should pick it up or not, so I left it. Shall we start there? See if this thing will work?"

Tom nodded. "Best not to confuse scents." He grabbed a lead and opened the kennel, standing in front of it to keep the anxious dog from escaping. "This boy's keen enough, but who knows how he was trained." He fixed the lead to Baver's collar. "Let's go see what happens."

Baver struggled to go to the Hall, but Tom forced him along the trail until they reached the crypt. Whether he caught the scent of a fox or rabbit or man, they didn't know, but Baver started to sniff hard. Then set off on a short jog before stopping and sniffing again. Soon he was running so fast they were hurrying to keep up. Tom wanted to slow him, but Summerton was spurred on by a worry he couldn't explain.

"Let him have his lead." It helped that the bloodhound was heading straight for the family tomb.

"He's on to somefin," Tom agreed. "Though I couldn't tell you what."

Again, an ill shiver ran along Summerton's spine. As if he, too, had caught a drift of some scent, he lifted his head and looked behind him, anxiety building to near madness.

Baver bayed at the closed door of the crypt.

"It's unlocked." Summerton told Tom, who was already opening the metal gate.

The hound shot in and headed straight to the squashed cloth behind the sarcophagus of the first Baron St. Martins.

"He's got it!" Tom shouted.

The dog's muzzle was buried deep in the folds of cloth, his body shivering with anticipation. He turned and followed some unseen trail. The men hurried along, allowing him to guide them.

"He's going back to the Hall!" Tom snapped. "I thought we had him off that track."

"Or maybe that *is* the track!" Summerton shouted, as he grabbed the dog's lead, urging him to pick up speed, rushed along by his own billowing anxiety.

THE CARRIAGE SHUDDERED and drew to a wrenching stop. Lady Eleanor struggled with the window, and then managed to push it down. She stuck her head out of the gap. "We can't afford a delay."

"It's Wills, your lady." Coachman pointed to one of Summerton's liveried riders, looking worse for the wear on the side of the road. "He was sent to ride ahead."

"What happened?" she called out. "You should be there by now." They were less than a mile away from the Hall.

Wills pulled his forelock. "We were riding like the devil, m'lady, across the field. Hit a hole, the horse lost his footing. He's back there—leg's gone, I'm afraid. I started running, fast as I could, along the road, hoping someone would come by, get me there faster, but..."

"You'd best climb in." She tapped the window frame, forcing down her fear. She'd done what she could, and fretting would only make matters worse.

"She'll be fine," Liz soothed. "That lass's got a right good head on her shoulders."

"She can't outfight a man!" Eleanor fretted.

"Perhaps not, but she can outwit one."

Eleanor sat back. "I do hope so. I dearly hope so."

ROGER HAD THE ADVANTAGE. He'd spent time above stairs. Caroline had not. If he thought she was caught, she probably was. She should have taken that tour, but there had been so many distractions.

Unlike the lower floors, with their grand rooms, this was a warren of hallways and...

Stairs. There were stairs ahead. She stretched out her legs and ran faster. One side of the staircase was walled, the other open. She swung onto the balustrade and pushed away to slide down the railing, but Roger, feet away on the landing, grabbed her arm, laughing.

Time turned to molasses as he jumped onto the steps. The railing tipped drunkenly to one side.

Straddling the balustrade, she lifted her leg over, precariously swaying with the listing rail. She looked down at the set of steps below, wondering if it would hold her. Despite his fingers digging into her wrist, she jumped, giving him all of her weight. She caught him off-guard, and her sore arm twisted free of his grip. He took a step and fell halfway through it.

She landed hard, but the stairs held firm, even when the heavy wooden railing crashed down after her.

A miracle.

She ignored Roger's angry curses, his hiss of pain, and scanned the area, immediately below her. A vestibule with more rooms. She must be a whole floor away from the worst of the rot. These would be the rooms for lesser guests, companions, and nannies.

The staircase cut back around and continued down.

Roger was stuck, his legs kicking out through the ceiling over the lower stairs. She rushed away as quietly as she could, counting on the fact that Roger could not see her. She was certain the doorway to the original keep would be near. If she could find it.

A dangerous 'if.'

Roger would expect her to continue down the spiral of stairs. She went the other way instead, holding her breath until she rounded a corner to a wider hall. Larger rooms in this section, if the spacing of doorways meant anything. At the end, a wall of windows overlooked the grounds, to its left a pair of double doors.

The original square hall.

She'd found her escape, and none too soon. A crash reverberated through the hallway. He was close, so close. And she was standing in plain sight, bathed in sunlight. She shot for the double doors, grasped the lever, pushed down, and pulled.

Locked.

She looked over her shoulder, but the hallway was empty.

There was no place to hide. She looked out the window, hoping there would be a ledge, and caught sight of Baver, powerful and determined, bounding across the lawn.

Summerton and his steward broke from the woods, racing after him, heading toward the study!

If Roger caught her, they would be too late.

She pulled the door again, yanked. It didn't give. Sobbing, she fell against it, pushing it open. She yelped, struggling not to fall in her surprise, and slipped through the opening. As quietly as she could, she eased it shut behind her, saying a little prayer of thanks to Hitches for making sure those hinges had been oiled.

She was in the gallery. The ground floor was below, the fireplace and the spiraling staircase to her right. She needed to get down there, but Summerton had warned her the wood would not hold, not on the stairs and not on the floors.

She tested the give beneath her feet, as close to the wall as she could, wanting the security of the stone. It bowed, springy and rotten. She looked up at the strong walls, stained from decades of rain.

She side-stepped—cautious, testing—to the balcony side, praying the support for the arches had fared better than the stone walls. It felt stronger, but she didn't dare trust it, not after what had happened before. Not after seeing the drop to the floor below.

She refused to look at anything but the floor as she slipped her feet gently over the wood, her heart easing its beat with every sure step. Time ceased to mean anything. With the same caution she had used to get to the stairway, she made her way to the bottom, tears streaming down her face.

She hiccupped with relief as she turned toward the far wing.

Roger stood leaning against the curtain wall.

"So cautious." He *tsk*ed. "But not quite cautious enough."

His laughter echoed around her, but she refused to go down without a fight. She ran, he followed and tackled her, both of them tumbling to the ground.

She scrambled to get free from the tangle of limbs, but he held her fast, with anger. He dragged her toward him. She kicked and flailed, but to no avail. He sat on her, pinning her.

His hands wrapped around her throat, squeezing, pressing.

She fought against him, fought so very hard, but then she saw Jeremy's lanky form and Biggs's massive bulk looking over either side of Roger's shoulders. Jeremy, her friend, and Biggs, her uncle's bodyguard, were in on it, too.

There was no room for wondering. There was no time for questions.

Hope slipped away on the heels of consciousness.

THE HOUND LED THEM into the house, to the study, and then up two flights of stairs, into quarters that had long been closed. These quarters were used in a day and age when St. Martins hosted so many guests they needed separate quarters for commoners and companions and governesses. A balustrade hung at a drunken angle, and there was a hole in the staircase where a foot had broken through.

The animal didn't stop, not for a moment, but pulled them with greater force. He seemed torn when they entered the open gallery lined with doors to bedchambers on the one side and a balcony overlooking the grand staircase on the other. Summerton's heart raced wildly.

The dog sniffed and howled, nearly yanking Summerton off his feet, and charged for the staircase, his nose close to the carpet. Even as they headed down, his aunt rushed in through the doors below.

"Summerton!" Her call rang through the Hall. Panicked, frightened sounds he'd never thought to hear from her.

“Here,” he shouted, as he ran behind the dog.

“Summerton! Caroline is not with me! She could be in mortal danger!”

Those words, the dire fear that had been running down his spine these past hours, the broken stairs, balustrade. Caroline would not go quietly or meekly. She would take the whole search on her own shoulders, and in so doing, become a victim.

Without saying a word, he gave the dog his lead, bounding toward the doors to the old Hall. The doors were ajar.

His stomach plummeted at the sounds of shouts and running feet. They crossed the threshold.

CHAPTER 21 ~ Thresholds

Angry cries rent the air. Summerton pushed past three of Sir Michael's men, tracking the sounds to the west wing.

He raced into the old hall, to the screen wall.

Caroline's limp body lay in another man's hold. The man's weeping stalling Summerton from moving any closer.

She couldn't be dead.

She couldn't be.

Baver pulled free, bounding over to Caroline, shoving his muzzle into her neck. Footmen were pulling the man away from her. He looked familiar, but Summerton didn't care about who he was. Not now.

Baver pushed at Caroline, stopping to lick her face, just as he had the night she'd tried to run away. She was even dressed in the same urchin's clothes, her hair a snarled halo. Her beautiful, delicate hands, ripped and bruised, the promise of another bruise on her cheek, beneath one eye.

The duke knelt, wrapping his arm around the dog, burying his face in the folds of his neck, unwilling to face the reality before him.

"Summerton." His aunt took his arm. "I don't think she's dead."

He looked up. Even with Baver pushing her, licking her, she lay limp and unresponsive, a rag doll of a woman. "Are you certain?"

Baver used Summerton's moment of distraction to pull free of him, and shoved Caroline with his snout.

She moaned.

Baver licked her face again.

She gasped, her eyes opening but not seeing, the whites turned blood red, her wild fear as terrifying as a demon. She flailed against Baver. The dog sat back on his haunches and howled. A footman, who'd come to take Baver away, scurried back, crossing himself.

Fool. She could have four eyes and Summerton would still love her. She was alive! That was all that mattered.

Eleanor slumped back from where she had crouched beside him. "I didn't think she was dead." Her hand shook as she raised it to brush away a greying tendril. "Her complexion wasn't mottled enough."

"Her eyes?" he asked, worried for her.

"Broken blood vessels. They will mend."

He thought his aunt might cry. He didn't blame her. Caroline had given them quite a scare.

"Caroline," he soothed, "it's me. You're safe." He reached for her, pulled her onto his lap. She whimpered, tried to cough, and whimpered again, curling into him. He felt her tears against his shirt, unable to see them with her face buried so deeply against him. He rocked her, speaking over her head.

"What happened here?" he whispered, finding rips in her clothes, pieces of wood and plaster in her hair.

What had she gone through, fighting for her life?

"I will kill this man," he promised. "I will see him hung as he hung Alice, but first, he will be sorry for touching you." He brushed a kiss on the one small portion of her hand that was not torn or bruised. "You are safe now," he promised. "I am here, I won't let anyone hurt you." He opened her hand, kissed her palm. "You will be safe." He pressed his lips to her ear.

"We need to move her, Summerton," Eleanor told him.

Caroline nestled in, as though she could burrow right inside of him. "Be still, my sweet," he soothed. "Not just yet. She's not ready."

He wanted someone to blame.

"You!" he said, to the man being held by two footman. "What do you know?"

"It wasn't me!" he pled. "We caught him at it. It wasn't me."

Caroline's head shot up. Wild-eyed, she looked at Jeremy.

"Oh, God!" Jeremy tried to back off, "Oh God, oh God what did he do to you?" He collapsed, weeping and calling for God.

"Who is 'he'?" Summerton demanded, caught between billowing fury and calming Caroline, her breath coming in short, panicked hitches. "Shhhh," he calmed her. "You're safe." He shot Jeremy a look, letting him know he'd best start talking.

The man wiped his nose on his sleeve, hiccupped a sob. "Roger Little, that's the man. We caught him doing..." He pointed at Caroline. "I thought...we thought...."

"Where'd he go?"

"Biggs ran after him. If he doesn't get him, no one will."

"Biggs, that's Robert Howlett's man?"

Jeremy nodded, twisting his cap in his hand, rubbing his eyes with his sleeve. "Is she...you know...going..."

"She's going to be fine," Eleanor told him, "but we need to get her upstairs. Hitches has sent for the doctor."

Caroline sat up slowly. Summerton started to lift her, to carry her, but she pushed away, using him for support to stand on her own. Tremors wracked her body, visible to all. She ignored them, refused his wish to carry her, though she did take his arm.

No one said a word, but stood at attention as the duke and duchess slowly made their way through the Hall. Her knees buckled more than once. He caught her from falling but didn't try to do more than that.

"I don't know why," he whispered, his voice thick with emotion, "but if walking on your own is what you want, so be it."

Although shaky, she made it to the duchess's bedchamber on her own legs.

"There you are!" Mrs. Beechum hurried out of the duchess's dressing room. "I've a bath prepared for you, your grace," she promised Caroline. "Nice and warm with plenty of salts to ease sore muscles. And we've Hilda here," she gestured to a robust little woman who stood beside a table topped by a traveling apothecary cabinet. "She'll see to you until the doctor can arrive."

"Hilda?" Summerton asked.

"I will take good care of her, sir," Hilda told him, offering Caroline her arm.

Caroline rebuffed her help, looking to Summerton for assurance.

"I'll be in your sitting room," he promised. "We'll all be there." He was loath to leave.

"No need to wait," Hilda told him, practically pulling Caroline away from him. "She'll need her rest."

"Gently!" the duke reminded her.

"You'll have to trust me," Hilda told him, though she gentled her hold. "But she needs to get into that water. It will help."

"Cara?" Summerton asked, pouring all the questions he wished to ask her into that one word—was she all right, did she want him to stay, did she feel safe?

Would she ever feel safe?

She offered a pathetic smile—no doubt merely a show for him—but then nodded and turned to walk with the other woman, giving him the answer he needed.

"Be gentle with her," he reminded them, hesitating in the doorway, uneasy. Of course he was uneasy, he'd nearly lost her.

"Come, sit down, Summerton," Eleanor beckoned from the sitting room.

He tapped his fingers on the side of his leg. The reason for fear abated, even though the feel of it lingered. "Just a moment," he told his aunt, and went to knock on the dressing room door.

Eleanor stopped him. "Really," she huffed. "Don't hover, Summerton. It's unattractive."

"Of course, you're right." He sighed and joined her.

Caroline was safe and sound, and he'd do best to let the ladies fuss over her.

CHAPTER 22 ~ Potions

How does one communicate without a voice?

Hilda prodded and poked, and barked orders at the two maids until they were running in circles.

Oddly enough, Mrs. Beechum's earlier disapproval seemed to have evaporated. She poured cupfuls of her scented water over Caroline's aching body. The soothing texture of the salted water, sloshing about, running over her, soothed her to doze in the warm bath. Gentle as could be, Mrs. Beechum worked the knots from Caroline's hair, brushing it from top to bottom. Hilda gave the housekeeper an unguent to work into Carolyn's scalp. It burned and soothed, all in one.

In that hour—or two, or however long it lasted—Caroline loved the housekeeper like a babe does its mother. But Hilda stopped the care with abrupt efficiency, sending Mrs. Beechum off, telling her they didn't need two nurses.

She had Caroline stand, cold and shaking, naked beside the tub as she pressed every bruise, pulled apart every wound, inspecting them.

Who looks deep into wounds?

In the end, the woman used ointments and unguents on every sore before allowing the maids to drop a night rail over Caroline's head.

"Did he have his way or are you still a virgin?"

The maids ducked their heads, distancing themselves from the question.

Caroline shook her head.

"He didn't have you, or you're not a virgin?" Hilda pressed.

It wasn't worth answering. Caroline ignored her and walked to the bed.

"You'll need your draught," she said, flicking her hand toward one of the maids. "Did you prepare it, like I asked?"

The younger maid nodded, hands behind her back, standing as far from the apothecary box as possible.

"Well, give it to her then," Hilda prodded.

The girl was young, no doubt brought in from the village with little experience serving. Having run her father's household, Caroline knew the sort, just as she knew exactly why the maid was in the room. Mrs. Beechum would have brought her to help with any manual chores—filling the bath, carrying towels. For her, it was likely a privilege just to be here. The young maid had clearly not expected to deal directly with her employers.

While Caroline felt for the poor girl, she was about to refuse the draught. No doubt that brew was laudanum.

She would not have it. Roger was out there, somewhere. She refused to be made vulnerable by drinking something that would put her in a stupor.

Hilda shoved the girl, who was clearly terrified, but more so of Hilda than of Caroline. She took the glass and carried it to Caroline's bedside.

Caroline shook her head. The lass put it on the table, for Caroline to take if she wanted it.

"Give it to her," Hilda demanded.

Caroline pressed her lips together, shaking her head.

"Make her drink it."

Both the maids and Caroline looked at Hilda as though she were mad. "You need to drink it," Hilda told her.

Caroline shook her head again, in no uncertain terms.

Hilda conferred with the girls, low enough that Caroline couldn't hear.

In truth, Caroline could easily fall asleep without help if only Hilda would leave her alone. She felt safe with that. A normal sleep she could wake from and be alert. But not the sort of sleep draughts produced.

She didn't feel safe enough, not here, without someone she trusted. Even Mrs. Beechum, who'd become a mother figure to her, had left.

Hilda crossed to the bed. "You need to take the draught," was her only warning before she pushed Caroline back, her beefy arm pressing down on her injured throat. Startled by the pain, by the bullying, Caroline fell back gasping.

Hilda poured the thick brew into her mouth. Caroline spat it out, sputtered and spewed, spraying the woman with a gush of the drink. She thought the woman would hit her—she raised her fist, as if planning to do just that—but one of the maids gasped, "No!" and Hilda eased back.

Caroline jerked her head toward the door, signaling for one of the maids to go find Summerton, but Hilda stopped the girl before she could take a step.

"It's a'right, you don't need ta go getting the duke. Leastwise, not before cleaning her up."

This the maids seemed to understand. They scurried about—changing Caroline into a dressing gown, helping her to a chair, getting clean linens, changing the bed, and carrying the dirty piles of laundry out of the room.

Woozy, senses dulled from the little bit of draught she hadn't been able to spit out, Caroline fought to stay awake, not to fall out of the chair. Her attention drawn by the maids' departure, Caroline looked at the door, watched it shimmer and sway.

Hilda was fussing about her, but she couldn't understand what the older woman was doing

"There we go," Hilda tightened the sash, tying Caroline to the chair.

I won't fall over. Caroline wanted to explain, but couldn't speak.

Confusion turned to fear when Hilda pinched her nose shut. Caroline tried to kick, tried to pull free, but the sash held her up in the heavy chair. Nothing budged.

When she couldn't hold her breath any longer, Caroline tried breathing through clenched teeth, willing the maids to return, for Summerton to check on her, for anything.

Hilda poured the bitter, bitter brew into Caroline's mouth.

Even then, much of it poured out, streaming down her chin. Neither of them won or lost that battle.

Hilda dressed Caroline in a fresh nightrail before the maids returned. As if, once she could speak, Caroline would keep her bullying a secret. As if she were a child, too intimidated to tell anyone what had happened.

Caroline would tell, once her voice was back. Barring that, she would write a note. She would let Summerton know how badly she'd been treated. He would champion her.

"You will sleep now, which is what you need. And this..." She roughly slapped a poultice around her neck. "Doctor would expect I do that."

Many healers were odd. But they didn't set out to increase the damage. This grizzled, gray-haired, heavy-eyed healer appeared set on doing just that.

Somehow, Caroline had to get the maids to understand, or the duke or Lady Eleanor. She needed protection.

When the maids returned, Caroline pleaded with her eyes, trying to stand, but her legs gave way as her eyes drooped.

"Here, your grace, let me help you." The older maid helped Caroline, who was no longer capable of helping herself, to the bed. Desperate to convey some message, Caroline tried to squeeze the woman's shoulder, but she couldn't. All power had left her, her strength melting away.

The other maid had pulled the sheets back. They both helped tuck Caroline in.

"You'll be right as rain," the one said.

"The duke's just outside your room, he's that concerned for you," the other whispered.

Outside her room? Too far away.

She did not want to sleep.

The pain leeched out of her. Thoughts washed away, a tumble of them caught in a tide. She tried to race after them in distorted dreams, but kept getting caught by ugly words, black and sticky questions wrapping around her ankles.

A gruesome mass rose up out of a tomb and hovered over her, hands outstretched. She tried to scream, but pain lanced through her, shuddering her awake.

Caroline opened her eyes, disoriented. Her chamber was filled with nightmare shapes melting and shifting around her.

Laudanum.

Everything was alive, swaying, but she refused to allow fear its sway. She'd been given a sleeping draught, that was all it was, and she'd managed to spill more than she'd drunk.

She rolled to her side. She would stand and find her legs.

She grabbed the bedside table, clutched the lace doily.

"No, no, you must rest." The bully witch forced her over onto her back, and then bustled back to her box of horrid poisons.

All of it so slow, but Caroline kept her eyes on the bedside table, her fingers tangled in the lacy table cover.

"Shhhh," Caroline warned the candlesticks dancing in a little candelabra, crying to be lit, and their companions, the jug and glass. They would help her escape, but they mustn't tell the witch.

She pulled, the lacy doily still clutched in her fingers, shifting the little candelabra, the jug, and the glass.

She watched them cascade to the floor and felt herself fall with them, deep into a dream.

SHE KNEW WHO HE WAS. Or had known. She wasn't alive. Not any more.

Except he couldn't be sure.

He'd not felt death with her. Missing the ending was far worse than the interruption of amorous congress. One merely engaged the body, while the other—killing with one's bare hands—fed his very being.

Power.

Every life taken gave him more power.

This missed opportunity enraged him.

He had to get back there. Feel her lifeless body; see those bulging, glazed eyes, knowing that he was the last thing to be seen with them. Her last moments focused on him, and him alone. Finish her.

Seething anger stopped him from running. He was *the ambassador*. No one crossed him. He toyed with others, played with their innocence, and chuckled at their confusion when his darker self surfaced.

He studied his long, narrow hands. How deceptive that they appeared so delicate, almost feminine. She'd scratched his hands.

He'd go back. Imagined the fear in her eyes if she lived. He would take his time destroying her, watching her life ebb away.

Nostrils flaring, he looked back. He'd easily outdistanced the men, even after fighting the heiress, but his lead would not last for long. That baying hound would not give up.

He hated dogs almost as much as he hated cats. In truth, he hated all animals, especially the human sort. He felt in his pocket, found the packet of rat poison he'd meant to feed to the reporter, and sprinkled it along his path. He stepped in it, and reached down to smear it into the hem of his pants.

Let that scent get up the bastard hound's nose.

SUMMERTON CHARGED INTO the duchess' bedchamber, summoned by an almighty crash, eerily similar to his wedding night.

"It's nothing, your grace," Hilda rushed at him, stopping him, stammering. "Just an accident."

There was a scattered heap beside the bed. The water jug and Waterford drinking cup remained intact, but the delicate reading candelabra had shattered.

"She's just a wee bit upset." Hilda left him to push a struggling Caroline back down. "She needs her rest, poor mite."

"Leave her alone." Summerton waved the maids aside, scowling when Hilda held firm. "Leave her," he ordered, prepared to shove the woman aside if she didn't move. It appeared she wouldn't.

"Hilda!" Eleanor warned. "You do not want to upset his grace."

"She needs rest," the woman argued, blocking Summerton from reaching her. "She must rest!" The panic in her voice set off a chain reaction she couldn't have anticipated.

Summerton grabbed around her ample middle, picked her up, and set her aside, but the moment he let go, she rushed past him, covering Caroline with her body.

"Good God, what's the matter with you?" Summerton bellowed.

"She's my patient," Hilda cried. "Mine!"

Eleanor shook her head at Summerton. Reluctantly, he stepped back, turning to one of the maids, who stood rooted, eyes wide. He whispered for her to get some footmen.

Eleanor moved up beside Hilda.

"Tell me what you think she needs." Eleanor moved around the woman, efficient but calm, distracting her from the comings and goings at the doorway.

"She needs me," Hilda sniffed, easing up and away from Caroline. "I know what she needs better than anyone."

"Of course." Eleanor nodded. "But surely you could use our assistance?"

Hilda shook her head, easing her defensiveness. "She just snagged the doily there, see." Both women looked at the lace cloth, still entwined in Caroline's fingers. Caroline was twitching and whimpering in a restless sleep.

"Ah, I see," Eleanor agreed.

Summerton met two footmen at the door. "Go to either side of her," he explained in a whisper. "Slow and gentle. She's not quite right." He remained by the door, still and quiet despite the hectic beat of his heart.

Eleanor was still speaking with the nurse. "Shall I sit with her, while you rest?"

"No." That one word was practically shouted.

Hitches could be heard in the duchess's sitting room, overseeing preparations for the meal. Summerton had asked to dine alfresco, upstairs, so they could be near Caroline.

Hilda's hand hovered over the poultice covering Caroline's neck.

"The doctor's here," Eleanor's lie reminded him the doctor was due to arrive. Where the hell was he? "Let Dr. Graham look at her."

Hilda snapped around, eyes narrowing on the advancing footmen, who knew enough to go still, even as Hitches's voice drew near enough for Summerton to hear him say, "...nearly strangled her grace. Hilda's with her now."

"The doctor is here," Summerton said from the doorway, watching over his shoulder as a man with a black satchel approached them.

Abruptly, Hilda stood tall.

"I've taken good care of her," Hilda informed Dr. Graham, "but these silly girls tried to dose her up with the tincture. Treated it like it was a tonic." She glared at the maids, whose eyes grew even wider, one shaking her head.

"Thank you, Hilda," Eleanor took her arm, "Dr. Graham can take over."

"He'll need me—" Hilda tilted her head toward the doctor, "—if only to watch her."

"I'll watch her." Summerton stepped further into the room. "She won't be alone."

"Go with these two men." Eleanor released Hilda to the footmen. "They'll take you to the kitchen, see that Cook takes good care of you."

"My medicines."

Dr. Graham chimed in. "Not to worry, Hilda. I'll see that one of these boys takes the box to your cottage."

"No!"

The doctor stepped back.

"I'll take it myself," Hilda said.

"Have something to eat first," Eleanor suggested. "You've been here a while. No doubt you're hungry and the doctor would like to see what you've given the duchess."

Hilda waddled toward the door, a footman on either side. "Not me," she accused. "The maids."

The minute she went through, Summerton closed the door. “Where did she came from?”

A maid rushed forward to pick up the broken candelabra.

“She’s not so bad,” Dr. Graham said as he approached Caroline. “Been here for years, your grace. Married one of the game keepers.” He lifted Caroline’s eyelid. “The man died.” He looked at the other eye. “Hilda sometimes works up here, when needs be. Not much. A bit off, but she understands herbs and the like.”

“She’s from up north?” Eleanor asked.

The maid on the floor blurted, “Tha’ woman wasna’ right. She were cruel-like. It weren’t truth, about the tonic. We poured it, helped give it to her grace, but Hilda, she told us what to do.”

“Beth!” Hitches reprimanded. The doctor consoled, “Of course she did,” shooing the girl away from the bed. “Hilda can be gruff, but she knows what she is doing and wouldn’t let anyone touch one of her patients without strict supervision.”

Eleanor wasn’t paying attention. Summerton thought he knew why. “I know what you’re thinking, Aunt. She’s from the north, but what are the odds she is connected to this?” he argued.

Eleanor merely tilted her head and tapped a finger to her lips. “It won’t hurt to speak with her, once Caroline is settled.”

Summerton sighed, preferring answers to yet more questions. “I don’t want her near Caroline again.”

Summerton sat beside a sleeping Caroline, opposite Dr. Graham, who disentangled her fingers from the lace edges of the table cloth.

“She pulled everything off the table.” Eleanor joined him.

“On purpose?” He frowned.

Caroline’s brow furrowed, her head jerked. She was uneasy in her sleep.

“Do you know what she was given?” Eleanor asked the maid who’d been willing to speak earlier. “Do you know what that woman gave to her grace?”

"Tha' bottle over there." The girl pointed to a bottle by the box. "Nearly full when we started."

Summerton left Caroline to go through the woman's healing supplies. "Laudanum?"

Eleanor lifted the amber glass to the light and then sniffed the bottle. "She told you to give her this?" The younger maid nodded, tears on her cheeks. "That's an undiluted tincture. You say she gave her nearly a full bottle?"

"Rubbish!" Dr. Graham joined her at the apothecary box. "Hilda wouldn't allow that. It could have killed the girl."

"What are you two saying?" Summerton asked.

"Most of it ended up on her clothes," the maid explained. "That's part of the reason we changed her nightrail and the bed linens. She had a terrible time swallowing. Poor thing."

Eleanor crossed to Caroline, leaned over to smell her breath, and then looked to the maid, who stood wringing her hands. "Did you give her any more after she was changed?"

"No, m'lady. Nothing else except the poultice around her neck."

Dr. Graham shook his head. "Hilda is usually very good at nursing."

Eleanor ignored him. "Was Hilda ever alone with the duchess?"

The two maids exchanged a look before the older one started to nod. "When we took the dirty linens away."

The younger one spoke for the first time. "I found a soiled dressing gown on the floor. It's wet and sticky."

"Your grace should leave, and you as well, Lady Eleanor," Dr. Graham ordered as he pulled Caroline to a sitting position, her head lolling to the side. "Send me some strong footmen and water for a cold bath."

"Will she survive?" the duke asked.

"If I have anything to say about it," Dr. Graham told him.

“Eleanor,” Summerton snapped. “Get coffee, strong coffee and see to those footmen. I’ll help out here.”

CHAPTER 23 ~ Missing Pieces

Lady Eleanor stepped out into the night. She hoped the threatening rain would fall and clear her thoughts.

Caroline had awoken. They still didn't know whether or not the overdose of laudanum had been purposeful. The doctor considered it a mistake, noting that the poultice had been very helpful. Caroline's throat was better than any could have expected after such a trauma.

Summerton was not convinced either way. He had trouble believing the woman would intentionally harm Caroline without motive, and there wasn't one.

None that they knew of.

Unfortunately, that Hilda woman had left. They couldn't find her. But Caroline had told them about Roger Little and his cruel, cruel past.

"I—" She had whispered, pausing briefly to clear her throat and take a sip of herbal tea.

"You aren't supposed to be using your voice, not yet," Summerton had protested.

Caroline had brushed that aside. "I can speak." Faint and raspy, but she could do it.

"If you can..." Eleanor hadn't been as considerate. They needed the information. "We need to know more about this Roger fellow."

"Very bad," Caroline tried, then gave up speaking. Leaning over the lap desk they'd brought in earlier, she dipped the quill into the ink and wrote.

played cruel tricks, on children in mills

"Dangerous?" Summerton scowled. Caroline shuddered at the memory.

A boy died, little girl was scalped
Very, very wicked

Summerton had risen, pacing away. Eleanor would have left it like that, Caroline watching him, her eyes for him alone, but this was very serious business.

"What happened?"

No proof. Denials. Father barred him from Howlett properties

Eleanor shook her head. "But he didn't stay away, did he?"

Left awful things for me

"For you?" Summerton asked. Caroline nodded, writing,

On my swing, buried in my sand box, or in my fairy garden.

"Fairy garden?" Eleanor asked. Caroline shrugged, a bit bashful. It was Summerton's turn to study her, a small smile of interest.

Eleanor hated to end his smile, but she'd had to press. "What sort of things, Caroline? What did he leave you."

Tears pooled in her bloodshot eyes, she sniffled, blotching her writing with tear drops.

Animals, pets, with the cruelest of endings.

"Good God," Summerton shouted. "You were just a child. Did no one do anything?"

He was sent away after that. Never saw him again.

Until now. Eleanor had left Summerton to console the poor girl while she went outside to think.

Something, some memory teased just outside her grasp. They were so close, all they needed was to find Roger Little.

Surely that was all.

Surely.

Of course, his father could have been involved. Most probably was. Then again, this Mr. Little had been terrified. Did he fear for himself, or his son?

Something did not quite add up. It prickled her skin and would not leave her thoughts. She could feel it out there, threatening.

The young man could not have orchestrated the whole thing. Not on his own.

He would have needed help. Some way to blend in, even before the reporters were summoned to create a diversion. Because the reporters hadn't been there when Alice was murdered.

Jeremy had been the only stranger noted in the valley when Alice was murdered. Which meant one of two things—Roger either hid very, very well, or he wasn't considered a stranger.

What were the odds of that? And when else had she had that thought, about odds and coincidences? She shook her head. Really, she was getting too old. She just couldn't remember.

Eyes closed, she tilted her face to the sky and breathed deep.

Kahki, the cat, curled around her legs. "Ah, sweetie." She bent over and picked up the three-legged feline. "I thought you were comforting your mistress."

The cat nuzzled her shoulder. She stroked the length of it, poor three-legged animal.

Three legged.

Three legs.

Of course! There were three. Someone up north, or in London, would have contacted the reporters. Someone down here to offer a local home. And then Roger Little.

Three of them. If they got one, the rest would tumble.

She gave the cat a squeeze for helping her solve part of the riddle.

Now who would the three be? The two Mr. Littles and who else?

Biggs was not clever enough to be a part of this scheme. His size would allow him to kill, and he hadn't returned after chasing Roger. But Jeremy didn't believe he was guilty.

Of course, there was Jeremy. The baying of the dog would have warned him that others were coming. His appearance of innocence could have been an act.

Eleanor considered herself a rather good judge of character, however, and Jeremy had seemed so earnest, so deeply worried about the mills. The rest of the Howlett Empire did not appear to interest him.

This killer was ruthlessly greedy. Roger had shown his hand in his attack of Caroline. Strangulation was nothing new to him.

Mr. Little had distanced himself from his son in miles, but had they stayed close in other matters? And what of Mrs. Little? There'd been no mention of her.

With a deep breath, Eleanor pulled her mind from the whole affair. If it had been daylight, she'd be fussing in the garden, digging in the loamy soil, deadheading flowers, or raking up leaves. Nothing cleared the mind quite like good manual labor.

Instead, she headed for the stables, drawn by the sound of voices. Perhaps it was the others, Jeremy and some of the guards, waiting for the steward and his men to return. The need to know if Roger had been found drew her to them.

"Aunt?" Summerton stood in the glow of the open doorway.

Of course he'd be there. That's why Khaki was outside. He'd brought the cats out for their dinner. Most likely an excuse to be near at hand when Tom and his men returned.

She'd nearly reached him when a stable lad came running from the other side of the Hall, yelling, "Clear a table in Tom's office. The hound is goin' ta need tendin' somethin' bad!"

ROGER LITTLE DUCKED under the low-slung lintel and stepped into the kitchen of the small cottage. She'd been expecting him. Two places were set at the table, and a stew or some such was heating on a banked fire.

No sign of her. He ducked out, moved across a square little vestibule, no wider than the narrow stairs opposite, and looked into the sitting room. Empty as well. He stood on the slate floor, a hallway between door and stairway, listening.

No sounds. The hag snored like a wallowing pig. He already knew she wasn't out back, in the privy. He'd come past it.

Foolish woman. She should know better than to make him wait.

After all he'd done to get here, the least she could do was serve him, take care of his wet clothes, soothe him. She'd be sorry she hadn't. She'd pay, of course.

Little tortures. Nothing to actually harm—he still needed her—but he could frighten her enough that she'd scramble to please him up until the day he was done.

Then he would finish her. Not that he wanted to. Hesitation flickered, but after this, she would be a liability. At least he would be considerate when he ended her life. Incapable as she was, she did try and she always put him first. He would honor that.

The stew proved savory, and the beer strong and smooth. He took his time, refreshing his reserve. Heady though it was, strangulation took impossible amounts of strength. Even so, it was worth it. He'd decided she couldn't have survived. Impossible. He'd gotten her. The snotty little heiress was dead, long live the assassin.

Everything else was in order. He'd wooed the heiress's maid, the one who took over for Alice. A silly little thing, full of tittle-tattle; so much so, she'd been lucky to keep her position for as long as she had. The aristocracy did not like their soiled linen made public. Or, rather, their lack of it.

The stupid girl had even divulged the duke's failure to consummate his marriage.

Caroline was the man's possession and he had not yet possessed her.

Either the man was not interested in women, or he held far too many scruples. Roger didn't care much for women, himself. In truth, Roger didn't care for anyone, but somehow he didn't think the duke was of that ilk.

Replete, Roger pushed back from the table.

His first chore was to steal Caroline's body, so he could prove she'd died a virgin.

Next he'd kidnap Lady Eleanor.

He went to the cupboard drawer and pulled out a thick fold of papers, carefully wrapped in leather. Annulment papers. The duke would sign them if it meant keeping his aunt alive. Besides, it wasn't as though he could argue the matter in court if the girl's body proved the marriage had not been bonded in flesh.

The duke would be allowed to live so he could stew in his misery and self-contempt. How wonderful to be responsible for tumbling a man from such great heights.

Invigorated, Roger stood, rubbing his hands together. Oh, what a night this promised to be.

Fools, the lot of them. Playing right into his hands, giving him the tools he needed to manipulate and destroy. He savored the feel of victory, so close, so very close. No one could stop him now.

CHAPTER 24 ~ 'Til Death Do Us Part

Jolted awake, her heart thumping, Caroline strained to see beyond the shadows cast by a lantern on the mantelpiece.

A crash had roused her. A loud, shattering noise. She strained to hear footsteps or shouts, but there was nothing.

A dream. It must have been a dream.

She eased back down.

The bed shifted. Her scream lodged in a painfully swollen throat and her whole body tensed. She slowly swiveled to see the other side of the bed. Summerton lay atop the covers, fully dressed. Asleep.

Who will take care of him?

In her dream, the one on the other side of that crash, no one had. She sniffled against the memory. He'd been dressed in rags, his home a shambles, while his faceless bride danced about in expensive finery, ignoring him. Ignoring St. Martins and all the people of Summerton.

A dream. That was all...just a dream.

She rolled over, free to look and admire without anyone being the wiser. How would it feel to be his wife in truth, to have the right to reach out and touch him, wake him so he would wrap his arms about her, put his lips to hers?

A wayward curl hung over his forehead. She eased it up, away from his eyes. It was softer than imagined. Her father's hair had been brown and coarse. Nothing like Summerton's silky mane. Hair had been Samson's downfall, but she was no Delilah.

The curl fell again, too soft to control. This time she let it wrap around her finger, like a tendril of honeysuckle to an arbor.

"Are you going to pull it to wake me?"

She did. Jerked back so quickly it tightened on her finger.

"Ouch!" He caught her wrist and studied her with wary blue eyes.

She should look away, tell him to go...but she did not want him to leave.

"I didn't mean to stay." He released her, sat up, and ran his fingers through his mistreated mane. "I merely wanted to check on you."

"And yet you laid down?" She was curious. No one had ever slept by her side, not in her memory. Perhaps her mother, gone too long to remember that.

He offered a smile, but it was weak. He was embarrassed. He stood and tucked in his shirt, disarrayed by sleep. "I watched you," he offered, looking for his shoes.

Busy, active. He was disturbed. He always moved like this when he was disturbed. But why? What was so alarming?

"I liked waking up to you," she admitted.

He stilled, looking down at his cuff, fiddling with the link. His other sleeve open and dangling. She reached over and skimmed the bed to find the missing link. When she did, she held it out.

"Thank you." He took it without looking at her.

"What's wrong?" she asked, surprised that speaking didn't hurt nearly as badly as it had mere hours ago.

He offered his back as he slipped on his shoes. "This was a mistake, but I doubt anyone would know."

Her reputation.

"I'm not trying to trick you." He turned now, anxious for her to understand. "No one saw me come in here."

"But they may have seen you here."

He didn't say a word, just looked at her with eyes full of misery and regret.

She'd promised *in sickness and in health*, never intending to honor it. She'd promised *I thee wed* and *'til death do us part,* fully intending to leave him. She'd broken those promises and yet he still honored her. Didn't bully her to stay.

She'd been a fool. If she wanted to rescue the mills, he'd not stop that, wife or not.

He'd honor her.

He'd take care of her.

All he'd asked of her was a month, possibly two.

Who will take care of him?

She would.

"Don't go." She held out her hand.

He shook his head, his jaw flexing.

"Be my husband?" she asked, less sure of herself.

"I need to leave." He stepped back, fussing with his sleeve as if his delinquent cuff was more important than her request. "I didn't mean to force the situation." Lips pursed with determination, he lined up the opening and pushed the link through. "There's a good chance no one has seen us."

She blinked.

"Yes. I see..." She would not cry.

She heard him move around the bed, coming closer, but she dared not look up.

"Leave me," she snapped, as he sat beside her. He reached down to cup her face, but she jerked away from him.

"I will not have you cornered," he told her.

"I'm not!" she retorted, lifting her chin, looking down her nose, even as she brushed away her falling tears. "Do you think I give a wit for what your sort thinks? They can gossip about me all they would like." She shrugged his hands from her shoulders. "Which is precisely why I would probably not make a good duchess. Is that why..."

"Stop it." She'd roused his anger.

"What?"

"Stop what you are going to say, and don't think I don't know, because I know you, you headstrong little minx." His anger softened.

"If you did, you would have accepted my invitation."

"An impulse, fleeting as those are?"

"That just proves you don't know me," she denied. "I've never felt this way before."

"Fleeting," he assured her, relaxing for the first time since he'd awakened.

"What? Something the witch gave me, perhaps?"

He laughed. "The witch? Could be." Though he was trying to keep his mouth pressed in a line, it kept sneaking into a smile. He took her wrist and felt the beat in the tender skin beneath her palm. "Have you ever felt this way before with me?"

She nodded, despite a welling of timidity. Aware of where this game could lead.

"When?"

She almost missed the question, a teasing breath of air that slipped inside her, stirring up those strange feelings. Why wouldn't he kiss her?

"The night by the stables and in your study." She wrapped her free hand around his wrist, felt the turbulent beat of his pulse.

He swallowed. "The witch didn't give you anything then."

"No." She shook her head, wondering what it all meant, his refusal to stay *or* leave. The leap of his pulse, the new tension that gripped him.

"Caroline, will you look at me?"

She did, a quick glance. She was not bashful by nature, and yet she felt...embarrassed...there was so much to lose.

She wanted him, to herself.

He was not someone for another woman to neglect. No, for he was not a single carefree man. He was her husband.

In name only. Her fault, until now. She clutched her hands to hide their trembling. The blood pounding in her ears almost made her miss what he said next.

"A duchess is not a proper duchess if she cares a wit for what others think."

Her head snapped up. "A true duchess is part of the ton, part of the aristocracy," she insisted.

Slowly, he shook his head. "A duchess leads the ton, my love. Top of the heap, so to speak. Not that it matters, of course," He hooked her hair behind her ear. "I don't give a wit what anyone thinks, either. Not if I have you by my side."

"You've turned me down."

"Only for tonight. Prepare yourself, I will be forever hounding you until that invitation is re-issued."

"You may be sorry," she admitted.

He laughed and pulled her close. "That goes two ways, my love."

She looked up at him. "Stay."

He groaned. "Not tonight. I wouldn't be any kind of gentleman if I stayed tonight. I'd be taking advantage of a weak moment. And you need your rest. I'd rather not seduce you to *oohs* and *ahs* of pain. Much better they be of pleasure."

She pulled away. "I may change my mind," she teased.

"Exactly." He sighed and stood. "Exactly."

She should have seen before now how worn and weary these past days had made him.

He needed sleep, rest. She'd been selfish.

"Go then."

He scowled.

He ran his hand down his face and stood, pausing just inside the door. "Good night, my love."

"Good night," she whispered.

He did need his rest. He'd been carrying too many worries on those shoulders of his. *She* had rested all evening and most of the night, except for the time she'd gone out to Baver. She wouldn't be able to sleep any longer.

Baver.

Ned, the old stable man, had promised to stay the night with him. She would go and help. She got out of bed, slowly, so many aches and pains, and prepared to go to the stables. With so many men out looking for Roger, he wouldn't be anywhere near at hand. She'd be safe.

HALF A DOZEN MISSIVES were sent back and forth before she was finally set free. Hilda didn't like walking through the woods at night, but she had to get home. There was a cow to milk and chickens to coop, if the fox hadn't already gotten to them.

And her boy. Her wee boy needed to be cared for. It had been a rough day for him. Worse than he even knew. There would be tantrums. She wouldn't blame him.

She waddled along the path, made anxious by how long it was taking her to get to her cottage. Frustrated by the dark. She knew the path, but not every hole and root.

Something rustled in the bushes to her right.

"Who's there?" she cried out. Feral pigs could be mean.

No one responded. She hurried along faster. Whatever it was, it kept pace. Not a pig, for she heard his breath. It had to be a man.

She stopped. "Roger? Is that you, my boy?" He loved to tease her. "I've news." She turned in a circle, searching through the darkness for something, anything. "They called me up to the big house, to tend to the new duchess."

Roger stepped out of the brush.

"Ah." She smiled and brushed at the debris that clung to his shirt. "I knew it would bc you."

He pushed her hands aside. "The new duchess?"

"Well, yes." She started walking again, but he grabbed her arm to stop her. She *tsk*ed as she peered up at him. "She lives, my boy."

"Lives?"

Hilda smiled, nodded. "I wouldn't steal your fun, but she can't talk. I forbade her to do so for a week and gave her enough laudanum so she'll sleep for a day, maybe more." At least, that had been her intention. The girl had not been able to swallow much of it. But surely she would sleep through the night.

He grabbed her arms. "You didn't kill her?"

"Did you want me to?" He usually didn't want her to finish off his games.

He shook his head, offered her that lovely smile of his. Such a handsome boy. Her boy. She may not have borne him, but she'd raised him.

"No, you did right." He kissed her forehead. "I'll go get her."

SHE LOOKED OVER HER shoulder, as if worried he would harm her.

He'd thought about it, but he always thought about killing. Fantasized it. Though he wouldn't kill her. Not tonight, anyway.

Maybe, one day, when she was too old. When living was a burden to her. He'd do it fast, when she wasn't expecting it. A quick, sharp snap. He'd heard you could do that, from an old man from the orient.

Not tonight, though, His father wouldn't like that.

"SUMMERTON!" LADY ELEANOR rushed into the family dining room. "There are carriages coming down the drive. Sir Michael's returning."

The duke stood. "He would have barely reached Manchester, if that."

Hitches hurried out of the room, to prepare for new arrivals.

"Did you say two carriages? Sir Michael only took one carriage."

"I know," his aunt agreed, "but it's him, I am certain of it. Perhaps your messenger caught up with him."

"All the more reason for him to continue." Summerton headed for the entrance hall.

"Has Caroline been down yet?"

He looked over his shoulder. "I thought to let her rest."

"Send her coffee. She will want to know what is happening."

"I already have—" he smiled, taking his aunt's arm, walking with her to greet their visitors, "—and I believe you will be wishing us happy, very soon."

Eleanor nodded and gave him a sideways look. "I rather thought you two were getting to that point." She patted his arm. "Congratulations."

"Not so quick. She's contrary enough to back off rather than agree to a fait accompli."

"Don't let that happen. She will make you a smashing duchess."

"Yes," he agreed, "I rather think so."

A footman opened the double doors of the outer balcony. Before they crossed the threshold and headed out onto the front steps, a maid ran down the stairs calling, "Your grace, your grace."

"Mind yourself!" Hitches warned the girl.

"But it's her grace, sir. She isn't there. Her abigail's been looking all over for her and the room's torn apart, like a demon thrashed it."

"Caroline?" Summerton asked.

"Nowhere to be found, your grace." The maid curtseyed.

Lady Eleanor was halfway up the stairs before he caught up with her. "We'd had an argument."

"You are not to blame for this."

He was. "She wanted me to stay with her. I should have." He remembered the balustrade hanging, drunkenly, broken in her fight for freedom the day before. She'd not have the strength for another battle.

"Don't," Eleanor commanded. "Don't even think it. Go down and tell Sir Michael what's been happening,"

"I want to find her," Summerton demanded.

"The maid said she's not there."

He called down to where Hitches and the maid were now in deep discussion. "Did they look up in the nursery?"

"Yes sir, they checked all of your chambers and above stairs. No sign of her," Hitches told him, and went out to greet the arrivals.

"The dog." Summerton shook his head. "She could be with him."

"God hope!" Eleanor exclaimed. "Go get Sir Michael and check the stables. She could be there."

By the time he was out the front door, Sir Michael was already descending from his carriage. Rather than help him, Hitches was at the lead of the team, speaking with a stable boy who held the horses.

"Your grace," Hitches said.

Summerton slowed.

"Her grace is with Lord Baver."

He stopped completely, and laughed. The little minx—she was safe, she was in the stables. He changed course, changed mood, took the last stair and turned to Sir Michael.

"Where's Bevieann?" Summerton asked. The reporter had left with him. He'd helped her into the vehicle himself.

"She wanted to keep going. I gave her funds to catch the next mail coach."

"And why are you here? Perfect timing, but I hadn't expected it. You couldn't have known the developments here," Summerton asked.

Sir Michael tipped his head toward the large traveling coach pulling up behind his.

"Caroline's uncle, in a right state. He's heard about what's been going on down here. Thought I had better come back to keep an eye on him."

"Ah," Summerton murmured. "He'll find Caroline in the stables. Most likely not dressed for greeting others, but her dog was injured in the night."

"Drool?"

He nodded. "And Caroline was attacked." He slapped Michael on the back. "She will be fine. I'll fill you in later."

"Howlett won't like this," Sir Michael said, as they watched the man descend from his coach. "He'll smile like a market barker while he's ripping you apart."

Summerton didn't doubt it. Robert Howlett had always struck him as someone who held his cards close to his chest. At least they now knew he'd had no part in their trials these past few days. He'd been too far away to orchestrate matters. Besides, what could have motivated him? He'd gotten his share of the dowry, and there was still the business. Sir Michael had no need of Caroline's portion.

"I've had my fill of him." Sir Michael turned away. "I'll walk to the stables. Shake out the kinks."

The duke stopped him. "What is he doing here?"

"He's been hearing rumors, that's all he's said. Hearing rumors."

As he left, Summerton turned to see just what Sir Michael meant. Although not obese, Howlett was muscular, making him large in both girth and height. The sort who would have made a fine boxer, if his brother hadn't secured him a fortune.

Unfortunately, a fortune did not translate into a sense of fashion. Today he wore a color combination often seen on the streets of London, but not with such jarring hues. His yellow vest and matching trousers glowed brighter than the sun. The hue of the man's jacket was blue enough to dazzle a peacock. Unlike his own starched white cravat, Howlett's looked to be steeped in fresh blood. The end effect reminded him of a tropical bird he'd once seen in a friend's aviary.

"Ho, there, young man," Robert Howlett bellowed. "Where's that niece of mine?" He winked, patted the duke's back with enough force that Summerton grabbed the wagon wheel to keep from flying forward.

"I believe she is in the stables," he explained, hoping he was right.

"Ah, with her flea-bitten pests."

"Her dog, the hound, was injured."

"Injured? Heard worse than that was happening here," the man said with a smile.

"Yes, a trying time." He signaled to Hitches. "Mr. Howlett will need a room." To Robert, he said, "Breakfast is still out in the dining room. Get yourself something to eat, freshen up. Caroline and I will meet you in the study."

"You said she was in the stables." Howlett placed an unwelcome arm around Summerton's shoulder. "Why do we not go find her there? Eh?"

One did not touch a duke.

Summerton looked over at the man. Howlett removed his arm. Cleared his throat. Brushed his hands and launched into a string of complaints from carriage to stable. The journey had been rough, and country inns were filled with fleas, greasy, gristly food, bad wine. What trials he'd had to endure because the duke couldn't take care of his little girl properly.

All was somehow delivered in a light, jovial tone.

The stables consisted of four blocks of stalls. Sir Michael stood at one, its top door open. The two men joined him.

Caroline lay curled up on a heap of straw, bruised and mussed, Baver nestled beside her. Old Ned sat on a bale of hay, pipe in hand. Gnarly and ancient and sent out to pasture, so to speak, Summerton had pulled him back into service last night. Ned didn't care much for people, but he had a canny way with animals.

"Gawd, he's an insult to nature." Ned pointed his pipe at Robert Howlett. "Could stop hens from laying, he could."

Robert Howlett took no notice, his eyes on his niece. "What have you done to her?" He scrabbled with the lower door, trying to get it open. "By God, she's been murdered!" Robert Howlett cried. "This is exactly what I feared! What have I done, having her marry you? You've had her murdered!"

"Keep your chin shut," Old Ned snarled. "She's only sleeping."

Caroline shifted, rolling away from the sound, covering her head with her arms. Summerton smiled. That was his girl. Whatever had happened in her room earlier, she was safe and sound and with her animals.

A fox paced nervously in a cage on the floor, growing increasingly skittish in the presence of so many visitors.

Robert Howlett shoved Summerton, who'd leaned over the stable door to open it. He held up a hand in warning, but the man backed up as if Summerton had punched him, shouting, "Caroline! Caroline! Wake yourself!"

What a nuisance Howlett was! Summerton unhitched the bottom half of the door, stepped inside and closed it, daring the other man to follow. He didn't want him disturbing Caroline with his clawing presence.

Her groan pulled him around as she curled into a tighter ball.

"Leave her be," Summerton told her uncle. "She deserves her rest," Though he'd rather she did it above stairs.

Or possibly not. What had happened there?

Robert continued to shout. "Come on, girl! Haven't you caused enough trouble?"

"I said to hold your tongue," the duke ordered, considering the very real temptation of having the man taken away by force.

They all watched and waited. Caroline blinked, opened her eyes, and then looked over at where he stood, in the corner of the stall.

Howlett and Sir Michael gasped, the magistrate turning away from the sight. Howlett leaned in closer, appalled. Summerton had forgotten how shocking her eyes were. It hurt to look at them.

Sir Michael shot Summerton a hard look. "What's been going on here?" he demanded.

Caroline rose, pushing her hair from her face and straw from her hair, ignoring the other men. Or perhaps she hadn't noticed them. He didn't care. He just liked the way she looked at him.

"Ah, the intrepid duke!" She shielded her eyes from the sun, not that there was much of it in the shadows of the stall.

Ned looked to the cage. "Best get this fellow out of here, he'll 'ave a heart attack, what with all the attention."

Caroline leaned toward the cage. "No, no, no, you don't want to do that," she slurred.

"Caroline?" Summerton knelt beside her, peering into those hellishly red eyes.

"Good mornin'..." She burped, held a hand to her mouth, eyes wide, and giggled.

Giggled?

"Ned?" Summerton eyed the older man.

"She was summat in pain, your grace. So I gave her a wee dram."

"And another, I think." Caroline giggled again. "And another and..." She fell backward laughing.

"You're alive," her uncle said, with far less enthusiasm than he'd used to proclaim her death. "And drunk, at nine o'clock in the morning!"

"Uncle Robert?" Caroline asked. "Why are you here?" She swished her hand in the air. "Deed is done, money in the bank, and all that." She tried to stand, wobbled, and then toppled. "Oh my."

Summerton wrapped an arm around her shoulders, earning him a dreamy-eyed stare. If getting foxed made her look at him like that, he might just take to plying her with liquor.

"I like it when you hold me."

Summerton ignored the embarrassed shuffle of feet behind him.

"Right, oh." Sir Michael turned on the old groom. "Not well done, Ned."

"No, sir, but she seemed a might upset, worried after the dog and all. Been here since the early hours, your grace," he explained. "Since well before daylight. Thought 'twould help her sleep."

So she'd been here since he left her.

"Come on, you." She sighed and rested her head on his shoulder when he lifted her into his arms,

"You left me," she pouted.

"I'd best not do that again."

"No," she said with a sigh, nestling in only to lift her head again, swiftly, hitting Summerton's chin, both chiming, "Ow!"

"Sorry," she offered, rubbing the hurt spot, "I just thought of..."

"What," he asked.

"Liz, where's Liz?" She looked around the stableyard, as though the newspaper artist should be there.

"Left, to find Bevieann, though she was torn about it. No doubt Bevieann will berate her for missing a good story, but the poor girl took one look at you and thought better of staying. Aunt let her take your carriage."

Caroline sighed, her head back down on his shoulder. "That's good. I'm glad."

"Glad?" Her uncle blustered, pushing forward. "Look at you! You're bruised, your throat. What has he done to you?"

"Tried to kill me," Caroline said, over Summerton's shoulder as he carried her from the stables. "Roger."

"Roger? Roger who?" Robert's face went red. "Summerton was supposed to protect you."

Caroline squirmed, but the duke held her firm. "Protect me, Uncle? How'd you know?" She looked at Summerton. "Did you know you were supposed to protect me? Before...before, Alice?" No, he hadn't. It would have been a damn site better if he had. "Did you know?" Her fuddled brain was starting to work. He needed to get her indoors. "Was that part of the settlement?"

Her uncle marched alongside of them, through the courtyard. "No, he did not know."

Caroline pushed free, bracing herself with the duke. "What was he to protect me from?"

"I don't know!" Robert bellowed. "I haven't been able to find the source, but everything pointed to you. Something, *someone* meant to do you harm." He rubbed his eyes. "I didn't want anything to happen to you." He looked away, reining in emotions, but they held sway. Summerton almost felt sorry for the man.

"He was supposed to take you away, far away, where no one could touch you." He cupped her face in his large, square hands. "I chose him for that, I couldn't let..."

"You *chose* him?" Caroline stepped away from Summerton, wobbled, but refused his help.

"Only the best for my niece," Howlett puffed out. Summerton wanted to squash him, one hard jab at the face, but Caroline was watching him. "Offered him a deal he couldn't refuse!"

He knew exactly what she was thinking. The look on her face… No, he hadn't noticed her on his own, but how could he? She hid behind palms at balls. She wouldn't have been seated anywhere near him at dinner. His world had been designed to protect him from commoners.

Only she wasn't ill-bred. She'd been born with power and intelligence. He should have noticed. Wanted to tell her he had, but he wouldn't lie to her.

"You never even considered me, did you? My uncle came to you with an offer."

A lifetime ago, yes, Robert Howlett had approached him, and a deal was struck. None of that relevant any longer.

She pointed at her uncle. "That's why you forced me to marry the duke?"

Forced me to marry the duke. She couldn't even say his name. *The duke*. Not Summerton, not my husband, but *the duke*.

He stepped back, leaving niece and uncle to discuss the unpardonable sin of forcing her to marry someone she did not want. An old argument that meant nothing now.

"He's a duke. Look at this place. They may call it a hall, but it's closer to a castle. Places like this can be fortified. But you weren't supposed to need that. He was supposed to take you to safety! Why the hell *didn't* you?" Robert's brash scold reverberated through the stable yard. "What, did you want her dead? You have her money and now you want her dead?"

"Stop," Caroline croaked, her throat too raw to shout, sobering with anger. "People have been murdered! Summerton is not the sort to abandon his people at such a time. He's not about to run off and leave them to die."

"Well, he should have! He should have run off to ensure your safety!" Robert turned in a circle, like a ringmaster to his audience. "He means to do her in, doesn't he?"

"Don't be ridiculous." Sir Michael stepped in. "Utter rubbish." He took the other man's arm. "About time we move this discussion indoors."

"I don't know if it's safe in there," Robert bellowed, stomping toward her. "I think you should come with me, Caroline. Get clear of this place."

"You said I was in danger," she told her uncle. "Well, that danger was Roger Little. Not the duke. I brought the danger with me."

Her uncle stopped in his tracks, stunned. "Impossible. Roger Little is dead."

"He can't be." Caroline shook her head, side-stepping, as if his news were a physical blow.

"Died when he was twenty. No more."

"Caroline," Summerton had enough. "Let's go inside."

"Roger Little is not dead," she murmured, though she sounded a mite unsure now. "And I will not have you saying anything against the duke." She wouldn't look at him, even as she defended his honor. "He's a good man." She stepped backward, toward the house. "Good and kind and fair, which is more than I have been."

"Enough, Caroline." Summerton reached for her, but she brushed him away.

"Uncle Robert offered you a fraudulent deal. He didn't tell you your life would be at stake, that I was a pariah, bringing death. Misery..." She stood with the exaggerated stiff posture of a drunk pretending to be sober. "The duke deserves better than the drama we have offered." She lifted her chin imperiously. "Let him have the money you promised him, and then you can take me home."

Drunk talk. That's all that was. A little too much of Old Ned's elixir.

She turned, with extra care, and headed for the house. They all watched her weave her way, none daring to challenge her pride.

Don't go. Be my husband.

Words he'd walked away from only hours before. He'd meant to be fair. To give her time to heal aches and pains. Time for her heart to recognize, without trauma, without force, that it wanted him.

He'd been a fool.

CHAPTER 25 ~ Vandals

Eleanor and Sir Michael eyed each other as Summerton followed Caroline into her chamber. Having seen the damage first, Eleanor had stopped Caroline from entering her chambers until the two men could join them.

Summerton walked by Caroline's side, but neither of the young people spoke to the other.

"I didn't do this," Caroline blustered, though no one had suggested otherwise.

"She was too foxed to have done it," Summerton told the others.

"I'm not foxed." Caroline hiccupped and skirted around bed linens and broken vases, stooping down every so often to pick something up. An embroidered handkerchief, a miniature of her mother.

"If you would look in the dressing room," Eleanor suggested, "to see if anything is missing."

Caroline sat on the bench at the end of the bed, not going anywhere. "Alice would have known."

Summerton stifled a curse, and went to stand in the open doors to the balcony.

"This is not my fault." Caroline buried her face in her hands, her neck exposed by her bent head.

"You say a 'Roger' did this to your neck?" Sir Michael hesitated as he moved closer. "Like the others, only she survived," he said to Eleanor.

Eleanor leaned over her as well. Caroline started to raise her head, but Eleanor stopped her. "Just a moment, this is important. The swelling is going down." She pushed at Caroline's throat. Caroline pulled away.

"Please, Caroline, we need to look at this." Eleanor pulled a small magnifying glass with an inlaid wood handle out of her pocket. "The bruise is coming out. Do you see this, Sir Michael?" She outlined a band of blue going to purple. "Narrow fingers, narrow hands, and no ring? There's no widening, and the imprint is darker here." She traced the bruise.

Sir Michael leaned in close. "He may have taken it off?"

"No, very different." She straightened, only to catch Summerton scowling at her.

"She is not one of your corpses, Aunt."

"No, I didn't think she was. My apologies if I offended you, Caroline."

"It doesn't matter." Caroline walked unsteadily to her dressing room. "I'll have Bitsy pack as she straightens up." Dazed, she looked about. "He must have pulled everything out of the trunks. Most of my things were in trunks."

"Caroline," Summerton said.

She did not respond to him, but turned in the doorway to ask, "Why did he do this? Why would anyone..." No one could answer.

She left them for the dressing room.

"She intends to leave with her uncle," Summerton informed the empty doorway. "She might just do it, if he leaves soon enough. Can we forbid him to leave?"

"Don't be foolish. He won't go before tomorrow," Eleanor said. "A decent meal and a good sleep; she will see sense."

"This whole business is enough to send anyone running," he argued.

Eleanor raised her eyebrows and shook her head. "Don't be a fool, Summerton. It doesn't suit you."

Sir Michael was surveying the damage. "This was done in anger," he said. "Do you think whoever tried to strangle her came to finish what he started?"

"That makes sense," Eleanor told him. "He would be furious to find she wasn't here. But how did he get in? With all the men we have walking the grounds and the hallways, you would think this could have been avoided."

"That's just it," the duke told them. "We've pulled in men from three counties. Too many strangers, no doubt easy for the murderer to move about..." Summerton surveyed the chaos. "Maybe she *should* go with her uncle. She'll be better off away from here."

"Except she's the draw, Summerton. She's the one the killer is after," Eleanor reminded him.

A low guttural noise filled his throat, like the cry of a wounded animal.

"What do I do, Aunt?" he asked, running a hand through his hair. "How do I keep her safe?"

"I may have an answer for that, Summerton, and a plan."

Both men looked at her, but she wasn't quite ready to divulge her growing suspicions.

"First, you will have to convince Caroline to stay."

"OH, YOUR GRACE, LOOK at this." Bitsy held up a delicate muslin sleeve, savagely ripped in two. "And your blue evening dress!" Tears bloomed in her eyes. "If only I hadn't unpacked your things, they might have been spared, but now..." She shook her head. "Ruined, miss, just ruined. I hardly know where to start."

"One thing at a time, Bitsy, that is all you can do."

This had to be Roger. It had the feel of him. The sooner it was set to rights, the sooner she'd feel safe.

"Over there," she pointed, "start a pile of anything you deem impossible to mend. And here—" Caroline stood near the washstand, "—whatever might be salvageable. Anything he didn't touch, pack." She doubted she could wear anything he'd touched.

"Serviceable dresses are the most important." She lifted one. "It looks like he ignored them."

"But your evening gowns, and all this..."

"I won't be needing them. Not straight away. Not in Manchester."

"Manchester?" Bitsy asked.

Caroline lifted a mangled bonnet. "Yes, I'll be leaving in the morning."

"Another trip? Like the last one?"

Poor Bitsy. The thought of a temporary trip to the continent discomfited her. She'd never be happy with a permanent move to Manchester.

"You needn't join me. I can hire someone else up there."

"Will the duke be going?"

Caroline admired the girl's intelligence. If the duke went, they would be returning. "No, he will not be going." She picked up what was left of a silver silk dress, sliding it through her fingers.

"If the duke fails to convince her grace to stay," Summerton said from the doorway, "then he will most certainly be joining her."

She didn't dare look at him. "You can't," she said.

"Ah, but I can, and I will." He raised an eyebrow at the maid, who scurried from the room.

"Caroline," he prodded her. She wouldn't respond. Hard enough to go without him nudging at her.

"Caroline," he tried again. "Don't leave me."

His words slipped inside her as gracefully as the silk slid over her hand. He'd convince her to stay with one look, one touch, and then someone else would die.

She dropped the silver silk in the impossible-to-mend pile and picked up a delicate chemise, folded it over her arm. She lifted one white stocking with purple and gold clockwork. The other hung lazily from the fire grill. "Could you pass that to me, please."

He did, making her smile. She doubted he'd ever picked up after himself, let alone someone else.

"Caroline?" Soft as kid leather, his voice lured her. She ignored it, ignored *him*, and grabbed a blue muslin dress from the floor.

Summerton took it from her, held it up, revealing huge tears in the delicate fabric. "Thank God you weren't here when he arrived."

"If I leave, he will leave."

Like a cat on a window sill, waiting to pounce, he watched her.

"He won't get to you, if you stay close to me. Sleep in my chamber tonight. I'll watch over you."

"No."

She wanted him to stop asking her for the impossible. She was poison, anyone with her risked death.

But he was so, so tempting, and she could only be so strong.

"I want you here with me, Caroline."

Did his words cause it, or perhaps the book she picked up with all the pages ripped out? She didn't know, but one moment she was fighting the chaos and the next she was on her knees, curled around the tiny volume of poetry she'd yet to read. Insanely, she tried to piece together the ragged, scattered pages, growing frantic in her desperation before she hurled it across the room.

"Why did he do this?" She gestured to the destroyed room.

"Because he failed."

"This is his failure?" She sniffled. "Ha. And I don't care what my uncle says, he is not dead!"

"You haven't seen him in years. That's what you told us. Looks can change."

"But I know him."

Summerton crouched beside her.

"No two men could have that same cruel look."

"One would hope not, my love. One would hope not." He pulled her into his arms.

She should have fought him off. Kept her independence, but he stroked her back, offered comfort and strength. Exactly what she needed to fight her growing fear.

"You need to rest."

"I have to set this to rights." She dabbed at her running nose with a scrap of fabric. Looked about at all that needed doing. "Where did Bitsy go?" And remembered the look he had given her maid. "You sent her away."

"She'll take care of this better without you getting in the way."

"I still have decisions to make," she argued.

"Later," he stood, helping her rise. "Now, you need to rest. You can use my rooms."

She shouldn't.

She wanted to.

She needed to leave.

She did not want to go.

"I can't think."

"No, not now. Quite rightly. Come with me. You can sleep and I will watch over you."

"You are awful." She pushed away. He pulled her back.

"How am I awful?"

"I shouldn't even like you." She slapped his shoulder, not so hard as to create separation, but enough to lodge complaint. "You were arrogant and dismissive and greedy. You didn't even choose me."

"You didn't choose me either. Do you still feel that way?"

She turned away.

"Well? Do you?" he pressed.When she didn't respond, he took hold of her shoulders. "Caroline, I've not held to any of the conditions of the marriage settlement. Legally, I'm in forfeit. But as long as I have you, I don't care. We'll find a way, some way, together."

"I did choose you," she whispered.

"What?"

"I chose you, but you only wanted me for my money." She bit her lip to stop it from trembling.

"I didn't know," he whispered.

"I've my pride," she grumbled. "When you married me, I promised myself I'd not love you." Irretrievable words. So much for pride.

"Did you succeed?"

She rolled her eyes. Foolish man.

"Because I've been in love with you from the moment I tackled you on our wedding night. I was jealous of Baver, licking you, when all I could do was sit back, knowing you didn't want me."

"Ha!" she snorted.

"What does that mean?"

"You are a foolish man," she told him. "Foolish, foolish man."

"Will you stay with me? Work through this together?"

There, before them, a door to a sitting room and beyond that...there would be no turning back if they crossed that threshold.

He pulled her up against him, his lips pressed against her head, smiling. She could tell without seeing them. She knew even before the whisper of his words washed through her. "It doesn't seem fair that I should love you so desperately while you are trying *not* to love me."

She tried to hit him. He chuckled.

"Do you really?" She didn't mean to sound so timid.

"Caroline, have you ever known me to lie?"

"I think you did, when you invited me to sleep just now."

His laughter reverberated against her, teasing her. "You can sleep if you wish."

"You'd not try and seduce me?"

He didn't laugh any more, but turned her into his arms, tilted her face, to look into her eyes. "It's time, my love. Past time for us to love each other."

Why had she fought this? Why had she thought she should go away?

"I want you safe," she told him.

"Ah, my fierce little protector,"

She nodded, and he lifted her into his arms. "Broken glass on the floor. You're shoeless," he explained. "Let me worry about protecting you." He carried her away from the chaos.

ELEANOR SAT UPON THE worn velvet of a straight-backed winged chair hidden from the door. The positioning, against the wall, concealed her in plain sight. She waited.

Robert Howlett did not disappoint; entering the room with keen interest, he did not once look back over his shoulder.

He studied the undersides of figurines and vases, hefted the weight of pieces made of precious metal. She couldn't fault that.

St. Martins may have been ignored by its owners, but even with the threat of impoverishment, they had not sold off generations worth of valuable objects. Perhaps Robert thought to change that.

She was impressed he had the knowledge to discern what was valuable.

She waited until he put down a delicate piece of china. "Mr. Howlett."

He jerked upright, tugged at the hem of his immaculate jacket, and smoothed the front.

"You startled me." He chuckled and stuck his thumbs in the pockets of his vest, patting his thickening belly with his fingers. "Thought I was the only one down here. Not used to waiting for gongs and such."

She'd asked Hitches to withhold her presence. He'd threatened his niece. It didn't matter that the girl's menagerie of animals lived, or that the old mill worker had been sent into retirement rather than released from his job. That didn't forgive the pressure this man had forced his niece to face.

She was very close to understanding just what was happening, but she wanted to be certain. She'd only met him once or twice, years ago, and paid scant attention.

"Mr. Little arrived below stairs early, as well. I take it dining practices are different in Manchester."

"Yes, absolutely. We are, after all, progeny of working folks. Used to having dinner on the table when we get home after a long hard day." He flipped his tails and took a seat opposite Eleanor.

Mr. Little had not looked at figurines or studied the artwork. He'd shifted curtains, peered out windows, and twitched with every sound. Truly afraid.

That was the day after the first murder.

"I couldn't help noticing that you like attractive things, Mr. Howlett," she said. "That was a very handsome vest you had on earlier. Very handsome. What shade do they call that?"

"Canary yellow." He puffed up. "Rather fond of it. Tailor told me that the color is quite the thing. Caught your eye, and all."

"Oh, yes, very handsome. Original, too. And your cravat pin? Quite striking."

"Not another gem like it in all of England." Howlett looked down at the ruby. "Except for my ring." He held out his hand so she could admire the large gem. "A pair, they are. Rare."

"You can find so many unique items in London. You were there, just recently, before returning to Manchester?"

"Manchester's home. Caroline's home."

"And a busy place for you, no doubt. Admirable of you to take the time to check on your niece." She smiled. "And how remarkable that you and Sir Michael would find yourselves in the same inn, at the same time, on the same day. I must say, our magistrate was quite amazed."

He relaxed and leaned back. "Wild coincidence, isn't it?" He craned his neck toward the liquor trolley.

"Sherry?" she asked.

"Yes, please."

"Help yourself. One for me as well, if you will."

"Of course!" He rose to pour them drinks.

As he leaned over the trolley, she noticed a long, rectangular shape bulging from the outer seam of his trousers. Whatever had the man thought to stuff into his pockets before dinner?

They were not the only two to arrive early. Sir Michael, who had been waiting in the study, came in shortly after them. Without even knowing why, he did exactly as she'd prompted him to before they went to prepare for dinner. He went straight for the sherry, griping, "I hope the youngsters don't keep us waiting too long."

"Youngsters?" Mr. Howlett asked.

"Your niece and my nephew, Mr. Howlett," Eleanor explained. "You know how newly married couples can be. Time gets lost."

Mr. Howlett studied his sherry. "Mr. Little was of the impression..."

"Yes?" Eleanor asked.

"Nothing." He looked up with a smile. "Misinformed, no doubt. Man gets things wrong, even with all his fancy education."

"Of course." She looked at her sherry, ran her finger around the rim of the glass.

"What do they do with the land around here, Sir Michael?" Howlett asked. "Anything under that soil? Anything mineable?"

"No, we don't have those resources here. Not like up north, or to the west."

"Mars the countryside," Mr. Howlett boomed. "Doubt the folks down here would allow it, though it brings a pretty profit."

Eleanor set her sherry down, and caught Mr. Howlett watching her with narrowed eyes. At least she thought so.

Hard to say, as it transformed quite quickly to a genial, "I agree, though I hope the children don't take too long. It was a long hard journey, wasn't it, Sir Michael?"

"Very trying," Sir Michael agreed.

Caroline stepped into the room on Summerton's arm. Despite massive bruising, and the red of her eyes, she had a subtle glow of rest. Deep rest. Summerton held her hand to his arm, closer than was entirely proper. Eleanor would have applauded, if she could have gotten away with it.

"Uncle," Caroline offered her cheek to her uncle, who rose to greet her while Summerton went to the sherry tray.

"Lady Eleanor, Sir Michael." She blushed, barely uttering a greeting to them before swiveling to look at Summerton.

Considering there was a murderer out and about, they were both amazingly relaxed.

The Dukes of Summerton never relaxed. Not entirely. Nor were they the sort you would call content. However, he was doing a fine imitation of it tonight.

Eleanor raised an eyebrow. Perhaps she hadn't needed Sir Michael to throw about innuendos. The evidence was right before them.

Mr. Howlett noticed as well. His eyes narrowed, his nostrils flared, but the tight look passed in a moment. It happened almost too quickly for her to notice. But notice, she did.

Of course, there could be any number of explanations. Perhaps he didn't trust Summerton.

"Are you almost packed?" Howlett blurted. "No doubt most of your things can follow."

"Actually, uncle, there was an upset." She looked over her shoulder. Summerton stood behind her chair, his hand on her shoulder.

"A vandal went through her rooms," the duke explained. "We haven't found anything missing, but it will take some time to sort out. Thankfully, the duchess was not in the room at the time." His fingers tightened on her shoulder, and she tilted her head into his hold.

"What? How?" Robert Howlett boomed. "Outrageous. Someone breached her rooms and you stand there, calm as can be?" He stood. "You need to come home, Caroline. Things like this don't happen in Manchester." He strode to the door.

"Uncle," Caroline argued. "These things don't usually happen here. There's no precedent whatsoever."

"Caroline," Howlett cajoled. "I thought you wanted to come home. You said as much outside, when I arrived."

The girl blushed again.

Eleanor smiled at her nephew's bride. "I believe you can put that down to a lover's tiff, Mr. Howlett."

"I see, well, be that as it may, you can't deny the threat of this place."

"Do you know? I've been thinking about that." Eleanor jumped in, before Summerton could challenge the man. "You mentioned you had arranged this alliance between Summerton and Caroline because you felt she was in danger. Surely it's no safer in Manchester."

"Of course it is!"

"Then why do you have a guard? I don't walk around with a guard, do you, Summerton?" Sir Michael asked.

"No, never until now," Summerton confirmed.

"What do you know about my guards? Prosperous men have to be careful."

"Father never had a guard," Caroline said. "I never thought about that before, but you have Biggs. You've always had Biggs and Bart."

"Biggs?" Eleanor considered. "I had forgotten that Mr. Biggs was your man. Didn't he try to catch Roger Little after you were attacked?"

"It wasn't Roger Little," Howlett snapped. He tugged his coat down, smoothing the front of it.

"Whoever it was," Summerton said. "Biggs was there, and he chased him. He's not been seen since."

"Perhaps he did this man in," Howlett suggested.

"Or the reverse," Sir Michael speculated.

"Oh, my," Lady Eleanor actually leaned back in her chair, ignoring years of deportment. "Oh, my."

"I don't like this." Howlett stood firm, "I want our girl safe. Look at her—covered in bruises, and her room was violated. Her very room! No comfort in that for me."

"Aunt Eleanor is correct. Manchester is no safer," Caroline said. "And St. Martins offers more security. You said as much earlier. I'm very sorry if it offends you, Uncle, but I won't leave."

"No, no." He bowed his head, as though the idea weighed against him. "It's not a matter of offending, but I won't have you in danger." He looked up. "That's all there is to it."

"That decision does not lie with you, though, does it?" Summerton asked. "If you had warned me of the danger, lives could have been saved. Trust me, Caroline's safety is my highest priority."

Howlett's scowl reiterated the accusation he had made earlier in the day—that Summerton could very well be the source of the danger.

Hitches stepped into the room. "Dinner is served, your grace."

Caroline sidestepped Summerton and took her uncle's arm. "I will be perfectly fine," she promised, as she led her uncle to the family dining room.

Eleanor, partnered by both Summerton and Sir. Michael, held back.

"Her uncle seems quite concerned with her care," she noted.

Summerton snorted.

"You don't agree?"

"He was glad enough to be rid of her. Couldn't push the wedding forward quick enough."

"He thought you'd keep her safe," Sir Michael said.

"And out of the way," the duke reminded them.

Eleanor studied the two walking ahead. "I tend to believe her father really did want his daughter to have a tour. She said so herself."

"Possibly."

"Quite a hodgepodge for any man to swallow," Sir Michael said. "These have not been happy days for St. Martins."

And wouldn't be, until they found the culprit...or rather, culprits. She knew who they were, she just wasn't certain how many "theys" were in the mix.

Worrisome.

Worrisome, indeed.

CHAPTER 26 ~ Gentlemen, My Wife

He could not stop looking down the table at Caroline. His wife. In flesh as well as in name. No turning back from either. She would not be leaving with her uncle, and God save him, she would not go on the journey without him.

He would have to keep her safe. Yet the situation seemed fully out of his control. He had guards, damn it. But that posed its own problem. He'd hired every available man, who was not mired in planting, to walk the forest. He had his own servants and Sir Michael's minions watching the house. Their servants' cousins, friends from other counties. Known to a few, but not to all. Too easy for a stranger to slip into the mix. Unacceptable.

"No!" Caroline held firm. "We will not leave until the murderer is caught."

He studied Howlett. Calmer now, trying a different tack. "I didn't mean to anger you, Caroline, but can't you see what's before you?"

"Yes," she admitted. "I brought death to St. Martins."

"Don't be ridiculous!" Summerton snapped, earning a fierce glare.

Did she believe she was solely responsible for all that had happened?

Eleanor argued. "Apportioning blame is a foolish activity. If you fall from a ladder, do you blame the man who made the ladder? The tree the wood was taken from? Or the rain that watered the tree? Really! A ridiculously fruitless exercise."

"Couldn't agree more," Mr. Howlett dabbed his lips. "No one is trying to place blame. I just want to set matters right. You didn't want the marriage, Caroline. I never should have pushed you, so back you come. To Manchester..."

"No." Summerton slapped the table, pulling all eyes to him. "We will not be separated."

Again, Howlett tried to soothe. "Now, now, your grace. Think of how selfish your words sound. One heiress is as good as another. You'll be free to find one who wants you."

Was Howlett insulting him intentionally?

"Uncle Robert," Caroline broke in. "You don't understand. We are both settled to the match."

"Now, now, Caroline, neither of you chose this arrangement," Howlett soothed.

"Marriage, Howlett. Let's call it what it is." It was time to stop this foolish wrangling. "And you are very much mistaken on one count, Mr. Howlett. From the moment you brought her to my attention, I have been settled on Caroline. There could be no other."

Caroline put her fingers to her lips. He thought she might cry. That was not his intention.

"You're being frank? Then let me be direct. We all know she is not a suitable duchess," Howlett dabbed his lips with his serviette. "Not really."

Everyone stared at him.

"Well, she ain't."

"Quite the contrary," Eleanor interrupted. "Caroline has all the qualities of a duchess, a rare find in this day and age of self-indulgence."

"She stinks of trade!" Howlett argued. "And don't pretend you don't know the term." He jabbed the air with his finger. "I just learned of it," he appealed to Caroline, "after you was married. Heard people talking. They've no right. You deserve better."

"Oh, Uncle," Caroline cried, and Summerton could see the man wrapping her up in his own misconceptions.

"I learned how they treated you at school. Those girls with their hoity-toity airs, looking down their little noses at you, who could buy and sell them ten times over. You need..."

"How can you know about school?" Caroline asked, bewildered.

"Mr. Howlett," Summerton challenged. "No one will ever look down on Caroline again. No one. She is my wife. The Duchess of Summerton."

"She's good enough on her own!" Howlett barked.

"But she isn't on her own, is she?" Summerton told him.

Howlett backed down. "I didn't mean to imply she was. But I'm here for two reasons. Word is, it's not safe here. And tongues are wagging that there will be an annulment."

Even the breeze, so prominent in this room with its leaks and drafts, stilled.

"That would be impossible," Summerton told him, dismissing the subject by dipping into his dessert.

"Impossible?"

Summerton looked to Caroline. "Much as it becomes you, you needn't blush, my dear. In our station, dynasties depend on such information."

Howlett's mouth worked like that of a fish on dry land.

"Summerton." Caroline's blush deepened.

Eleanor pinned her nephew with a glance. "We are not usually so crude as to speak of such things at the dinner table."

He'd let Howlett get the better of him. Or perhaps he just wanted to shout to the world that she was his. Either way, though he knew it was not well done of him, he wasn't, truly, sorry. "My apologies, Aunt. Caroline, please forgive me."

"Well, then," Sir Michael lifted his glass to the silence. "Perhaps we could turn to the port a bit early?"

"Yes, of course." Caroline nodded to a footman, who eased her chair back. "Shall we, Aunt?" she asked Eleanor.

"She ain't your aunt," Howlett bit out with a little too much aggression.

"She is, through marriage," Summerton amended. The older man snorted, then lifted his glass and downed what was left in it.

Hostilities simmering barely below the surface, the men joined the ladies after only one drink. Summerton headed for Caroline, who stood at the piano forte, tapping idly at the keys.

"Do you play?" They were married, bonded for life, and there was still so much he didn't know about her.

She shook her head, "Not well enough to play in front of others. But I enjoy listening."

"Do you sing?"

She shrugged, looking up at him through her lashes. "Passably."

Ah, she could sing. "I prefer vocalizing, myself." He hesitated, not wanting to frighten her. "Caroline, will you stay close tonight? Where I can see you?"

She lifted her face, leaned into his touch as he traced her cheek.

"Are you...comfortable...after this afternoon?" he whispered, not knowing how to be more specific or delicate, but she must have understood, for she nodded, her cheek growing warmer.

"You can't go back to your rooms tonight."

Her eyes snapped to his, wide. Surprised.

"Are you worried for my safety?" she asked, her voice low, intimate.

He chuckled. "Yes, of course, but that's not why I mentioned it."

Her blush deepened. He wanted her in his arms, to feel her softness pressed again him.

Later.

He sighed, stepped back. "We are poor hosts." Which he didn't care two figs about, except plans had been made. "Shall we join them?"

She took his arm. Eleanor sat on the settee, needlework in her lap. Sir Michael beside her. Mr. Howlett stood looking out the French doors.

"Care for a game of whist?" Summerton asked, the question directed at no one in particular.

"Not me, thank you," Eleanor declined. "I've a bit of a headache."

"I'm sorry to hear that," Caroline said. "Does your abigail have something she gives you for that?"

"I'll be fine," Eleanor promised.

"If no one objects," Howlett said. "I'll just step outside."

Summerton had expected as much. Howlett was damn fond of his cheroot. "I'll have a footman light a torch on the balcony." He went to the bell pull.

"No need," Mr. Howlett said, and opened the door.

"I'll join him," Caroline offered, lifting her shawl.

"It's been drizzling," Eleanor warned. "I just checked."

"Not raining now," Robert said from the threshold. "But suit yourself, little one. Wouldn't want you to catch a cold."

They watched as he crossed into darkness, clouds having obscured any hint of stars or moon.

Summerton was unsettled by Caroline joining the man. Something wasn't right. Eleanor sensed it, too, for she said, "A night like this, the rain comes and goes without warning."

Eleanor never let anything as mild as rain keep her from a walk.

Summerton stood between the door and Caroline, unintentionally blocking her.

Caroline sighed, possibly torn as well. "He manipulated me terribly, before the wedding," she tried to explain in a soft voice. "Wrong as his methods may have been, it appears he did it for the best of reasons. I was so hateful at the end." She looked to Summerfield. "This might be a good time to apologize."

"You'll have plenty of opportunity," Sir Michael suggested.

"I'm not so certain of that. I think he means to leave in the morning, and who knows when we will next see each other," she added.

"You'll be in communication about the mills, your father's enterprises," Summerton reminded her.

Caroline shook her head. "Uncle Robert will never accept a woman interfering in business. Offends his manly sensibilities."

"A little too easily offended," Sir Michael quipped.

Caroline smiled at the baron. "So true, but I'll be able to help. If Mr. Little is still the man of business, I'll work through his people. They will speak with Mr. Little, who can make Uncle Robert think it's just two men considering options." She stepped reluctantly toward the door. "It's such a dark night."

"He'll understand if you don't join him," Eleanor eased.

"Most probably," Caroline agreed. "I'll just walk a little way with him, talk."

"Don't leave the path," Eleanor admonished.

"Don't go out of sight," Summerton added.

He walked her to the doorway and then watched as she joined her uncle. Eleanor joined him. "We should have stopped her," he said softly.

"I dare say you are right." Eleanor agreed. "I hadn't accounted for this."

No one spoke, all deep in thought, until Eleanor said, "You should follow them, Summerton. It would be prudent to make sure no mischief happens."

"Spy on them?" Sir Michael blustered.

"Discreetly. I'm afraid I don't have much faith in Mr. Howlett's concerns."

"You doubt him?"

"Don't you? Mr. Howlett is a man familiar with charming. But he's revealed his temper this evening." She put her needlework down on the piano bench. "I fear he is at his wit's end, and he could be dangerous."

"But we've already ruled him out. He hasn't been here and he appears genuinely concerned for Caroline," Sir Michael argued.

"Has he?" Eleanor looked up. "Are we certain of that?"

"I saw him," the magistrate confirmed, "at the Fox and Hound, shaking off the dust just as we were."

"Did you see him pull into the yard?" Eleanor asked.

"Can't say as I did, but what difference does that make? Only reason to be at the Fox and Hound would be traveling between here and Manchester, and he hadn't been here."

"You must be right." Eleanor nodded absently. "But perhaps it would be best if Summerton observed them."

"I'm going to do just that," he agreed. "But Aunt, we've plenty of men around the grounds. Nothing should happen."

Before he quit the room, Eleanor suggested, "Take a footman or two with you."

He stilled in the doorway to study Eleanor. She did not waver.

"That worrisome?" he asked. "Despite the men already there?"

"I'm afraid it might be. Don't dawdle."

He called for Hitches as he hurried to the back of the house, where he could slip out unseen from the back gardens.

"And me?" Sir Michael asked.

"You and I—" Eleanor rose, "—will have a word with Mr. Little. I expect him at any moment."

THE AIR WAS MUSTY FROM the ground they disturbed, and the scent of apple blossoms filled the night.

"Thank you for suggesting a walk." Her leash had been too short these last few days. Caroline hadn't realized how much she missed walking outdoors. "Spring is so rich and full of new life."

"That it is, pet, that it is."

"I'm sorry you had to come all this way for nothing."

"It isn't nothing, Caroline. Very important business, these marriages and settlements."

It shouldn't be. How awful it would have been to share what she and Summerton had shared that very afternoon with someone you loathed. She shuddered. "I was awful to you, uncle. I had no idea you were that worried or that he would turn out to be such a wonderful man."

"Is he? Barely spoke two words to you before you married." He turned down a tunnel of a path, trees arching overhead, high and green.

"I've never been this far." She hesitated. Summerton had asked her to stay in sight, but her uncle had already demonstrated that he cared for her safety. Apologies could be shown, as much as said. She needed to trust him.

She took his arm. "Summerton faced heavy demands. Even if he'd wanted to, there was no time. Not then." She squeezed his arm. "If the two of you sat me down and talked to me..."

He *tsk*ed. "Caroline, you are a woman. You need to trust us men to know what's best."

"Without any say?" She looked at him.

He shook his head, chuckling. "And you tell me you're happy, so it appears it did all work for the best, which means we were right, weren't we?"

"Father always gave me the opportunity to consider options..."

"Your father spoiled you, and it wasn't well done of him. The world does not work that way."

"He trusted me with his interests." They were a long way from the Hall, far from sight. She looked back, over her shoulder, into total darkness. "Uncle."

He ignored her tug. "That was badly done, Caroline. Very badly done on his part."

What was badly done? "I think we should return."

"Do you? But it's been so long since we've had the chance to visit."

"Uncle." Again, Caroline tried to pull back, but he held her tight.

"Do you remember the Robinson affair? The boy who lost his arm?"

They'd had a row, she and her father, her uncle teasing her for being too soft. In the end, her father had relented, grudgingly. They'd reimbursed the family for work lost and found the boy a job he could do with one arm. "It was our responsibility."

Robert smiled. "It was his responsibility to do his job so he didn't get hurt. Yet you set the business on a course it should never have taken. An example was set."

"He did his job right. The machine broke."

"Life isn't always fair."

She tried to pull free again. "You're hurting my arm, Uncle."

"I was with your father from the beginning," he said, ignoring her. "Before you were a sparkle in his eye. I made things easier for him, softening folks he'd insulted, easing situations he'd turned into battles." He patted her hand on his arm. "Getting rid of people in the way. He never appreciated that." His sigh whispered on the night air. "All this, I did all this, but he listened to you."

"He took your counsel, had you by his side..."

"On a leash. He had me on a leash." Anger twisted his smile, more malevolent for the deep shadows.

She stopped, firm. He'd have to drag her to get her further. "Uncle Robert." The tunnel of greenery grew ominous. "We've come a long way."

As quickly as fury rose, it settled. Malevolence transformed to cosseting concern. He released her, adjusted the shawl on her shoulders. "Come on, then. Let's get you back inside." And offered his arm again.

They didn't speak. The chirps and croaks of frogs around them were the only sounds as Caroline considered her father, her uncle, and their relationship. "You've been angry with him for a long time?" Caroline asked.

His hand tightened on hers, then relaxed. "Anger is such a harsh word, Caroline. We were brothers. There's always a little rivalry with brothers. Pay no attention. I said too much."

"I never realized." But on some level she had. Robert had moods. That's what her father called them. *Your uncle is going away for a time, pet. He's in one of his moods.*

"Water under the bridge."

He let go of her and stepped back. "Brotherly rivalry," he mused, shaking his head. "Ruined everything. The whole reason I never married."

She stilled as he stopped to remove a thin silver cheroot holder. Foolish to be afraid, he was taking her back to the Hall. There was nothing to worry about.

Even as she thought that, she worried over wearing skirts that would tangle if she needed to run.

He held up a cheroot. "Do you mind? I know—" he chuckled, "—terribly lower class, but there you have it. I never took to snuff."

She shook her head. "How will you light it? No candle or tinder to be found out here."

He snapped the silver lid closed with a decisive click. "Instantaneous lighter. I'll show you, if you'll give me a moment. The idea is not quite perfected, but I believe I've got the hang of it."

A bird rustled, twittered. Disturbed by them or something else? Caroline looked around, tried to peer into the wood, further down the path.

Robert tapped the end of the cheroot against the case, drawing her attention. When she realized he was watching her, studying her, she stepped back. He stepped forward, as though her walking backward and his advancing were a perfectly normal way to conduct a conversation in the middle of the woods on a dark night.

"Your mother was supposed to be mine," He *tsk*ed and tilted his head, smiling. "But then she was, in the end." He held the tobacco. "To think, you could have been my daughter."

"My mother?" Her mother had been strangled by highway robbers. Uncle Robert had been out of town. In one of his moods.

Hadn't he?

"Of course she loved me." He lifted the cheroot to his lips, patted his coat. "Ah, here it is." He pulled a vial from an inside pocket. "But she was as much a whore as any woman," he said, with such ease, as if discussing the most mundane of topics. Caroline questioned her hearing. "And your father with his bloody Midas touch." He put the cheroot to his lips, his face scrunching, nostrils flaring, and snapped the glass vial apart.

Flame surged from the broken glass, which he lifted to the tip of his cheroot. The light cast his features in sepulchered shadows, creating a monster behind him in the night.

Only, it wasn't a monster. It was Biggs, revealed in the halo of light, looming over him, arms spread wide, ready to engulf him.

Caroline screamed, then turned and ran straight into Roger Little's arms.

"Put him down," Roger demanded, holding Caroline tight. One arm pinning both of hers, the other wrapped around her neck.

"No, Roger!" she warned. "You won't get free this time. There are men everywhere."

"And I'm one of them." He laughed. "I've been hired as a guard."

"That's my boy!" Robert Howlett smiled with pride. "You can let me down now, Biggs."

Biggs did not release him.

"What do you mean, 'my boy'?" Caroline asked.

"He's my father, isn't he?" Roger explained.

"Your father? What about Mr. Little?"

Roger tightened his hold on her. "Quiet, you, or I'll break your neck," he whispered in her ear.

"True," Robert cooed, as if she were a toddler. "He will, little Caroline. Best keep mum." Then to Roger, "Go ahead, tell her, my boy. My heir."

Mad. They were both mad.

Roger chuckled. "Mr. Little had to go to London with your father, didn't he? Took your ma, too. But they didn't take Mrs. Little or my father. Deed done, and here I am. Spitting image, wouldn't you say?"

And he was. Of course he was. How had she missed that? He looked exactly like her Uncle Robert.

"Roger Little died, son. Do you remember? After that girl in Edinburgh?"

"And Edward Howlett was born."

"Exactly." Robert Howlett struggled to get free, barking, "I'm warning you, Biggs, I don't like it when you interfere with my games."

"Mr. John pays me to interfere."

"But Mr. John is dead. I'm the Mr. Howlett you must listen to now."

"Mr. John may be dead, but he's still paying me."

Roger was watching the confrontation and had loosened his hold, but Caroline didn't think, for a moment, she could pull free. Even if she could, her blasted skirts would keep her from running far.

Instead, she went limp, dropping like dead weight, taking Roger by such surprise, she easily pulled him with her when she tucked and rolled.

Down they went, her skirts falling indecently as she landed on top of him, both of them on their backs. He'd been winded by either fall or the shock of falling, she neither knew nor cared which.

She flipped over, and with a swift, hard jerk, she raised her knee between his legs, then scrambled free of his convulsive curl to protect himself.

Breathing heavily, she stood and brushed her hands as Robert howled and Summerton plowed through the undergrowth, six men fast on his heels.

"You screamed!" He looked as ready to kill as the footmen who'd surrounded the whimpering, prostrate form of Roger Little, who'd curled in on himself, gagging.

"Your lordship?" Biggs said. "I've got him, just like I told you I would."

"You were there?" Caroline asked.

"Shh, my love, I'd not let anything happen to you."

"You were there?" She couldn't quite fathom it.

"Just in time to see you topple him," he admitted. "Good Lord, I've never been so...amazed, proud, afraid, in the whole of my life," he admitted, pulling her close for a quick, hard kiss. "Now, let's get these men back to the house so we can hand them over to Sir Michael. I don't ever want to see them again." He winked at Caroline, "And I don't think this one—" he shoved Roger with the toe of his boot, "—will care much for seeing you."

"I haven't done anything wrong," Mr. Howlett wailed.

"Aye, you have, Mr. Robert. Lady Eleanor says you killed those girls. Says she can prove it, besides," Biggs told him.

"What, a woman? They are going to take the word of a woman over..." Biggs ignored his blathering, put him out with one punch, and slung him over his shoulder. "That will keep 'im quiet for a bit."

As the footmen looked down at Roger, one of them shook his head. "Don't think we can move him yet, your grace."

"You've rope?"

"Just like you said." Another of them held up a coil.

"Tie him up. Bring him when you can." Summerton flinched.

"Did I injure him badly?" Caroline asked.

"The cad deserved that and more. You took your lesson to heart."

That very afternoon, Summerton had explained a few facts about male anatomy and suggested reliable ways she could protect herself. In the most dire of circumstances, of course.

"You weren't the first man to suggest that defense," she told him.

"There was another?" She couldn't help but smirk. She'd shocked him. Obviously, he'd forgotten she'd been raised by a man who didn't share his refined sensibilities.

"My father knew the dangers of mill yards and factories." She frowned, realizing he may have been more concerned about the danger of his brother. "He was very direct. Told me it was my best defense, but that I would only have one chance."

"To use it in the direst of situations."

Caroline bit her lip. "This felt rather dire."

"It was, my love. I just don't want the power to go to your head."

"Ah," she smiled, a secret little smile, knowing it would worry him for years.

CHAPTER 27 – Loose Ends

As was their habit, they gathered in the study for tea and port. Summerton chose to forego his usual spot—standing in the shadow, leaning against his desk, to sit beside Caroline on the settee. Lady Eleanor and Sir Michael took their regular places and Mr. Little, who had not participated in this part of the evening on his last visit, had been invited to take a seat in a spare chair, pulled up to the group by Summerton.

"They're secured for the night," Sir Michael announced, referring to Roger Little and Robert Howlett. "We've spoken with Jeremy and Biggs. Appears Biggs' function was to watch over Robert Howlett, not watch out for him. Stop him from hurting others."

"Well done," Summerton said, squeezing Caroline's hand. She squeezed back.Even Lady Eleanor offered a smile.

"What I want to know," Mr. Little asked, "is how Lady Eleanor knew I was at the Inn?"

"You knew?" Caroline asked.

"Oh, yes." Eleanor, with her ever-present needlework in hand, said, "I knew he wouldn't leave until Roger was found."

"Yes." He scratched his jaw. "Well, he was supposed to be in Scotland, but one never knew for certain, not once he matured, and once I heard about Alice, well, I feared the boy had a hand in it.

"My father was quite harsh with Roger, banning him as he did. Do you think that affected Roger, perhaps turned him bad?

"Harsh? I don't know what I would have done if he hadn't stepped in. And it was his responsibility, by Jove. Roger never would have existed if your father had taken his brother in hand."

"What do you mean?"

"Robert Howlett wanted your mum from the moment he set eyes on her. Caroline's father had just started courting her, but when Robert showed his hand, John didn't waste any time before wedding her. That's when we were young, our futures no more than dreams in our heads."

"But Robert didn't take it well?" Eleanor suggested.

Little snorted. "John called them 'Robert's Moods.' Each time he fell into one, John would send him off to the old farm where Robert's mother lived. She was not the sort of woman who made good company. Being around her probably made it worse."

"I'd forgotten they were half-brothers, the two Mr. Howletts. But are you saying their father never married Robert's mother?" Sir Michael asked.

"Never. Didn't even know that he had another son until the lad was four or five years old. But looks told out," Little said.

"He looks just like my grandfather did," Caroline confirmed.

"Bitter about it, then?" Summerton asked. "Even though he weathered better than other boys born out of wedlock? At least he was recognized, cared for."

Little snorted. "Not that he sees that. Matters grew worse when John's Ellie took with little Caroline here. John's excitement over the expectation only deepened Robert's bitterness."

"But he always seemed so jovial!" Caroline said.

"Oh, always the life of the party, was our Robert, but he stuck more daggers in a chuckle than other men could do with a sneer." Sad-eyed, he reminded her. "Actions, Caroline, always look to actions rather than words. Your father knew that. So, though your mother was carrying you, he risked taking her with us on business rather than leave her at home alone. Didn't dare with Robert about."

"Oh, dear." Eleanor's hand went to her mouth. "So he struck out at the closest woman he could get."

Little nodded. "My wife's happiness was destroyed for new equipment. The sort of business that made John the man he became. I had to go to negotiate contracts. None of us suspected he would turn on my Ellie."

"And during that trip," Summerton suggested, "Roger was conceived."

Little rose and walked to the French doors overlooking the yard they'd crossed to capture Robert Howlett. "We were gone a month. He kidnapped my Ellie. She did not go voluntarily. I came home to a house full of toppled furniture. There was blood on the floor and strands of her beautiful hair, yanked clear out of her head." He leaned against the doorframe. "I was standing amid that mess, lost to the world, when Robert brought Ellie into the house. He said they'd had a nice visit with his mum. Out of town. Hoped I didn't mind." His fist crashed against the door frame. "I wanted to kill him, would have, but Ellie stopped me. The look of her... I don't think she would have survived if I hadn't thrown that man out of the house then and there. So, so fragile, my poor girl.

"She never told me what happened there," he gritted. "Swore me to secrecy, but she was never the same. Never." He wiped his eyes, shoulders shuddered, tangible ripples of agony.

Yet he continued. "My Ellie never took to the child. Perhaps he'd have been different if she had, but she didn't. She gave him to a wet nurse, who kept him on the teat well past time."

"Mr. Little," Sir Michael softly reminded him of the mixed company.

"My apologies to the ladies, but it's the God's honest truth. Worse, Robert Howlett was beside himself. He had a son. Crowed about how his son and Caroline would marry. Keep it all in the family now, right?"

"I would never marry Roger," Caroline said with vehemence.

"No, that became clear. So he had to find another way to make Roger heir to the Howlett fortunes."

Summerton rose. Caroline had been expecting as much. He'd be itching to do something, to feel that he could turn to right something that had gone so horribly wrong.

"Ring for tea, would you, Summerton?" Caroline asked, offering him direction, even as she mulled over Little's words. "The wet nurse? Would that be Hilda?"

"Very good!" Eleanor beamed.

"Is that true?" Sir Michael asked.

But Little had turned back, stunned. "You know about Hilda?"

"She's here, in the area," Eleanor said. "Obviously helping Roger, but I didn't know why until now."

"Well, if she's here, that explains everything," Mr. Little said.

"Yes, I dare say it does." Eleanor lifted her needlepoint, as if everyone understood now.

"Aunt?" Summerton asked, from his spot in the shadows, leaning against his desk.

"Well, you see, that is why Robert Howlett was so keen to have Caroline marry you, rather than another aristocrat. If his son was a regular visitor to the area, Robert Howlett must have been one, too." She put down her sewing. "What a boon it would have been to learn you were looking for an heiress to take residence in a community where he and Roger had the freedom to come and go without anyone taking note. They'd be as good as local."

Summerton opened the door to Hitches and a maid. "But how did he know I needed an heiress? I'd barely learned of the situation myself."

Mr. Little shook his head. "My fault entirely," he said. "Your man of affairs made a quiet mention to me. It was well known that Caroline offered a sizeable dowry, and I was on the search, anything rather than have her under Robert's guardianship."

"Why was that?" Lady Eleanor asked. "Surely John Howlett would never have allowed such a thing."

Mr. Little accepted a glass of port. "Yes, well, to that—" he fortified himself with a sip, "—a will was found, forged no doubt, but I've been unable to break it. While it's in debate, he is considered her closest family and until her marriage, he was her legal guardian." He offered Caroline a sympathetic smile. "I've been fighting it, my dear, but to no avail. That's why I was so eager to see you married off."

"And Robert would be eager, too," Eleanor offered.

Summerton signaled Hitches, who had arrived with the tea, to stay in the room a moment. "Your grace?"

"Had you ever seen Mr. Howlett about the town?"

"I'm afraid I don't go into town much, your grace," Hitches answered. "But Mr. Howlett did seem rather familiar to me when he arrived. There is a similar fellow, a Mr. Telly. Rather a loud gentleman. Story teller. Said he came to town to get gentleman tonics and such from Hilda."

"Gentleman tonics?" Caroline asked.

"Nothing for you to worry about, my dear," Summerton told her.

Eleanor's wink confirmed they would speak later. She slipped the phrase away for clarification after the men were gone.

"A familiar face?" Sir Michael asked. "Someone you wouldn't consider a stranger?"

"No, I wouldn't consider him a stranger."

"So why call in the newspapers?" Caroline asked, as soon as Hitches and the maid left. "If they didn't stand out in town anyway?"

"To create chaos," Summerton offered. "A bigger crowd. They knew there would be a death, so they needed to make the waters as murky as possible."

"So Uncle Robert encouraged Roger to murder..."

"No, no, no," Eleanor *tsk*ed. "Roger tried to hurt you, my dear, but not the others."

"They were killed by strangulation!"

"Your uncle."

Sir Michael sat up, blustering. "But he was in Manchester."

"Was he?"

"I saw him on his way..." Sir Michael sat back. "Ah, I see. He knew I was on my way and deliberately met me."

"It was a risk, his coming here, but things were getting out of hand." Eleanor took her tea from Caroline.

"You were right," Caroline remembered. "Robert rarely lost his temper. He could be cruel, but he always seemed jovial. But from the moment he arrived, he was very angry."

"You didn't do what you were supposed to do," Summerton told her.

"Which was?"

"Run away or go on the bridal journey, where you would be more vulnerable. You thwarted him at every turn," Eleanor explained. "He wanted to be rid of you in a place where no one could accuse him of anything. But you were not so easily removed."

"But wouldn't it all go to Summerton?"

"I think your uncle was assuming there would be a...a grace period in your marriage."

"What about the attempt on Summerton?" Caroline asked.

"Ah, well, you two were growing closer. Thankfully, between your quick thinking and Jeremy's presence, Howlett only had the one thwarted opportunity. He had to get away or risk capture."

"Couldn't Jeremy identify him?"

"Oh, my dear, your uncle would not have left himself open to be seen. He might have worn a scarf, a hat, any number of items to hide his identity."

"How do you know this?" Caroline asked.

"Observation and logic," Eleanor admitted. "And we don't know all of this as fact. It is pure speculation until we speak with Jeremy and Biggs again."

"Two people dead, a whole community terrorized, because he wanted me out of the way." It didn't seem fair. So many hurt, frightened.

Caroline looked at her husband, only to find him already studying her.

"It appears your father's enterprise will need you," he said.

Too true, but with Robert out of the way, they had a chance.

"Mr. Little, how bad are things at the mills?"

"Ah—" Mr. Little brushed his hands, as though shaking off the earlier conversation, "—your uncle turned everything upside down. It's not the business your father ran. His ideas burdened the workers without earning more. In fact, production has dropped. There have been more accidents."

"I'd heard as much."

"Did he reimburse families? Find new work for injured..."

Little shook his head, stopping Caroline from asking more. "No, he stopped all those policies the moment he got you out of there. But I've kept track of who was injured, how, and why. With your permission, I can follow up."

"Absolutely." She leaned forward. "And Jeremy, he can oversee the actual running of the mills."

"If that's what you want."

Eleanor looked up. "But I thought you said Jeremy had been released because he stole money."

Little cleared his throat. "He left at the same time as Howlett and Roger. I had men investigating, but we didn't know if Jeremy had joined forces with Roger or not. They may have offered him a lucrative arrangement."

"Howlett had you chasing him?" Summerton asked.

"Howlett liked his shell game, baiting and switching, so you never knew where you'd be hit," Little admitted.

"If the man was so evil, why didn't he just carry out his threats about Caroline's animals?"

With a very unladylike snort, Eleanor said, "I rather think he liked the idea of you suffering with them."

Little nodded, chuckling. "That was his favorite part of the negotiations. Cheered him immensely, especially the parrot."

Summerton rolled his eyes.

"The installments for the dowry—" Little cleared his throat, "—I'm afraid that was my fault. I told Howlett that it was in the paperwork."

"What?" the other four all asked.

"But I added that to the dowry arrangement to ensure you left the country, went away, beyond his reach."

"And he let you do that?"

"He liked the idea of you not receiving the full jointure. I believe he never thought it would reach the point of you getting more."

"And now?" Summerton asked.

"I think you've proven yourself. I'll sit down with your man of affairs and release the whole of it."

The money. It was always about the money.

"Well," Caroline stood, a bit disheartened. "I guess that's all there is." She smoothed her skirts.

"Caroline?" Summerton's voice slid over her like rich velvet, "You truly believe that's it?"

"There aren't any more questions, are there?"

"You tell me." Summerton caught her arm and pulled her back to the settee.

"Really, Summerton, this is not the place." Eleanor objected.

"Then why don't you all leave? It's time my bride and I had some time alone."

"Alone?" she asked, as everyone rose, busy straightening vests and skirts, looking anywhere but at the settee. Sir Michael murmuring about how he'd best have Old Hilda questioned.

Summerton ignored them. His soft words for Caroline alone. "Yes, like a bridal journey without the travel."

"We aren't going now?"

"We'll go," Summerton promised. "We'll go, once everything is set to rights."

The door clicked shut behind the last of the others.

"But I have another little journey planned, for just the two of us." The words were whispered along her neck, followed by a kiss.

"Now?" She smiled, curious, willing.

"Yes," he stood held out his hand. "It means traversing the wilds of a hidden staircase..."

"A frightening place." She whispered against his neck, willing it to affect him the way he had affected her.

"Ah," he said, "then you will have to stay close, very close. I will keep you safe."

And he did, through that whole adventure, and many more to come. Adventures in the Hall, adventures along their journeys. A duke and his duchess's quest for life, until their explorations led to two sons and three daughters.

Ah, the grand scheme—a wonderful thing they would never take for granted.

Don't miss out!

Visit the website below and you can sign up to receive emails whenever Becca St. John publishes a new book. There's no charge and no obligation.

https://books2read.com/r/B-A-HUQG-CNIV

BOOKS 2 READ

Connecting independent readers to independent writers.

Did you love *Summerton*? Then you should read *The Gatehouse* by Becca St. John!

A deaf aristocrat fights to protect the woman he loves from a killer he cannot hear ~

Found standing over the lifeless body of his twin, the Earl of Longford, Christopher knows what everyone will think. That he killed his brother in a beastly rage. For Christopher is deaf in a society that condemns the silent as half-wits, quite capable of murder. Especially when he loves his brother's bride. Beyond caring what the world thinks, Christopher searches for a killer he cannot hear as he fights a love he believes he is unworthy of.

Left a spinster at the altar, her groom murdered, Helen has no time to mourn. Her best friend, and confidant, Christopher, is in danger and so, it appears, is she. Born to marry the Earl of Longford, whoever that may be, Helen ignores her own risks and crosses into the line of fire to protect the only man ever to hold her heart.

Lady Eleanor solved crimes as a young child, and never stopped. This one is personal. Condemned without evidence, her godson, Christopher, is threatened with the barbaric asylum that destroyed his youth. She must act quickly before unjust convictions steal him away and cruel deception shatters a love, hidden and denied for far too long.

Read more at https://www.beccastjohn.com/.

Also by Becca St. John

Lady Eleanor Mysteries

Summerton

The Gatehouse

The Handfasting Series

The Handfasting

Seonaid

Women of the Woods

The Healer

The Protector

An Independent Miss

Watch for more at https://www.beccastjohn.com/.

About the Author

Writing was a tool, not a toy, until a stay in a haunted hotel and a bookcase full of dog-eared romances. Hooked, Becca read old romances, new romances, both sexy and sweet, until her own tales begged to be written.

Living in Florida, Becca divides her time between dreaming up stories, diving deep into history, kayaking, and swimming. Her husband gives her the space she needs by fishing in the mangroves and waterways or watching football (the English sort) with his British buddies. Becca and her hubby break the routine with adventure travel; though, at heart, Becca is a homebody believing there is no greater playground than inside the mind.

Read more at https://www.beccastjohn.com/.

Printed in Great Britain
by Amazon

64669307R00180